OF WOLF AND MAN

Other Works by Christopher Andrews

NOVELS

Pandora's Game
Dream Parlor
Paranormals
Hamlet: Prince of Denmark

COLLECTIONS

The Darkness Within

SCREENPLAYS

Thirst
Dream Parlor
(written with Jonathan Lawrence)
Mistake
Fighter
(written with Roberto Estrella)

WEB SERIES

Duet

VIDEO GAMES

Bankjob

OF WOLF AND MAN

A *Triumvirate* Novel by
CHRISTOPHER ANDREWS

This *Triumvirate* novel is dedicated,
solely and entirely,
to my wife, editor, and Imzadi,
Yvonne Kristina Isaak-Andrews.

You are the world to me.

The following story takes place approximately
eighteen months after the events depicted in
the short-story, "Connexion," and approximately
two years after the events depicted in
the novel, *Pandora's Game*.

The hunter fled through the forest, and the wolves followed.

Scott Gerrard wasn't sure which was louder: The heavy clumping of his booted feet through the underbrush, the thudding of his heart (which felt like it would explode at any moment), or the gleeful yet malevolent *barking* which trailed him.

Stealth was not an issue. Scott did not bother to "creep" his way through the foliage. He had no delusions. The wolves knew *exactly* where he was. They were toying with him, playing games with him like they were *more* than animals ...

Watch it, Scott, don't go down that road — if you go down that road you'll crack and then you're a dead man, you hear me?

... and his only hope was to reach the campsite ahead of them. *Let* them play their games, if that's what it took to get him there first.

His favorite hunting rifle lay in the dirt, hundreds of yards behind him. It would have done him no good even if it were in his hands right now, as *they* had torn it to pieces — ripped the wooden stock to shreds and even bent the metal barrel, if he had seen correctly — just as they had the other members of his hunting party.

Brandon. Monty. Patrick. Rick.

Dead, all dead. Not even faithful ol' Tanner — that poor, wretched Retriever of Monty's, who was way too old to be out here with them, anyway — had been spared.

Only Scott was left. And it was *his* fault they were out here to begin with ...

The five men, and Tanner, had been hunting together for years, usually in Colorado or Montana. But it wasn't as *fun* as it used to be. It seemed like every season, the fucking Liberals got new laws put on the books — you can't do this, you can't do that; you can't shoot this, you can't shoot that; oh, you can shoot *this*, but only while you're standing on one foot under a cloudy sky with a corncob up your ... whatever.

Then Scott got a big idea: They take a trip up to Alaska, where everything is nice and spread out. Sure, they've got National Preserves out the whazoo, all protected under Federal and local law, but any bleeding-heart Liberal would whine to you about how bad the budget-cuts had gotten, how understaffed these areas were, especially as you pushed north into the Arctic regions.

Understaffed meant fewer park rangers.

Fewer rangers meant bigger holes in security.

Bigger holes ... *bigger game*, licensed or not, protected or not.

It would make for an expensive trip, of course, but even that cheapskate Monty had caught on to the possibilities by then. Hell, Brandon and Rick started talking about bagging a Kodiak, but Scott wasn't thinking quite *that* big. After all, if they bagged a bear, and if that animal *happened* to be on the protected list this year — who could keep track anymore? — how the hell would they get the damn thing home without getting caught? And what was the point of shooting something if you weren't going to bring home a trophy to show for it?

Nah, what Scott wanted was a *wolf.* An Arctic Wolf, the biggest wolves there were. Now *that* would make one helluva trophy ... and the skin would tuck nicely into a suitcase for the return trip.

So, they spent the next four months planning the trip. They arranged to arrive in the summer, because none of them wanted to freeze their asses off. Brandon and Patrick okayed it with their wives, and Rick got someone to watch his kids for the two weeks he would be gone. And Monty, whose first words on the subject had been to complain about the expense, insisted on bringing Tanner with him, which cost a pretty penny.

And Scott? Well, Scott had no one to ask, no one to worry about. He had never been married (though he'd come close once) and he had no children (that he knew about). All he had were his friends ...

... and those friends were all *dead* now ...

The barking grew more intense, and some of it even gave way to *howling,* straight out of a fucking horror movie. But the camp was close now, very close. Scott had another rifle there — thank God for procrastination, because he had never unloaded the bullets after Tuesday afternoon's target practice. There were at least four shots left in it — not enough to take out the whole pack, but once the shooting started and *their* blood was shed, he was pretty damn sure that these fucking coyotes-on-steroids would change their motherfucking tunes ...

When they had gotten as far north as Unalakleet off the Norton Sound, Scott and Brandon — the undisputed "nicer" looking pair of the five friends — began making subtle inquiries into the best known locations of the Arctic Wolves. They had to be cautious, to tread carefully, because while some of the locals were very practical about wolf-hunting and even hunted on the side themselves, others could be just as rabid Nature Lovers as those down in the lower forty-eight.

On Brandon's suggestion, they kept their guns tucked away while he and Scott carried around nice-looking cameras ... *implying* that they were here for the photography, without having to actually *lie* about it — Scott had kept the receipt and would be returning his overpriced Nikon as soon as they got home. Slowly but surely, talking to a white man here and an Eskimo there, they got the information they needed.

They made their way further north. It would have gone a lot faster without ol' Tanner along for the ride, but they knew the old boy wouldn't be around too much longer, and Monty would take it very hard when that day came. So they kept their peace and played with the white-muzzled Retriever instead of complaining about him.

They were making their way from Coldfoot to Deadhorse when they managed to get "lost," which would be the story if they got caught. With Brooks Range to the west and the Arctic National Wildlife Refuge to the east, they had a lot of ground to cover, but so did the park rangers.

Bigger holes, bigger game ...

Scott's boot snagged on something, and he almost went down, but at the last moment he managed to catch his balance and keep going. He could hear some of the barking and howling coming from in front of him now (*I knew they were playing games with me, I* knew *it!*), but that didn't matter. Those noises were coming from further ahead of him than the distance remaining to the camp, to his tent, to his other gun. The sons-of-bitches had outsmarted themselves this time. They should have killed him when they had the chance, when they killed his friends and Tanner...

The hunting grounds up here had thrown them all for a loop. For one thing, they weren't used to the tundras, and had to look harder than expected for the woods to which they were accustomed — they needed cover from the Feds as much as from the game. Their rented SUV had four-wheel drive, but that was still nearly insufficient once they left the main roads.

Another thing that messed them up was the weird daylight up here. As the season crept closer to the height of summer, the white nights were on the way. They were used to the usual pattern — you get up early, you hunt all day, you return to camp in the evening, you get drunk with nightfall, and then you sleep until the next morning. But up here, at this time of year ... well, it never really got *dark* dark. Oh, it wasn't like twenty-four/seven daytime or anything like that, but instead of the sun going all the way down like it should, it just sort of tucked itself right below the horizon, leaving the world stuck in a kinda-sorta "dusk" for a few hours, then started back up into the sky again.

This shouldn't have been that big of a deal, but it

messed with their internal clocks. They had trouble sleeping the first few nights, but eventually they adjusted.

Over halfway through the entirety of their trip, they set out for hunting for the first time. Monty and Rick were a little grumpy over the wasted days, but the land was beautiful, and when they did find themselves at the sudden edge of the woods and looking out over the tundras, Brandon started making use of his camera "prop" after all.

They didn't see any game all day — not the kind of game they were *hoping* for, anyway — but that turned out all right. Patrick shot a rabbit, Tanner chased a squirrel up a tree and then spent ten minutes giving it a what-for while the men laughed, and Brandon took a lot of pictures. As the day began to wind down, more according to their watches than from judging this weak-ass "nightfall," they made their way back toward camp, and Scott felt satisfied even without having so much as seen an Arctic Wolf.

That was when Monty stepped into the trap ...

Scott smashed through some underbrush, and *there* — there was the camp! But behind him, some of the wolves were now close enough that he thought he could hear their padded feet kicking up dirt, their furry bodies knocking aside underbrush.

Almost there, almost there, almost there ...

Scott had been leading out front, debating with Brandon about the merits of keeping his expensive digital camera after all, when they heard Monty scream. It wasn't a yell, it was a *scream*, and that sound coming out of a manly-man's mouth was never a good thing.

Hustling back a few dozen yards, they found Patrick panicking and Rick staring, Monty holding his right shin and crying, and Tanner whimpering.

Oh my God, Scott thought, *his foot is gone!*

But that impression only lasted for one tense moment. His foot wasn't gone, it was just down a shallow hole, out of sight. So what the fuck was the chaos all about?

"Monty, what the hell?!" Scott yelled over the bedlam as he stomped forward. "Did you twist your ... ank ... le...?" He just stared for a moment, trying to *un*see what his eyes were telling him.

Monty had stepped into a hole, that much was correct. But this wasn't like a gopher hole or any some such. It looked like the hole a dog would make when burying a bone. But then, to Monty's great misfortune, some branches had fallen over the top of the hole, hiding what would otherwise have been difficult to miss, even in the fading twilight that would last for the next several hours.

But all of that was neither here nor there. That wasn't the real problem.

The hole itself *could* have been dug by an animal, and those loose, thin branches *could* have ended up covering it by chance ... but how did any of that explain the two little *spears* that were poking up through the top of Monty's foot?

"Someone *help me!*" Monty cried as he squeezed his shin tighter.

"What the fuck ...?" Brandon whispered as he knelt for a closer look.

The spears were made of wood. Under most circumstances, Monty's hiking boot would have just crushed them, splitting them into pieces. But these two little bastards had been positioned with their points — their deliberately-crafted, unnaturally sharp points — straight up. As Monty's foot had come down and broken the loose branches, his full two-hundred-thirty pounds had come down right on top of the spears. They must have been well anchored not to have turned to the side when they met the resistance of his boot sole. Judging from their placement, one of them might — *might* — have only cut the sides of his toes as it stabbed between them. But the other one had emerged closer to the tops of his laces, and dead center; pretty much the thickest part of the foot.

Scott looked up, around, side-to-side. There were no trees close enough to this very spot for those loose branches to have just fallen so *perfectly* to cover the hole.

Someone had done this deliberately. But why? What kind of animal trap was this? Most game was too light for this to be effective, their paws or hooves too small for such a perfect fit.

This was a *man* trap. What kind of sick fuck would do this?!

Brandon touched the bloody tip of one of the spears. Monty screamed.

"What do we do?" Patrick huffed. "What do we do, Brandon? Scott?"

"We, uh," Brandon began, then spat on the ground to one side, as though he had a bad taste in his mouth, "we need to get his foot out of there. If we break off the two points, we'll have less—"

"No, no, no!" Monty cried. "Not two! *Three*, damn it, *three*!" He fell back, crying again but trying not to.

Three? Oh, Jesus, Scott realized, *that means there's another one we can't see, one that's gone into his fucking* heel.

"What do we do?!" Patrick started again.

"Patrick, calm down!" Scott snapped. "Monty's the only one here with an excuse to lose it right now, so *calm down*!"

Patrick nodded. Rick, who had been silent when the cavalry arrived, remained so. Tanner continued to whimper and pace, distressed by his master's pain but no more certain of what to do about it than his human companions.

"Okay, here's what we do," Brandon said with authority, but Scott had known him too long — he was making this up as he went along. "Patrick, I want you to haul your ass back to camp before it gets too dark to see—"

"Yeah, right," Rick muttered, staring up at the eerie glow in the sky. The full moon was visible, but only a few stars were bright enough to penetrate the overall radiance of the barely-hidden sun.

Brandon ignored the interruption, "Bring the first-aid kit *and* the tool kit. Can you carry both of those, or do you need—?"

Tanner suddenly barked, loud, and since Brandon was kneeling, it was painfully close to his ear.

"Jesus, Tanner!" Brandon groused, placing a hand against the side of his head as the old dog barked twice more.

Even through his haze of pain, Monty reached for his dog. "What is it, Tanner? What's wrong, boy?"

Tanner looked left and right, growling, his nostrils pulsing. He barked again.

"Shut up, Tanner," Rick muttered without feeling.

"Patrick," Brandon tried once again, "I need you—"

"No," Monty interrupted this time. He was pushing himself up onto his elbows, despite the pain it was obviously causing him. "Somethin's wrong." He reached for Tanner again.

"Monty," Scott admonished, "you should just—"

"*No*, you idiots!" Monty barked in his own way, looking around and reaching for his dropped gun. "Don't you dumbshits know anything? Pay attention to the dog! You *always* pay attention to the dog—!"

Scott was looking right at Monty, looking right at him, when the wolf appeared out of nowhere and sank its teeth deep into Monty's throat.

"*Oh, shit!*" Patrick cried, staggering away from the carnage. Brandon jumped to his feet with an inarticulate yelp. Rick just kept staring, his eyes wide and showing too much white.

Scott found himself strangely detached from what he was seeing. He felt no horror, or even dismay — hell, he'd been more upset upon seeing Monty's ruined and bloody foot. One of his oldest friends was dying before his eyes ... and somehow he felt *nothing*. All he could do was stare at the wolf.

It was huge. Of course, that's why he had wanted to come hunting up here in the first place — to bag a large wolf — but somehow he hadn't been prepared for just how damn *big* it really would be. He had always pictured a wolf in his mind as just being a burly dog, figured it would look like an Alaskan Husky.

But that was not the case, not at all. It had similar markings to a Husky, and it certainly wasn't as big as the black bear he and Brandon had taken a shot at a few years ago. It was the way it had emerged from the shadows like a grey-and-white bolt of lightning, the ruthlessness of its strike, the cold, inhuman gleam in its eyes.

Its eyes ...

Dear God, is it looking *at me ...?*

Monty spasmed and twitched as the wolf jerked its head from side to side, tearing his flesh like fingers through wet sand. Patrick was screaming and Brandon was fucking with his rifle and Rick appeared to have pissed himself.

In the end, only one member of their party took decisive action.

Tanner jumped on the wolf. He could not reach its throat, so his poor, old jaws with their two or three missing teeth tore into the wolf's left ear.

The wolf, which had remained uncannily silent during its attack, released a deep-throated *yip!* that was half pain, half surprise. It pawed and scratched at Tanner, but it did not release Monty's throat.

Scott heard Brandon mutter, "Son of a bitch," before he shifted his grip on his rifle — clearly, he was experiencing some kind of jam — and moved forward to smash the stock into the wolf's head. "Hold him, Tanner!" he yelled as he raised the rifle high. "Hold that fucker still!"

The wolf finally let go of Monty as Tanner came close to tearing its ear off. One look told Scott that Monty was beyond help at this point — steam rose from his gushing, mangled esophagus, but it was just the heat of the blood hitting the cool air ... Monty had breathed his last.

Brandon brought the rifle down, intent upon cracking the wolf's skull.

And, just as swift and silent as its predecessor, a

second, darker wolf leaped into view and bit Brandon right on the ass.

That's when Scott laughed. For however long he might or might not live, Scott knew that he would always remain baffled and feel guilty about his reaction to what had happened — *he laughed*. He laughed as though he were watching some screwball comedy instead of death and dismemberment. Some part of him knew that it wasn't *really* funny, that laughing was a disturbing and potentially dangerous reaction to have to such an event ... but he laughed anyway.

Brandon screamed and dropped his gun. The second wolf, every bit as big and menacing as the first, pulled and shook its head. Brandon's pants slid down his legs, and a significant chunk of his ass muscle came with them. And the glob didn't just break loose — no, it peeled downward, tearing a trench of blood and flesh down onto the back of Brandon's thigh.

A shot was fired. Scott thought it had come from Patrick, because Rick was *still* just standing there ...

What, and you're *doing any better than he is?*

... and now he appeared to have shit his pants, too. Either way, it didn't matter, because the bullet didn't hit either of the wolves.

The first wolf had turned on Tanner. Its ear was a dangling mess on the side of its head, but that was the extent of Tanner's victory. The wolf had the smaller, older animal by the hind quarters now. Tanner was crying out in pain, but unlike Brandon, he was still *trying* to fight. He might have gotten another bite or two in there if a third wolf hadn't joined the fray at that moment. Tanner was dead in seconds.

Patrick fired again, and now Scott realized that he had not been shooting at either of the first two wolves to begin with — he was aiming for the myriad of wolves that now emerged from the gloom.

It's not that dark, Scott marveled, *so how did so many of them get this close without any of us seeing them? And why are they so damn* quiet?!

Indeed, except for the first wolf's reaction to Tanner's assault on its ear, the pack had not made a single sound. There were eight — no, *nine* — of them now, and not a peep. Patrick fired once more before they dragged him down, and another wolf was approaching Rick with caution, almost as though his *lack* of action were making the animal suspicious.

Finally, *finally*, Scott began to move. He raised his rifle, taking measured aim at the wolf creeping its way toward Rick. Monty was a goner. So were Tanner and Brandon, and probably Patrick. But the least his pathetic, laughing ass could do was save himself and Rick, so that they could come back up here with every—

A tenth wolf (or was it the eleventh?), its fur white as snow, leaped in from the side and clamped its teeth down on the barrel of Scott's rifle. He was thrown off balance, and his finger twisted out of the trigger guard before he could fire the weapon. There was a brief tug-of-war, and then the wolf had his gun. It jerked its head, much like the first had done while biting into Monty's throat, and smashed the rifle onto the ground with each downstroke. The weapon broke apart, the metal barrel ...

no no that's not right no it can't be that strong

... crushed between the animal's jaws. The wolf gave one final toss of its head, and the rifle clattered to the ground, wrecked and worthless.

Scott stepped back and waited for the inevitable. His finger was hurting from where the wolf had yanked it from the trigger guard, but he knew that soon this would be the least of his worries. He, too, would be dragged to the ground, torn ... limb ... from ...

The white wolf did not attack, did not pounce, did not strike. It just stood there, licking its chops as though to rid itself of the taste of the gunmetal. Its amber, merciless eyes shined in the perpetual twilight, and its ears were pressed forward, its nose twitching as it studied Scott with multiple senses.

But it did not attack.

Other wolves made their way towards him. Only Patrick still struggled against his two attackers, but his efforts were ineffectual — little more than death throes. Soon, more than a dozen wolves stood facing Scott.

And *still* they were silent. One or two of them were snarling at him, but they made not a sound. Not a fucking sound.

"What—?" Scott began, before his dry throat croaked out on him. He swallowed hard, and this time managed to ask, "What are you waiting for?"

He expected no answer, of course. And yet ... he did. Sort of. After all, *none* of this was normal. The trap, the silent attack, this large pack of wolves managing to slink within striking distance with only Tanner being the wiser for it.

"So answer me," Scott said aloud at the conclusion of

his thoughts. "What are you waiting for? Huh? Monty didn't have to give you an invitation, so what do you expect from *me*?"

The white wolf in the lead raised its head slightly ... and *smiled* at him.

No. No, no, no. That couldn't be it. Monty always insisted that Tanner could smile, but Tanner was a *dog*, damn it — dogs were domesticated and had spent enough time around Man to have *maybe* learned the meaning behind a smile. But a wolf? No fucking way.

And yet ...

One wolf off to the left, with blood around its mouth like terrible war paint, pawed at the ground and took a tentative step forward.

Scott raised his hands. At this point, he almost *wanted* them to attack — that, at least, was something to be expected from wild animals.

The white wolf glanced at the advancer, then back at Scott. Then he barked. Barked *loud*. The pitch was lower and the volume was much higher than Tanner's, but otherwise, it was just a bark.

Nevertheless, Scott flinched.

This seemed to please the wolf ...

Damn it, that doesn't make any sense!

... who panted for a second, then barked again, even louder still.

Then the wolf who had advanced a step barked. It wasn't as deep, but was every bit as loud.

Scott took a single step backward.

This excited the wolves as his vocal challenges had not. They still did not attack, but now more of them began to bark, and more, until finally the entire pack was yipping and yapping and barking in an enormous cacophony of savage joy.

Scott covered his ears, taking another step back, away from them.

The white wolf slapped at the ground with its forepaw, like a bull preparing to make a charge. But that wasn't it. It was telling Scott something else — he knew it, could feel it.

It was telling him to *run*.

Scott took another step back. The wolf pounded the ground again, barking even louder.

Two more retreating steps from Scott. The rest of the wolves jumped up and down in place, so damned excited, many of them now licking their bloody chops.

If I turn my back on them, if I run*, they'll take me down in a matter of seconds.*

And what other options do you have, Scotty my boy?

The white wolf threw its head back, high into the air ... and *howled*.

And Scott ran ...

Now, he was seconds away from camp. Seconds away from his still-loaded backup rifle. His breath was burning in his throat and his heart was threatening to burst, but he didn't care — all he could think about was getting to that rifle before the wolves reached him.

He was even forming a plan, of sorts: He would dive into his tent, but he would not zip the entrance shut behind him — he had no delusions about how long it would take them to tear through the polyester walls to get to him. He would seize his rifle, aim it at the opening ... and wait. They had been having fun at his expense, but he wasn't going to play their game anymore. No matter how they barked, howled, or clawed at the walls, he was going to just sit tight and wait. Sooner or later, they would come in after him. Without taking the time to bite their way through other places, only one, *maybe* two, could get through the entrance at a time. They would bottleneck, and there would be no way he could miss.

Once one or two were dead, the others would most likely back off, giving him a few seconds to add additional ammunition. *Then* he would zipper the front flap, and they could tear at the tent all they wanted. For once, this never-night would work to his advantage — between the full moon and the lasting twilight, he would be able to aim at their silhouettes. And if he misses once or twice? So what — he would be sitting on all the bullets he and Brandon had brought with them.

Past the beer cooler, past Monty's bedroll, past the crushed and crumpled remains of last night's beer cans.

Behind him, a wolf bumped the beer cooler aside — they were *that* close!

Almost there, almost there, almost there ...

Scott threw himself toward his tent, brushing the front flaps aside with his outstretched arms—

The flashpoint of the rifle blinded him, and the noise didn't do his ears any good, either. Neither of those things really bothered him, though. What did bother him, what *demanded* his undivided attention, was the bullet that pierced his right kneecap, ricocheted up through his thigh muscle, and exited up near his hip.

He tried to scream, but for some reason, it wouldn't

come out. All he managed to do was wheeze heavily, spit leaking from one side of his gaping mouth, as he clutched at his devastated leg, hopped on his good left leg for about two seconds, then collapsed in a heap before the tent that was to have been his saving shelter.

The two wolves that had been right on his heels skidded to a halt. They did not tear into him, but tumbled to one side, rolled over the ground and each other, and then came to rest that way — huddling over one another, panting from their run, watching Scott but nothing more.

Scott tried to scream again, but all he got was another wheeze, this one even messier with drool than the first. He expected the horrible burning in his knee to get worse, but instead it actually got better as his entire right leg went numb. Some small part of him recognized that the bullet must have caused severe nerve damage, probably permanent ... but since he wasn't going to be around much longer, that didn't really matter, did it?

But ... *what just happened?*

The flaps of his tent parted, successfully this time. From the darkness within emerged a woman. A naked woman, who was holding the very rifle that had been his goal.

"What ... the fuck ...?" Scott mouthed, though as with his screams, very little sound actually came out.

Once outside the tent, the naked woman stood, holding the rifle loosely in one hand. Two of the wolves, including the white wolf that had destroyed Scott's other rifle and set him upon his final run, padded their way over to the woman. The white wolf stood on her right, a red-furred wolf stood on her left, and all three joined in staring down at Scott's bleeding form.

Fucking tree-hugger hippie, Scott thought, *fucking Liberal. That* has *to be it. No wonder the wolves were acting so strange — she* trained 'em. They're her fucking pets.

That was the only explanation that occurred to Scott, the only one that he would *allow* himself to consider. Nothing else made sense. Suppose, just suppose, that there were something *else* going on here. Something not so easily explained. Then, according to every horror movie Scott had ever seen, this woman before him should be *gorgeous*, right? She should be a gorgeous witch, or devil-woman, or whatever she was.

But this woman was not gorgeous, and she was exposed enough for Scott to tell. She was ... *earthy* may be the best word, if you went for that sort of thing. Scott, personally, preferred his fantasy woman more of the Kim Basinger-Michelle Pfeiffer mold. *This* woman was dark, very thick, muscular rather than lean, athletic. She also looked pretty damn tall, although it was difficult for him to tell for certain from his vantage point on the ground.

"What ...?" he finally managed to say with any volume. He was beginning to feel very strange, and with the blood gushing from his leg, he knew that could not be a good sign.

The woman smiled, or was it a sneer? It was hard to tell on her almost-masculine face. She stepped forward, and the wolves followed by half the distance. She squatted next to him, her legs splaying wide — under other circumstances, Scott might have forgiven her average looks in appreciation for such a sexually-exposed pose. It did not seem to bother her in the least that he could see her private parts, that her full breasts were close enough for him to touch. The look in her eyes was part anger, part disgust ... but mostly, it was dismissive and apathetic.

"Hunter," she stated in a deep-ish voice that matched her body and face perfectly. She did not seem to be asking a question, or even making a statement. It was as though she had simply classified him.

Scott said nothing, but his eyes flickered toward the rifle in her hand.

The woman saw the look, and the anger and disgust swelled to take a larger role on the stage of her face. She stood, stepped one muscular leg over his chest, squatted once more ...

... and pissed on him.

Scott started to react as one would expect, but she whipped the rifle around so that the barrel stopped bare inches from his nose. Gritting his teeth, he remained still and silent as she urinated on him. What else could he do?

The wolves drew closer, their snouts sampling the aroma of her handiwork.

Scott turned away, thinking that surely *now* it would end.

The woman finished, but remained squatting over him.

Slowly, he looked back, and gasped.

She stared at him with the amber eyes of a wolf.

"Hunter," she said again, more dismissive than ever, "no more."

And she shot him in the face.

ONE

Lupe sighed, then bowed her back in an attempt to relieve her aching and stiffened muscles. Her effort was hardly successful.

It had been a long day, and a glance at her watch revealed that it was going to be longer still. She reminded herself that she had volunteered for this duty, to supplement her regular paycheck, and she tried not to think about how small a supplement it was.

But she had not become a nurse for the money — if that had been her goal, she would have taken the necessary courses to become a full M.D. She wanted to work *with people*, something that her disappointed doctor of a father had never failed to ridicule. Her mother gave her support, but it was very passive ...

Lupe shook her head. What was the point of mulling *that* over again? She must be more tired than she thought.

"Next," she called out, preparing her checklist for the next person in line, a person who was a *true* volunteer, and whom she therefore admired sight unseen.

"Afternoon, lass. I hope ye've been havin' a good day so far?"

Lupe looked up ... and her day got a whole lot better.

The man was *gorgeous*. Dark brown eyes, dark full hair, killer smile ... he looked like a guy-next-door version of the actor Hugh Jackman. And that Irish accent was to *die* for! His thick sideburns were a bit dated, but Lupe could forgive that in a second if it allowed her to get her hands on the thick muscles of his arms and chest.

Very nice, Lupe. Reeeeal professional.

Oh, shut it! When was the last time I had a date?

Good point.

Lupe closed her dropped jaw and reached for his paperwork. "I guess it's been fine so far," she fudged.

He handed the completed form to her and sat down. "Glad to hear it."

"So, Mister ...?" Her eyes seemed to take a long time to find the appropriate box — after all, it was only *right at the top*!

" 'Mabrey' is the last name. But please, call me *Sean*."

"All right ... Sean. I'm Lupe. Thank you so much for volunteering today."

"It's my pleasure, Lupe," he said around that wonderful smile.

She looked over his form, and again found herself momentarily too stupid to read it properly. "Have you donated blood to the Red Cross before?" she asked, even though she knew the answer was on there *somewhere*.

Damn, girl, keep it together, would you? He's not that good looking!

Yes, he is.

"I've donated before, but not to the Red Cross. I usually donate plasma to the Bachman Foundation."

Lupe thought for a moment, and was relieved that at

least *that* part of her brain was still functioning. " 'Bachman Foundation.' I've heard of them. They're new, aren't they?"

Sean smiled. "New, and old. It's a long story."

"You do understand that the Red Cross does *not* pay its blood donors—?"

"Oh, yes. But when I heard ye were goin' to be here at the Convention Center," he gestured around at the large meeting room in an off-handed manner, "I thought I might drop by, anyway. It's been a while since I gave blood, and I don't do it *just* for the money, ye see?"

"Oh, of course," she gushed.

"Besides, gettin' to spend time with an attractive young lady like *yerself* has already been payment enough." He smiled again, and she melted that much more.

"I, uh, I'll need to test a sample of your blood. We need to check your blood-iron levels, and so on. I'm sure they do the same thing at the Bachman Foundation?"

"Aye." He laid his arm on the small table between them, his hand palm-up.

She pulled on some latex gloves and took his hand in her own ... his large, masculine hand ...

What *was* the Red Cross' policy on using a donor's phone number for personal reasons?

She was just about to pose that very question to him — as a sort of half-joking ice-breaker, so to speak — when something changed. His smile faded, to be replaced by a very forlorn expression. It was surreal. Just seconds ago, he had been ... well, she had hoped that he had been flirting with her. Had she done something wrong?

"Sean ...?"

"Ye seem very nice, Lupe," he said through a heavy sigh. He hesitated, then added, "I'm sorry."

"You're 'sorry?' I don't understa—"

Whoooop! "Your attention, please!"

Lupe jumped, the alarm and loud speakers catching her completely off guard. Sean just sat there, looking sad.

"There is an emergency in the building. Please evacuate immediately." Whoooop! "Your attention, please ..."

The prerecorded voice continued its loop. All around the convention room, donors stirred as nurses moved to free them from their needles and tubing. The donors who had yet to reach that stage of the process meandered toward the doors; the woozy ones who had passed through it already helped one another. It wasn't until the actual smell of smoke wafted into the room that people started moving at a more-than-leisurely pace.

Shaking herself, Lupe pulled off the gloves. "Well, Sean, looks like we'll have to continue this at another time."

Sean smiled, but while it was still charming, it lacked its previous glow. He said nothing.

She looked around again and saw that several of the donors appeared shaky enough that they might faint. They needed help, but the smoke in the air — which she could now *see* — was causing more people to jump ship and clear out.

"Sean," she asked, now all business, "can you please help me get some of these people out of here? I hate to ask, but you look like a pretty strong guy and—"

"No problem, lass," he said, "I'll be right behind you."

Taking him at his word, Lupe moved. In seconds, she

was helping two people, one on each side, as they steadied themselves. Thank God no one had passed out yet ...

Sure enough, just the thought jinxed it. A pale, skinny man stumbled against one of the reclined chairs and fell. Lupe recalled that his blood-iron had been borderline, almost to the point of turning him away.

But damn it, she couldn't just abandon the people she was already helping!

"Sean?" she called, turning one way, then another. "Sean?!"

She did not see the Irishman at first. She was about to give up looking when she finally spotted him, halfway to the convention room door. He appeared to be carrying something, but it was too small to be an adult, and children were prohibited from donating blood. He hadn't been carrying anything when he approached her table, so what ...?

Just before he reached the door, he angled his body to slip past a couple of evacuees, and Lupe saw that he was carrying a large red and white cooler.

The blood supply! He's stealing *today's blood donations! What in the world—?!*

"Sean, *stop!*" she yelled at the top of her lungs, which startled the hell out of the people leaning against her.

He paused in the large doorway, turning back toward her for just a second — he still had that dejected expression on his face. He mouthed the words *I'm sorry* once more, and then he was gone.

Lupe wanted to run after him, to tackle him to the ground and kick him until he explained just what the *hell* this was all about ...!

Except that she couldn't. People were depending on

her.

But you could bet your ass she'd be stopping by the Bachman Foundation to ask a few question. Oh, yes — count on it!

*   *   *

Sean Mallory loaded the stolen Red Cross cooler into the trunk of his car. The plan had been executed with perfection, the smoke bomb igniting right on time. It could not have gone smoother.

And Sean hated every moment of it.

He didn't fear getting caught at this point. He had given a false last name, a false address, and the staff at the local Bachman Foundation had already been advised about this "Sean Mabrey" fellow who had been causing some trouble in the area — when the Red Cross inevitably made inquires there, they would find sympathetic concern, but no helpful information.

What Sean hated was the very *idea* of it — stealing donated blood from a charitable organization turned his stomach. But what else were they supposed to do? The Bachman Foundation was still getting on its feet in this world ... and Alistaire could only go so long without blood.

Such were the complications of working with a vampire who never took victims.

Sean drove out of the parking garage and headed for his next errand of "grocery" shopping, this time a far more conventional destination: The local supermarket, one complete with an old-fashioned butcher.

Two years had passed since he and Alistaire — and

later, Trey — had emerged into this world, a world very similar to but far more *mundane* than their home. They had good reason to believe that they were far from the only supernatural beings to "cross over," and so they had to tread boldly into this undiscovered country, determined to continue their mission against their own kind as they worked their way west.

Things, however, had not been that simple.

Alistaire had to start from scratch. His business relations in the old world had been cultivated for centuries, and had *evolved* into their modern-day equivalents. Kathy Schaumburg, the sweet young girl who was one of only a handful of people who knew what they really were and where they came from, had given them a very small amount of money when they parted ways, and Alistaire had helped himself to a little "nest egg" that Neil Carpenter's family had kept well hidden at their trailer home by a nearby lake.

Still, it was barely enough to keep them sheltered at first. They were constantly moving, not only for lack of funds, but also to make sure that their host bodies were not identified — both Neil Carpenter and Mark Hudson were wanted for questioning in relation to the havoc that Bishop, another vampire who crossed over, had wreaked.

Things got a little easier once they located Trey. Sean had come across a newspaper article about a Doctor Melissa Kramer, a hypno-therapist who had been using her craft to help heal the sick, or at least bring relief to the terminally ill. Alistaire had one of those "feelings" of his, and so they shadowed Doctor Kramer for a month or so. Sure enough, as always, Alistaire's instincts were spot-on, and the two of them "rescued" Trey when he emerged into the body of

Travis Bekele.

Having Trey around to share guard duty while Alistaire slept during the day allowed Sean to get even more odd-jobs, and reduced their need for unfortunate-but-necessary petty theft.

It was also a tremendous help that every time Sean transformed into his wolf or Alistaire into mist, after they reverted to their humanoid form ... they found themselves looking just the slightest bit *different*, less like their hosts, more like their old selves. It was a very small, subtle change, one that neither of them noticed until Trey pointed it out a few months after rejoining them.

They did not know if they would ever change completely into their old selves. But after all, as Alistaire believed was no mere coincidence, he and Sean had already borne some physical resemblance to Neil and Mark. The important thing was, they now both looked different enough that they could relax a bit from the fear of Carpenter or Hudson being recognized by happenstance.

So ... they had help from Trey, additional funds through Sean's occasional work and Alistaire's increasing grasp of this world's economics, and a growing cloak of anonymity.

After many months of floundering, they began to find their way.

But Sean always got sullen when, even after two years, he was *still* forced to resort to the occasional crime. He was grateful that these instances were getting fewer and further between, but it made him feel *dirty*.

Pulling into the supermarket parking lot, Sean forced his mind back to completing his errands. At least, until he got home.

He had decided that he and Alistaire needed to talk.

*   *   *

Sean drove the car into the driveway of their modest Southern California house and popped the trunk. Moments later, he balanced the grocery bags in one arm and the stolen cooler in the other — a heavy load, but one that any werewolf could handle. He could *not*, however, get to his house keys with such an encumbrance, so he was forced to knock on the front door with his knee.

Although the door did not open right away, he heard movement from within. That would be Trey, tearing himself away from cartoons or, even more likely, his newest love these days: The Internet.

While he waited, Sean glanced toward the setting sun; by his educated guess, Alistaire would be up and about within the next thirty minutes or so. During the summer, his partner was forced to "sleep late," to match the greater length of daylight hours. Sean was grateful that *that* sort of limitation was not a part of his own curse.

A shuffling at the door pulled his attention forward again. The locks were unbolted, slowly — one of *Trey's* curses was impaired manual dexterity. Finally, the door opened ... but only a crack. One milky eye appeared. Far from the first time, Sean wondered just how it was that Trey's vision was unaffected by what *looked* like the world's worst cataracts.

Trey's eye disappeared, only to be replaced by his lips. "You raaaaang ...?" he drawled.

Sean groaned. "Trey Matthews, as long as I live, I shall *always* regret introducing ye to *The Addams Family.*"

The zombie giggled in delight, just as Sean had known he would, and opened the door.

It had become a ritual for them. In spite of his semi-regular flashes of adult-level intelligence, Trey was, as a whole, very childlike, and that included a childlike fondness of *repetition*.

Sean didn't mind. In some ways, Trey was turning into the younger brother that Sean never had ...

But that made Sean think of his sister, Theresa — he cut his thoughts off there.

With Trey taking his share, the two carried their bizarre "groceries" to the kitchen: Human blood for Alistaire, beer for Sean, extra-strength deodorant for Trey, and pounds and pounds of raw meat for both Trey and Sean. Sean would be cooking his own portion a bit — unless he was in wolf-form, he preferred his meat served at least *rare* — whereas Trey could only tolerate it if it were as raw as it could come.

Of the members of their Triumvirate, Trey handled his curse (in his case, the craving of living, human flesh) with the greatest mastery. While Sean was in almost complete control most of the month, during the nights of the full moon he lost that control entirely. Likewise, while Alistaire's steel will had prevented him from ever "taking a victim" in the traditional sense, he was still very much dependent upon human blood — he could sustain himself on animal blood for short periods of time, but the longer he pushed it, the more out-of-control his inherent thirst became.

But Trey — the lucky bastard — had never displayed

any real danger of attacking a human for cannibalism. Maybe it was the same inner strength that had allowed him to break free from his voodoo master. Maybe it was the advantage of having experienced guides in Alistaire and Sean to "leapfrog" him into greater self-control.

Whatever it was, Trey had thus far proven content to gorge himself on raw beef. It *had* to be beef — early experiments had eliminated pork, poultry, or fish as a substitute — and it had to be bloody raw, but otherwise ... well, Trey left Sean feeling *envious* from time to time.

"Did the Bachman Foundation send any blood today?" Sean asked.

"No," Trey answered, putting their meat in the refrigerator (not the freezer; they couldn't let the blood dry up). "Sent a ... e-mail. Should come ... Mon-day."

"I hope it gets here on time for a change." He gestured toward the Red Cross cooler. "I hope it's a while before I have to do *that* shite again."

Trey jerked as though Sean had fired off a shotgun. "Ali-staire ... doesn't like it ... when you *swear*, Sean."

Sean sighed. "I know. I'm sorry, Trey. I shouldn't have said— said a bad word."

Trey nodded his agreement and returned to putting away the groceries.

Sean shook his head. He didn't exactly consider himself a ruffian, but living with Alistaire's religion and Trey's childlike temperament sometimes made him feel like the world's worst "potty mouth," as Trey would put it.

"But ye know," he began again, "I can't help but wonder just how many sick or injured people are suffering every time we steal blood like this."

"Ali-staire ... has to eat, Sean." Trey then stood still for a moment, a confused and concentrated look on his face. He turned to Sean and asked, "Or is it ... 'drink' ... for him?"

Sean chuckled. "That's okay, Trey. I knew what ye meant. I think either 'eat' *or* 'drink' works for vampires."

"Oh. Okay." He closed the refrigerator.

"But it's not just the moral dilemma, either," Sean continued once more. "Sooner or later, I'm going to get *caught*. And what if that happens on a day of the full moon? What if I'm sitting in some jail cell when night falls?"

"That's why ... Ali-staire ... makes you stay home ... on those days."

"Aye. Ye're right." He glanced at his watch. Alistaire would be up soon, and then he could take this argument up with him.

Not that he expected to get much further with Alistaire, because Trey *was* right, and he knew it. He just hated doing things like he did today. Hated it so much.

Trey left the kitchen, so Sean followed him back to the living room.

It wasn't a long journey. The house was small — the most they could afford for now, nothing like their townhouse in Pittsburgh. There was a living room, dining room (which was more of glorified "breakfast nook"), small kitchen, full bathroom, and one bedroom. Since Sean was the only one in their group who slept in the traditional sense, the bedroom was his. Trey, who *never* slept, spent most nights browsing the Internet. And Alistaire, of course, retreated during the day to his coffin, which had been one of their biggest expenses in the beginning. The coffin rested in the crawlspace under the house, an entrance to which Sean had cut into the floor in the bedroom hallway shortly after their arrival here. That *same* coffin also served as Sean's impromptu prison on the nights of the full moon, until they could again afford a house with a storage cellar. It was more physically uncomfortable, and claustrophobic, than Sean would prefer, but it beat the alternative of breaking loose and mauling some innocent victim.

Before they could settle, Sean's enhanced hearing picked up the interior latches on the coffin being opened. He glanced at the clock, then at the windows — even with the blinds closed, he could still see the faintest hint of evening glow. Alistaire must have awakened and grown weary of being stuck in his coffin for the long summer hours. But with the dusk still in evidence, he would be groggy and sluggish for a while yet.

With a gesture, Sean led Trey into the hallway. He popped the surreptitious latches along the baseboard, and Trey opened the trap door.

"Thank you," Alistaire said when the door opened. He tried to pull himself out of the coffin and into the house, but he couldn't seem to get himself coordinated. *"Could one of you please assist me?"*

"Uh-huh," Sean mused aloud, "just as I thought. You're up too early."

Alistaire glanced at him as Trey helped him up and to his feet, then offered a self-depreciating grin. *"It is not just that, though I admit the lingering presence of the sun is not helping matters."*

"What is it, then?"

"I consumed the final ration of our current blood supply this morning before retiring. It has proven ... insufficient." He looked to Sean, a subtle pleading in his eyes. *"I sincerely hope today's operation was a success...?"*

Sean nodded. "It was. The cooler is in the kitchen."

Some of the tension seeped from Alistaire's shoulders. *"Thank G-God. And thank* you, *my friend."* He smiled and hurried down the hallway toward the kitchen.

Trey looked at Sean, who in turn rested his hands on his hips in annoyance. "I know, I know. Don't say a word..."

Here he had been moaning and groaning, both to himself and to Trey, about how difficult it was to steal from the Red Cross and wrestle with his conscience ... forgetting just how much *Alistaire* willingly endured in order to keep these instances as far apart as possible, specifically *because* he knew how much it bothered Sean to commit these crimes.

Yes, Sean now felt like a real ass — he didn't need Trey to point it out for him.

Honoring Sean's wishes, Trey returned to the living room without comment. Alistaire was in the kitchen now; Sean could hear him sifting through the donor bags and, a moment later, caught the scent of human blood in the air — so different from the cattle blood in the butcher's wares. He knew that Alistaire preferred a bit of privacy when he fed, so he stayed put.

Sean found himself feeling a bit lost now; he had been gearing up for a serious "No more" conversation with Alistaire, but he couldn't bring that up now. But as much as he had been dreading having a row with his friend, he now felt almost *disappointed*. How daft!

"Sean ...?" called Trey. "Can you ... come here?"

Eager for a distraction from his own absurdity, Sean stepped into the living room. "Aye?"

Trey sat in front of their computer, hunched over his keyboard and staring at the monitor. He two-finger typed a few words before answering. Whatever he was looking at, it really had his interest. "Someone ... sent a link ... to my blog."

"What is a 'blog'?"

Sean glanced over his shoulder, too familiar with how impossibly quiet Alistaire could move to be startled. "An Internet diary. Don't worry; Trey doesn't give away anything about us."

"Ah," was Alistaire's only remark. Although Alistaire had proven quite adaptive to the technological changes he had witnessed over the centuries, Sean knew that the Internet still boggled his mind a little. All Alistaire needed to know was that Trey's amateur, online sleuthing had turned up the trail of a legitimate vampire more than once (amidst *hundreds* of dead-ends, of course) — beyond that, he trusted the details to his two, more modern-minded friends.

"What did ye want to show us, lad?"

" 'nother blog ... from Alas-ka ..."

"What about it?"

"Looks like ... there might be ... were-wolves up there."

Sean stiffened. While vampires were a sadly common problem, they rarely encountered werewolves. Lycanthropes were able to blend in most of the month, and often went to painstaking lengths to avoid leaving living victims, even if it meant hunting them down *after* the full moon to finish the job. Vampires took similar precautions, but since the masters loved to have servants to lord over, their kind still "procreated" far too often. Trey once compared them to cockroaches, and Alistaire did not disagree.

"What does it say?"

Trey was clicking the mouse now. "There's a ... doctor up there ... who thinks he has ... were-wolves." Another Internet window popped up. Trey leaned forward and read some more.

Sean's instinct was to push Trey aside and read for himself, but Alistaire's calming hand on his shoulder held him back. *"Trey, would you mind terribly if Sean were to take your seat? This is, after all, his area of expertise."*

Trey swivelled his chair around to look at them, confused — Sean and Alistaire usually let him handle everything online. But then that hidden spark of intelligence flared, and he understood. "Sure ..." The big man lumbered up out of the chair and let Sean take his place.

Sean's attention came into sharp focus as he read, his entire body tense. Forgotten were the stolen blood and the lovely Lupe, the theft and feelings of guilt. This was business.

The doctor in question kept his name to himself, which was common enough — after all, who in their right minds would go blathering about the supernatural in the twenty-first century? If anything, this lent credibility to the man's account.

The doctor worked somewhere up in northern Alaska

— some towns were mentioned, but Sean was not familiar with any of them. Over the past few months, there had been a stunning increase in the number of wolf attacks. Contrary to popular belief, wolves tended to be quite timid of humans — why would they bother tangling with such large prey when there were plenty of smaller mammals upon which they could feed? Wolves would normally have to be starving (or ill in some manner) to behave otherwise.

Therein lay the doctor's bafflement. Wolf attacks had increased over one-thousand percent since the beginning of the year; even more shocking was that they were all *fatal*. The fact that the majority of the victims were poachers kept many of the locals from shedding too many tears, but the Alaskan officials were tearing their hair out. The very questionable decision had been made to *cover up* the situation for now, as summer was by far Alaska's largest tourist season. Every family or group of families were being led to believe that their loved ones were the *only* ones recently killed, as though this were a freak situation, a thousand-to-one tragedy.

According to the doctor, it was a lot like the movie *Jaws* — the authorities refused to "close the beaches," so to speak — only the dark secret involved wolves rather than a shark. And a lot more deaths.

Even with his anonymity, the man never actually said the word "werewolf" — that summation had come from Trey's faceless online friend who sent him the link. In fact, the first four paragraphs were just a straightforward, off-the-record warning to any or all tourists who happened to read it. Nothing suspicious or questionable, just a Good Samaritan trying to do what he felt was best.

About midway through his blog entry, he started making hints between the lines. He observed how fascinating it was that the majority of the killings took place during the full moon. He commented on the wolves' "uncanny intelligence" in evading traps as the local authorities *tried* to hunt them down as surreptitiously as possible.

Finally, he marveled on the biggest mystery of all: How forensic evidence insisted that a number of the wolves had been fired upon, and most likely struck, by hunting rifles during many of these attacks ... and yet not a single dead or even *injured* wolf had been found. Canine blood with some "unusual qualities" had been identified over and over, and yet the trails always ran out without leading to any carcasses.

For the sign-off, which was probably what prompted Trey's friend to send it his way, the man suggested that "if his old Russian grandmother were still alive," she would tell him and everyone to start taking silver jewelry and melting it down into knives and bullets. There was no "LOL" or winking-face graphic included with this final statement.

"Well?" Alistaire finally prompted him after he had read the blog a second time. *"What do you think, Sean?"*

Instead of answering his German friend, Sean swivelled his chair around to face Trey.

"How do we contact this man?"

Two

Arthur Petrov, the medical examiner in charge of the recent wolf attacks, gazed longingly over his glasses at the bottle of bourbon sitting on top of his office filing cabinet. He needed a drink, he didn't think he had *ever* needed a drink more than right now ... but that didn't change the fact that he was still on duty. He was treading on thin ice with Caster from the state police as it was; the last thing he needed was to be caught inebriated, however slightly, on the job.

Two things were contributing to his stress. The first was that damned, silly blog he had posted the evening before. He *had* been drinking then, heavily; if he'd had his wits about him, he never would have given in to such silly notions — to think that a man of science could even *consider* his dear-but-superstitious grandmother's nonsense! He kept his blog identity anonymous, thank God, but he still felt foolish this morning and deleted it as soon as he logged back on. Unfortunately, he saw that a number of people had already read it, but there was nothing he could do about that now.

The other thing stressing him out right now was the latest victims they had brought in, something that not only changed the pattern they had been seeing, but gave even *more* fodder to his already nagging imagination.

The remains of five men and a dog had been discovered early this morning. The postmortem suggested they had been dead for approximately one week.

Sometime during the last full moon, his grandmother's voice whispered.

Hush! he scolded it.

In the days they had lain out there, a lot of scavengers had taken their taste, but it was still very evident that they were victims of yet another wolf attack, especially that poor dog. Everything about this latest slaughter was the same ... except one of these victims had been *shot*.

There were other oddities, of course — the foremost being those obscene spikes one of the victims had buried in his foot. *Those* kinds of bizarre twists had been evident since the beginning, and it was one of the many inexplicable details that had Caster angry and Arthur spooked.

But for one of the victims to be killed by *gunshot* was new. He had been shot twice — once in the leg and once in the face. Caster was already pushing theories about the hunters turning on one another before the animals attacked, but that did not sit well with Arthur. The rest of the man's party had been assailed a respectable distance from their camp—

A knock sounded outside, and his office door opened without Arthur's reply.

Thank God I didn't indulge in the bourbon.

Raymond Caster appeared, his scowl firmly in place. Without any greeting, he demanded, "Have you finished those reports yet?"

"Not yet."

"What the fuck is taking so long?"

Against his better judgement, Arthur felt his anger rise. "Well, Mister Caster, I know that it may seem to you that by now I could just cut-and-paste the results from my *many* other reports, but I'm afraid it doesn't work that—"

"Watch your attitude, Doctor Petrov," Caster snapped. "I'm getting enough heat over this without having to put up with lip from you."

Arthur swallowed his ire. He could tell just from looking at the man that he wasn't sleeping well, and even in the summer, it was too cool this far north for him to be sweating like he was.

"I'm sorry," he said with sincerity. "I'll have the reports finished soon."

"What are you listing as cause-of-death for Scott Gerrard?"

Arthur took a deep breath. He removed his glasses and polished them with his tie, to avoid looking at Caster as he answered, "For the time being, I'm sticking with 'Death by Misadventure'."

Caster stared at him for a long, uncomfortable moment. They were both on uncertain ground here, as Caster's desire to log Gerrard's death as some sort of manslaughter was contradictory to his *other* directive of keeping this whole insane mess quiet.

Finally, at length, he grunted, "Fine. Send 'em over when they're done," and left.

Arthur slumped back into his chair and replaced his glasses. *Death by Misadventure?* It was a stretch, and they both knew it. If Gerrard had fallen, or succumbed to hyperthermia, or starved, or any of a dozen other deaths that claimed campers every year, then maybe ... but he had been shot and killed, and *then* the wolf had torn into him.

Wolf, not wolves.

Arthur shuddered, and forced himself back to his computer. His eyes flickered to the bourbon once again, but he compromised by promising himself another night of hard drinking in the privacy of his own home.

Two nights in a row. He hadn't done *that* since he was an undergrad at college.

Christ, this business would be the death of him.

*　　*　　*

Later, much later than he would have preferred, Arthur turned off the light and locked his office door. He had emailed the damned reports to Caster — the policeman would bitch about his not delivering hard copies personally, but right now he didn't care. When this business all came out into the open, and he had no doubt that it eventually would, he would be lucky to *only* lose his job. That would mean moving on, probably leaving Alaska altogether. As much as he dreaded returning to the lower forty-eight, he would not mind putting a little distance between himself and this insanity.

Arthur's house was barely a mile away, so he frequently walked during the warmer months. This time he regretted having done so — driving his car would have meant getting home, and drunk, that much sooner — but there was nothing to be done about it. Zipping his coat and picking up his briefcase, he stepped out into the gloom.

And that's all it was at this time of year: Gloom. The white nights were upon them. Still, with the sun low on the horizon and the moon waning, there were enough shadows to go around.

Arthur was halfway home when the strangest feeling washed over him. His pace slowed as the hairs on the back of his neck stood on end. His recent considerations notwithstanding, Arthur was not given to superstition, and so therefore felt more *bewildered* by the sensation than anything. Had he heard something, or seen something in the corner of his eye? What could trigger such an unpleasant feeling?

He looked around, but saw no one. This did not surprise him, as it was late and Danny's bar lay in the opposite direction from the coroner's office. He saw a single set of taillights retreating down the boulevard, but beyond that ... nothing.

So why did he feel as though he were being watched?

Shaming himself for giving in to even *more* silly notions, he continued on his way ... for about five steps.

The feeling was growing stronger.

"Hello?" he called out. Then, in an attempt to seem less vulnerable, he set down his briefcase, made a show of adjusting his watch, and asked as casually as he could, "Can you please tell me what time it is ...?" He hoped that whoever was there would believe that he had already seen them, that their stealth was pointless.

It didn't work; silence was his only answer. And yet, he felt more certain than ever that someone *was* watching him.

Picking up his briefcase, he continued on his way.

Then, just as he stepped off the curb into the next cross-street, Arthur spun around. He expected to see someone ducking out of sight behind a parked car or between houses. Perhaps it would even turn out to be Raymond Caster, tailing him for God only knew what reason.

But what he saw unnerved him far worse than any human pursuit.

At the other end of the block, standing openly in the street and displaying no inclination to dart out of sight, was a white wolf.

For several long seconds, Arthur just stared. It was the single most surreal moment of his life. Then he began to doubt his senses. After all, how could this be? A wolf, this far into territory dominated by humans, just *standing there*, staring at him? He blinked hard, then adjusted his glasses with his free hand.

Nope. Still there. Eyes locked on him, ears forward.

Perhaps it wasn't even a wolf. It was a good distance away, and Arctic summer or not, the light was not ideal. Maybe it was someone's Husky, or even one of those Husky-wolf hybrids; they often had white fur. Just someone's dog, sneaking out of its yard and wandering the streets, no more curious about him than it would be *any* passerby. Yes, he was sure that's all it was.

The big wolf took a single step forward.

Whimpering, Arthur turned and ran. He ran as hard and as fast as he could.

He hated himself for running, hated Caster for putting so much pressure on him, even hated his superstitious grandmother for ever putting foolish notions into a child's head. He was a grown man, a doctor who had fled to

Alaska when his marriage failed because he had always loved Nature. And now here he was, running away from a lone wolf like a madman.

But whether he believed his grandmother's stories or not, *something* had been making the local wolves aggressive, far more aggressive than they had ever been.

Arthur ran.

By the time his house came into view, he was gasping and wheezing. He had already fished his keys out of his coat pocket, but now that sanctuary was within sight, he began to feel foolish again.

Slowing down, he looked behind him.

The white wolf loped after him, not twenty yards behind.

Yelping, Arthur surged forward again, adrenaline shot afresh into his veins. But it did not matter; casual pace or not, the wolf would overtake him long before he could get into the house.

He acted without thought, which, for all he knew, saved his life. He used his key chain remote to unlock the doors of his car in the driveway, threw open the back door because it was closer, and launched himself into the backseat. He slammed the door shut, sealing himself in just as the wolf reached him.

Nearly choking as he struggled to draw breath into his exhausted lungs, Arthur stared out at the creature which had chased after him, however half-heartedly, for half a mile.

The wolf paced a little, sniffing at the ground and along the seam of the car door. It chuffed once or twice ... then stood up on its hind legs. Resting its forelegs against the glass, it stared through the window at Arthur.

Arthur was near tears now. Any self-chastisements about his education and grounded beliefs were forgotten. He felt like a terrified child, hiding under his blankets and knowing with total certainty that a monster was waiting to eat him. If anything, this was worse, for he could *see* the monster — it was not faceless, nor was it confined to his imagination. It was real, it was big, and *it was looking at him.*

"Go away!" Arthur yelled, his voice cracking with fear. "Go away, damn you!" He thumped the door with his fist. "Go out, get out of here!"

The wolf thought little of his impotent defiance. It continued to appraise him with cold, amber eyes. It was not even panting from its easy pursuit. It was as though it had turned into a furry statue.

Arthur's own breath was beginning to fog the windows, which caused further panic. What would happen if the glass fogged to the point he could no longer see the wolf? As unnerving as its stony gaze was, at least he knew exactly where it was. If the windows all fogged up, the wolf could sneak around to another door and wait for him there. How long could he wait out here in the cold before he *had* to make a break for the house ...?

It never occurred to Arthur to climb into the front seat, start the car, and *drive* away. He could only sit paralyzed in the backseat, clutching his briefcase in his arms like a security blanket, watching the wolf watching him.

After what felt like hours, the wolf made its first movement: It licked its nose.

Arthur cringed away as though it had bared its teeth and tried to bite him.

Upon seeing this, the wolf cocked its head to one side ... and *grinned* at him. People could say what they will, make whatever arguments they might want, it didn't matter. To his dying day, Arthur would know the truth — the goddamn thing had *grinned* at him; a mocking grin, to show just what a little man it thought he was.

Then, at long last, the wolf pushed away from the car and repeated its casual lope down the street, this time away from his house. If it had just disappeared into the shrubs or trees, Arthur might have stayed there all night, certain that it was lying in wait. But it remained quite visible, strolling away back down the center of the boulevard.

When it was almost out of sight, Arthur scrambled from his car and hurried into his house. Even so, part of him half-believed that the wolf would return with supernatural speed and eat him after all.

*   *   *

Arthur was on his third glass of bourbon, and his hands were still shaking. He was drinking so quickly that he already felt a heavy buzz, but it wasn't really helping — if anything, it was prompting his experience to take on an even more *ominous* quality as he replayed it over and over in his mind.

He had turned on his computer out of habit, but he wasn't really interested in browsing the Web just now. He wanted to calm down. He wanted to feel *safe*, damn it! He finished his glass and was pouring his forth indulgence when he noticed that someone was attempting to Instant Message him.

Arthur stared at the online identity the user had chosen, then barked an ugly guffaw.

IRISHLONCHANEY wants to chat with you, it said.

Arthur's first impulse was to hit the Ignore button ... well, that wasn't entirely true — his *first* impulse was to knock the monitor off the top of his desk, but luckily, he wasn't that drunk yet.

Without further consideration, Arthur typed out an unceremonious reply, then took another long draw on his bourbon.

ALASKADOC111 writes: What do you want?

Arthur kept drinking as several long minutes passed without a response. The icon showed that the person on the other end was still online, but perhaps they had stepped away from their computer. After all, it was late here, and Arthur had no idea where this "Irish Lon Chaney" might be located. It didn't really matter — he had planned on getting drunk again tonight, so he might as well do it at his computer as opposed to his living room couch.

Then, IRISHLONCHANEY writes: I want to help with your wolf problem.

If Arthur had read this message an hour ago, he would have groaned and rolled his eyes and kicked himself once again for ever writing that stupid, stupid blog, then thanked God that he kept his name anonymous.

But that was before the wolf chased him into the backseat of his car, before it *grinned* at him.

ALASKADOC111 writes: How can you help?

IRISHLONCHANEY writes: I am something of an expert on the subject.

Now Arthur *did* groan. He had returned to the point of

indulging his grandmother's beliefs — he had *not*, however, gotten so far as to accept that some werewolf-hunting Van Helsing was sending him Instant Messages.

But then, what other response had he really expected from that goddamn blog ...?

He typed his reply, stabbing the keys in anger.

ALASKADOC111 writes: Don't waste my time. We have a *serious* problem here. Go live out your fantasies somewhere else.

Satisfied, he dragged the cursor over to Logoff.

IRISHLONCHANEY writes: The alpha doesn't share prey.

Arthur froze.

This was a joke. It had to be. Or maybe it was Caster's way of teaching him a lesson? So few people knew the details ...

But his ID was *anonymous*. Sure, he wasn't so naive as to think that there weren't ways of tracing his location or cracking his IP address. But why would anyone have bothered to do that?

ALASKADOC111 writes: What do you mean?

IRISHLONCHANEY writes: There is always a victim who has been eaten by one, *and only one*, wolf. The alpha.

Normal wolves share prey with the whole pack, Arthur thought. *He couldn't have learned anything else from any book or video.*

ALASKADOC111 writes: And how would we know that?

IRISHLONCHANEY writes: Don't tell me you haven't made teeth casts from the bites.

Arthur wanted to laugh. He wanted to go to sleep and forget this whole mess. He wanted to tell this stranger to fuck off and to block him from further online chats. He wanted to tell his dead grandmother that he loved her but that she was full of shit, that's all there was to it.

He wanted to walk home from work tomorrow night without looking over his shoulder for a stalking white wolf. He wanted to feel safe.

He wanted the killings to stop.

ALASKADOC111 writes: Can you really help?

IRISHLONCHANEY writes: Yes.

ALASKADOC111 writes: How?

IRISHLONCHANEY writes: I and two friends can be there in about a week. We will need your help arranging for the receipt of a large crate. We will also need as few questions asked as possible.

ALASKADOC111 writes: This is crazy. This is insane.

IRISHLONCHANEY writes: You have been seeing "crazy" things for months now, haven't you?

A long pause, then, ALASKADOC111 writes: Yes.

IRISHLONCHANEY writes: Hang in there. Help is on the way.

Another long pause, then, ALASKADOC111 writes: Thank you.

IRISHLONCHANEY writes: My name is Sean Mallory. And you are ...?

Now Arthur paused for a *very* long time. If he answered this, he would be committed. There would be no turning back.

In the end, he compromised by giving only the Russian

version of his first name; he figured his grandmother would find it fitting.

ALASKADOC111 writes: Artur.

IRISHLONCHANEY writes: Pleased to meet you, Artur. I will be in touch again very soon.

And with that, "Irish Lon Chaney" a.k.a. Sean Mallory logged off.

THREE

"All I am saying, Sean, is that I would have preferred to have discussed *this matter first, before you committed us."*

Sean said nothing, merely grunted. His back was to Alistaire as he packed his duffle bag. He knew that it was a little early to be packing his personals; they still faced the cumbersome duty of arranging the transport of Alistaire's coffin. That would be neither easy nor cheap — moving freight on a moment's notice was never advisable.

As if reading his mind, Alistaire said, *"We cannot financially support this course of action at this time."*

"I don't think the shape-shifters are going to wait until our next payday," Sean quipped.

"If they are *shape-shifters."*

Sean turned to face him. "Are ye willin' to take that risk?"

"I 'take that risk' all the time. I discovered centuries ago that if I were to hunt down every single *report of vampire activity, I would run in endless circles. I deal with those which lie within my grasp, but I only relocate when I have thoroughly cleansed an area, or when I am* absolutely certain *that a serious infestation has germinated*

somewhere else."

Sean bristled. "If there *is* a whole pack of werewolves up in Alaska, it will be only the *fourth* pack we have ever encountered. Ye don't think *that* is cause for a temporary 'relocation'?"

"If this doctor, Artur, is correct in his assessments, then yes. But I fear his word is precious little to—"

"Fine." Sean returned to his packing. "I'll go alone. Ye can stay here with Trey. I'll deal with it myself."

"Sean—"

"Ye can just wait down here until a *vampire* rears its ugly head, in which case I'm sure ye'll be all over it—"

"Sean!"

Sean finally closed his mouth and turned back to his friend. Alistaire maintained his usual poker face (after all, he'd had half-a-millennium to perfect it), but Sean had known him long enough now to glimpse the hurt behind the German's eyes.

Sean's shoulders sagged. "Damn ... I'm sorry, Alistaire."

Alistaire blinked. *"There is no need to apologize. But an explanation would be appreciated."*

"What do ye want me to say?"

"I want you to tell me why you are so vexed."

Sean returned to his packing once more. "Look, we deal with vampires all the time, but we don't encounter werewolves nearly as often. And yes, I *know* that is a good thing. But they *are* out there, usually ending up in the wilds, and we hardly ever deal with them because we're always in the *cities* where the vampires so love to prey."

"So you feel dissatisfied with our chosen hunting

grounds."

Sean did not answer at first. He finally zipped up his bag, then folded his arms as he sat on the bed. *"Un*satisfied would be a better way to put it ... but aye, that is the way I feel."

"I see." Alistaire mused over this for a moment. *"And there is nothing else driving you toward this action?"*

"What do ye want me to *say*, Alistaire? That I've been restless since we came to this world? That I *hate* some of the actions we've taken, no matter how necessary? That I miss our old lives, and the blokes I used to drink with on Friday nights in Pittsburgh? That I can't even send a postcard home, because no one back in *this* Ireland would know who I am? And that maybe, just maybe, I *want* there to be werewolves up there so that I can take out my frustrations on something *other* than a bloodsucker? Is *that* what you want me to say?"

When he was certain that Sean had run out of steam, Alistaire replied, *"Yes, I believe all of that would be sufficient."*

Sean gawked at Alistaire for about two seconds before he broke down and smiled. With a small chuckle, he said, "Ah, Alistaire, ye hide yer sense of humor so well, I sometime forget that ye have one."

Alistaire, too, smiled. *"I have my moments."*

"So ..." Sean hesitated, uncertain where to go from here. Now that his huff had passed, he felt childish for having taken it out on his friend. He finally settled for asking, "Now that I've 'confessed,' can we go to Alaska?"

To Sean's relief, Alistaire nodded. *"That was never in*

doubt. I only ask that you be as forthcoming in the future when you select a spontaneous course of action."

"I promise to try."

"Fair enough.   I will contact the Bachman Foundation first thing tomorrow evening and request an emergency transfer of funds—"

"It is ... over ...?"

Alistaire and Sean turned to see Trey peeking around the doorway from the hall. Sean asked, "Is what over, Trey?"

"Are you guys ... done fighting?"

Sean and Alistaire shared a guilty look — they knew that Trey reacted poorly to any perceived tension between them (which, thankfully, was rare). Sometimes it prompted one of his child-like tantrums, but today it incited dread and sadness. Definitely the response that tugged more firmly at the heartstrings.

"Aye, Trey. We're all done fighting now."

"I will go with him," Alistaire told Sean sotto voice before moving out into the hallway. While Sean would be forced to soothe Trey with words alone, Alistaire could use his *influence* to calm him, one of the few vampire "gifts" which Alistaire admitted to appreciating.

Sean sighed with relief, glad that Alistaire had dropped the subject without pushing him further. Not that he had *lied*; everything he said had been true. He had just avoided, as always, the subject of Theresa—

Once again, Sean cut off his own thoughts.

Four

Arthur Petrov paced, partially to keep warm but mostly to quell his nerves. It wasn't working.

What am I doing here? he asked himself. *Seriously, what in the* hell *am I doing here?!*

Days after his "wolf" scare and free from the influence of alcohol, Arthur regretted every second of the past week — from writing that stupid blog, to allowing someone's loose dog to frighten him, to getting drunk and answering some whacko's request to chat, to actually following said whacko's instructions of arranging local transportation and lodging ... and finally, to not *canceling* these arrangements when he'd had ample opportunity to do so.

And *now*, here he was: Waiting at what served as the local airport (hours after he should have been home), waiting to receive that whacko, Sean Mallory — the Irish Lon Chaney himself — and a friend and "large crate."

What the hell am I doing *here?!* he asked himself once more.

You are here, Artur, answered his grandmother's voice, a voice he had been hearing often of late, *because you know that wasn't a "loose dog" that chased you the other night.*

"Shut up, Grandma," he muttered under his breath.

Then Arthur heard the first sound of the approaching prop plane. It drifted away as the winds shifted, but when it returned a few seconds later, it was more distinct.

For better or for worse, there was no turning back now.

Mallory had been a bit perturbed when he learned that no major airlines flew this far north, but Arthur had assured him that private planes made the run on a consistent basis — in light of recent events, they had been arriving with even more regularity than usual. Arthur didn't know what was so important about this crate that Mallory insisted on dragging along with him, but he had done as instructed and made sure to arrange for an airplane that was large enough to accommodate it.

As the plane came into sight on its final approach (which for these prop jobs meant a single bank around the nearest mountains and then straight in), Arthur tossed another nervous glance over his shoulder toward town. Part of him kept expecting the police to appear, ready to arrest him for something like Obstruction of Justice — Arthur didn't know the technical definition, but he was sure Castor would frown upon his bringing in bounty hunters, or *whatever* Mallory called himself.

The plane touched down, kicking up a light trail of mud behind it. It swerved a bit as it hit a slick spot, then straightened out and slowed its way over toward the small hanger. The pilot waved a greeting to Arthur, who waved back in turn. The two men only knew one another in passing, but since Arthur had arranged this little run, the pilot was inclined to be friendly for his latest meal ticket. The plane passed Arthur before coming to a stop, but he wasn't inclined to follow after it — rational or not, he wanted to procrastinate this face-to-face as long as possible.

The engine was still running at a low RPM, but the side door soon unfolded to the ground. Arthur saw the pilot's hand appear briefly in what he assumed was an "after you" gesture, then the first stranger appeared. He was a handsome, white fellow, but Arthur's first real impression was that he had not dressed for the climate; he wore only jeans and a windbreaker. Many people from lower in the hemisphere failed to appreciate how chilly northern Alaska could be, even in the summer ... but then again, if this man was really Irish — as in *from* Ireland — then he would be no stranger to cool weather.

The man looked around, spotted Arthur, and waved much as the pilot had. Arthur returned the gesture and, with reluctance, marched over to greet him.

"Artur, I presume?" the man asked as they came together, and even that brief phrase revealed enough of his accent to confirm that he *was*, in fact, from Ireland.

"Yes. You're Mister Mallory?"

"Aye," he answered with an endearing grin. He offered his hand. "And please call me 'Sean'."

Arthur accepted the handshake, but did not agree to the familiarity. Mallory absorbed this with a nod, then glanced back toward the plane. The pilot and a large black man were unloading the wooden crate that had caused such a hassle all the way up here. Arthur was again curious as to what in the world made it worth all this trouble, but as before, his desire to maintain *some* distance from this situation won out — with all the trouble he might be in already, he wanted to hold onto all the plausible deniability that he could.

The doctor in Arthur, however, could not help but notice the black man's sickly pallor. He wore sunglasses and a woolen cap pulled low over his ears, his coat was zipped all the way to the top, and his hands were covered in gloves, but Arthur could still see enough of his cheeks and neck to feel a wave of concern.

Mallory turned back and noted Arthur's attention. "I'm afraid Trey doesn't fly very well," he explained without prompting. "That's another reason I was leery of the propeller plane. He'll start feelin' better soon, now that we're back on the ground."

Arthur looked at Mallory, who stared back with a wry smile on his lips and a bland look in his eye. Something about the whole bit felt *rehearsed* to Arthur, as though Mallory had been waiting for the key moment to recite this spiel. After all, Arthur might just as well have still been staring at the large crate, so why assume that he was noticing the black man's sallow complexion?

Just drop it, Arthur. Stay out of it for as long as you can.

"Well," he said finally, "I hope he gets to feeling better soon."

"Aye," Mallory nodded. He glanced over at the sun, which hung low in the sky, then frowned and asked, "Beg your pardon, Artur, but what time is it?"

Arthur didn't need to look at his watch — he'd been stealing glances at it every minute for the last half-hour. "It's a little after eleven o'clock."

Mallory looked at him, then back at the sun. "I, uh, don't ..."

"It's the white nights. Normal for the season this far

north. The sun'll stay low for another couple of hours, pass behind those mountains, then climb back up. In the middle of winter, we barely get any *daylight* at all."

Mallory's expression grew very taut. Arthur knew that many visitors found the white nights unsettling — what could be more unnatural than the loss of day and night? — but Mallory looked as though he had just been told that a close friend had cancer.

"Mister Mallory, are you all right ...?"

Mallory hesitated a heartbeat too long before replying, "I'm fine. I ... suppose I should have done a little more research about this part of the world."

"Is there a problem ...?" *Like we need any more!*

"No, no problem," Mallory insisted, this time a little too quickly. "My *other* partner, the one who'll be followin' us up here on his own ... he's, uh, very light-sensitive. Turned him into a real night owl, if you follow me." He chuckled, but it sounded forced. "I don't think he'll be too happy, missin' out on real nightfall."

"Ah. Yes, I understand." But he didn't, not at all. *Oh, God ... they* are *just a bunch of kooks!*

Mallory stared over at the anemic disk on the horizon for a moment longer, then shook himself. "Right. Did ye arrange for the truck like we discussed?"

"Yes. It's right around the corner of the hanger. I'll drive it over."

Arthur ran back to the truck a little faster than necessary.

*   *   *

"Stupid," Sean muttered as he followed behind Artur's car down the bumpy dirt road. "How could I be so bloody *daft*?" He glanced out the driver's side window at the sun, low on the horizon but still clearly visible.

The pickup truck was old, and it creaked and squeaked over every rise and dip. The crate in the back was heavy enough to stay put, but Sean kept checking the rearview mirror to make sure it wasn't sliding around. It had been too long to allow them to close the tailgate, and Sean hadn't thought to bring any rope, which came as no surprise, seeing as how there was very *little* about this trip to which he had given proper consideration.

"Alistaire was right," he continued muttering. "He's *always* right. When am I gonna get that through my thick skull?"

In the cabin beside him, Trey sat forward, his de-gloved hands pressed close to the heating vents. Sean glanced over once, then again. Something about the sight was nagging at him, but he couldn't put his finger on what could be wrong with it. It was, after all, pretty chilly up here. It didn't bother *him* much, but Trey had grown up in the southern United States, where it was considerably warmer than Ireland or Alaska.

So why did the sight of Trey warming his hands bug him? If he weren't stressing out over how these bloody "white nights" were going to affect Alistaire, he might be able to think more clearly.

Might as well take the direct approach. "Trey, are ye cold?"

"No," Trey answered. But his tone of voice sounded odd, almost a wee bit *guilty*, like a child who was on the verge of getting caught doing something wrong.

But what could be wrong with wanting to warm his hands? If he felt cold, why wouldn't he admit it?

Sean started to press the issue further, but Artur made a sudden sharp turn to the left, and Sean hastened to follow suit. Biting down on a curse, he cut the corner, one eye watching the crate in the mirror the whole way. The change in direction brought the sun back into Sean's line of sight, and Trey's mystery slipped from his agitated mind.

After a few minutes jolting around on an even rougher road, Artur led them up to the cabin he had arranged for them. Sean appraised it with a pleased nod — it was a little small, but judging from the stilted front, he guessed that it came with the basement or fruit cellar that he had requested. All the better to keep Alistaire's coffin out of sight ... and Sean desperately hoped that his vampire friend wouldn't be *trapped* in that coffin for this entire investigation.

Pulling to a stop, Sean set the parking break. And as soon as he opened the driver's door, which screeched on a hinge that hadn't seen proper care in ages, he was afforded a brief distraction from his worries.

The smells! Dear God, he had nearly forgotten — having spent so much time in cities and suburbs — how the wilds exploded with dozens, *hundreds* of scents! He could smell plants, animals, and everything in between. Some of the scents he immediately identified, some were vaguely familiar, and many others he had never before smelled in his life. For a long moment, he just stood there, his left foot on the ground but his ass still on the truck seat, his eyes half-closed as he took a very long, very deep breath through his nose.

His olfactory was so exalted, he yearned to rip off his clothes, shape-shift right on the spot, and tear into the woods with abandon.

Then Artur opened his car door, and Sean came back to himself. This wasn't a vacation, this was business.

"Here are the keys," Artur was saying as he approached, holding them out to Sean at arm's length, as though he could not wait to get rid of them.

Even against the colorful scenery, Sean could smell the man's anxiety. "Thank you," he said as Artur dropped the keys into his hand. "You can go home and get to bed now, Artur. I'll be in touch with ye once I've done some preliminary research. Does the cabin have a phone ...?"

"What? Oh. No, I don't think so. I made sure you had electricity and hot water, but I didn't think about a phone. Cell phones don't normally work up here, but—"

"No worries," Sean assured him. "I'll walk into town and use a public phone if I need to reach ye."

"It's kind of a long walk ..."

Sean smiled. "I'm good for it."

The poor, nervous man kind of nodded and shook his head at the same time and shuffled back to his car.

"Artur ..." Sean called.

He froze, then looked back at Sean, an expression of dread on his face.

"I appreciate your situation," Sean told him. "I understand that ye want the killings to stop, but that ye don't have the slightest idea what to really think of me. Of us." He glanced back at Trey, who was sitting very still in the cabin of the truck. "We needed yer help gettin' here and gettin' set up, but I promise that I will keep ye as far from the 'dirty work' as I can. All right?"

Artur relaxed a little at that, the tension bleeding from his tight shoulders. He smiled at Sean, and it was his most sincere smile yet. Then he slipped into his car without another word, and was out of sight before the dust settled.

"All right," Sean said, clapping his hands together and moving around to the back of the truck. "What do ye say we get Alistaire out of that bloody box?"

The passenger door opened, and Trey got out. He glanced around as he joined Sean.

"Ready?" Sean asked, taking his side of the crate. Although they had gone through the motions of needing Artur and the pilot's assistance back at the plane, out here they could just pick it up together as they were truly capable of doing.

Trey took up position opposite Sean, and together they pulled the crate out of the truck bed ...

... and Trey dropped his side.

This in and of itself wasn't terribly surprising — after all, Trey wasn't the most physically coordinated person Sean had ever known. But Trey held Alistaire in such high reverence, he usually practiced extreme caution when handling his coffin, let alone when Alistaire was actually *inside* it.

Luckily, Sean shifted his grip in time to prevent the crate from crashing to the ground — he threw both arms around it in a bear hug and allowed it to come to rest on his bent knee. Even for a werewolf, it was no easy feat.

Biting his tongue, lest he bark an unkind and unfair rebuke at Trey, Sean wrestled the crate to the ground.

"I'm sorry ..." Trey mumbled, sounding miserable.

"It's all right, Trey. No harm done." Sean looked up and saw that Trey was staring down at his hands, clenching and unclenching his fists. "Are ye all right?"

Trey shook his head, and now he *looked* as miserable as he had sounded.

Sean brushed some wood splinters from the leg of his jeans and stepped around the crate to touch Trey's arm. "What is it, Trey? What's wrong?"

Trey still didn't answer, but now he pressed his palms together and rubbed them, as though he were trying to warm them. Though he gave them a healthy go, it must not have had the effect he was hoping for, because he was growing quite upset. His lower lip was puckering outward — a sure sign that he was on the verge of throwing one of his tantrums.

"Trey, *talk to me*."

"I can't ... feel my fingers."

"Trey, it's probably just the cold. It's normal ... to ..."

And finally it all came home: Trey warming his hands against the truck heater; Trey rubbing his hands together; Trey's fingers going numb.

Animate or not, Trey was, literally, a dead man — he shouldn't even *feel* the cold.

"And my knees ... are stiff," the big zombie complained. "And I can't ... feel my feet, either."

"I don't understand," Sean said, as much to himself as to Trey. "It's cold, but not *freezing*. Ye've been through colder winters than this in Pittsburgh. Why is the cold affectin' ye like this *now*?"

Was it even the cold that was causing it? He couldn't know for sure.

Trey stomped his feet, and it smacked both of a man trying to wake up a sleeping limb *and* of a child about to pitch a real fit. Sean needed to get Trey focused, and fast.

"Trey, listen to me, lad. We've got to get Alistaire outta this box. If I lift one end, can ye just *push* the other end for me?"

Trey wiped at a thin, dark tear that had rolled from under his sunglasses. "But it will ... mess up the grass."

Sean smiled. "That's all right. The grass will grow back."

Trey nodded, flexed his legs, and moved to help Sean as asked.

With far more tilting, banging, and jolting than Sean would have preferred, the two managed to get the crate up onto the cabin's front porch. It came as no surprise that the crate would not fit through the front door, and once Sean had retrieved the hammer from his bag in the truck, they were only a few minutes from setting the somewhat scuffed coffin down in the center of the nondescript single-room cabin.

"Trey," Sean said, "I need ye to draw all the curtains and shades." He glanced around — it was still going to be too damned bright in here! Once Trey had done as he had been told, Sean knelt beside the coffin and tapped on its lid four times.

No response from inside.

Swallowing against his growing nerves, Sean tapped again.

Still nothing.

"Why doesn't ... he answer?" Trey asked from across the room.

"I don't know," Sean said, but that wasn't entirely true.

If the sun never set, would Alistaire be able to wake up? If he did, would he be mobile, or even fully cognizant? And if he *didn't*, how would he be able to feed? How long could he go without any blood at all, even if he were in his trance the whole time?

Sean hated to break into the casket, but if they didn't get a response ...

Finally, there came a single thump, a sound that *could* pass for the occupant merely "shifting," if necessary.

Sean sighed with relief and repeated his taps, this time giving five of them. A few seconds longer than it should have taken, Sean heard the interior bolts being thrown.

The lid opened a crack, and a moment later Alistaire's fingers appeared, flexing — it was the closest semblance to Bela Lugosi that Sean had ever seen from his German friend.

"Sean ...?" he heard Alistaire whisper.

Resisting the impulse to open the coffin lid further, Sean settled for leaning closer to the thin gap. "Aye, Alistaire, I'm here."

"Why is it so bright?"

"We've closed off the windows as best we can. It's not that bright, really, it's just ye're so sensitive to sunlight—"

"It is still daytime?"

Sean could not tell if the vampire's tone indicated panic or anger. "No, Alistaire ... not exactly."

The coffin lid finally opened a few more inches.

Alistaire looked terrible. His eyes were squinted tight against the light, but it was more than that. It was like the worst case of waking a person from the deepest slumber, of forcing someone suffering from an intense hangover to rouse and greet the day. Although his teeth maintained their normal proportions, Sean knew that he was somewhat "vamped out."

"I don't understand."

Sighing, Sean relayed what little Artur had explained about these so called "white nights."

Alistaire closed his eyes and let his head fall back onto the casket's pillow. A low growl emanated from the back of his throat, something that was more customary of Sean than of Alistaire.

"I'm sorry, Alistaire ..." Sean began.

"It is not your fault, Sean. I have been around much, much longer than you, and I did not even take the season into consideration. I had heard tales of these white nights, and the dark days, as far back as my living years in Germany, but I have never traveled far enough north in Europe or America for it to have ever before been a factor."

"What do we do?"

Alistaire opened his eyes again, but as before, just a peek. *"I shall deal with this as I have all other obstacles: With Faith. Help me up."*

Sean wanted to protest, but this was Alistaire's call to make, not his. "Trey," he said, and only the name was required to bring the zombie to his aid.

Between the two of them, they supported Alistaire as he struggled to his feet. Again, Sean was struck with the impression of helping someone under the influence — although his speech had been clear, if a little weak, all other indications suggested that Alistaire was not fully awake ...

which, unfortunately, made sense.

Squinting a nettled glance at the windows, Alistaire tested his footing. Once he was certain that he could stand on his own, he waved them away — they let go as asked, but neither of them stepped back very far.

"It is not as bad as I first thought," Alistaire assured them. *"The sun may not have set, but I can feel that it is stifled, even more so than late dusk and first light. How did it appear in the sky?"*

"Weak," Sean agreed. "Ye can look directly at it without much discomfort."

Alistaire nodded, turning his back to the windows to face them. *"I will be able to tolerate this,"* he stated with finality. *"At least for the few hours I will have each night. I cannot guarantee that I will be able to venture* outside, *but if nothing else, I will be able to offer my counsel. And you will still have Trey to assist you in combat."*

"Ayyyyeee ..." Sean sighed, "About that ..."

Alistaire said nothing, merely looked inquisitive.

"Trey is having some trouble, too. My only guess is that it's the cold."

"The cold ..." Alistaire echoed, thoughtful.

"I'm stiff," Trey explained, still behaving as though he should feel guilty over the whole thing.

"But he's had colder weather than this," Sean countered his own suggestion. "It's not *that* cold up here right now. It *must* be something else."

"Not necessarily. I assume you are thinking of the winters in Pittsburgh?"

"Aye."

Trey nodded as well.

"My friends, that was in our old world."

Sean's head tilted back as the implications dawned on him. He was staring up at the ceiling by the time he finally said, "It never rains but it pours."

"I don't ... understand."

Sean turned away, pacing the room as he muttered, "Boy, did I bollocks this up," leaving Alistaire to explain it to their ward.

"Trey," Alistaire said, *"we are reminded once again that this world is different from our own. More 'mundane,' less imbued with the supernatural. Since joining us, you have spent the majority of your time in much warmer climates."* He paused, rubbing his eyes against the light coming through the edges of the drapes. He rotated so that, with his back to one side and Trey's bulk before him, his face was as sheltered as possible. *"If the temperature had dropped gradually, such as the natural coming of winter, you would have been granted more time to adjust. Additionally, I imagine the flight aboard the propeller aeroplane was even colder than the outside air is now, was it not?"*

"Yeah," Trey agreed.

Sean said nothing, just continued to pace.

Alistaire nodded. *"Lacking the normal bodily fluids of a living man, the cold put your system under quite a strain. While I shall be hampered by these white nights, you, Trey, are fortunate that we are here during the Alaskan summer. I suspect your body will adapt, though I cannot venture a guess as to how long this adjustment may take."*

"Too long, I'm sure," Sean growled.

Trey appeared stricken. "I'm sorry ... Sean."

Sean halted his pacing and counted to five before saying, "I'm not mad at *you*, Trey. But I *am* mad. Can ye understand that?"

Sean's voice was still sufficiently harsh that a shrug was Trey's only answer. The big man did not appear convinced that he was not, somehow, to blame.

Sean's usual patience was in short supply this evening, and so Trey's sensitivity grated on his nerves. This entire operation was already a disaster, and they hadn't even gotten *started* yet!

"I really should have come alone," he told Alistaire. "Maybe I was sulking when I said it before, but it looks like I was right after all. I've dragged the two of ye up here for nothing, and I'm sorry."

Alistaire turned toward him and opened his mouth to speak, probably to importune that the situation was not Sean's fault, that he had no need to apologize ... but the act brought him full face toward one of the shaded windows. He had relaxed his eyes a bit while facing Trey, and now he squeezed them shut, a hiss escaping him and his lips drawing away from his now-prominent canines as he recoiled in pain.

For Sean, the moment illustrated his point, driving it home like ... well, like a silver bullet. "Trey," he said as he moved to the door, "cover him up, and watch over him until I get back."

Sean hesitated only long enough to confirm that Trey had moved his body between Alistaire and the door, then he fled the cabin. It wasn't fair, leaving them like this. But his anger and frustration were reaching a boiling point — he *had* to let it out before he made any more foolish decisions!

He left his jacket on the porch of the cabin, along with his kicked-off tennis shoes; his shirt and jeans he tossed into the bed of the truck as he passed it by. Then he was running as fast as two legs could carry him.

As naked as the day he was born, Sean absconded into the woods.

Five

Sean should have felt like a royal ass for leaving Alistaire and Trey in a lurch like that. He really should have.

But he just felt too damned *good* to care.

Running through the woods, dashing under tree limbs and leaping over underbrush, Sean felt alive in a way that he had not since ... well, it had been a while. All of his senses were bedazzled by the call of the wilderness. It had been so long since he had allowed himself to just cut loose and *run like the wind*!

While he had thus far refrained from shape-shifting into his wolf form, he was no longer fully human, either. His body hair was thicker; his features were drawn, his ears in particular standing taller; his palms and the bottoms of his feet were tougher. He breathed deep through elongated yet broader nostrils; his lengthened tongue bobbed as he exhaled through a larger mouth.

Any unsuspecting observer would hardly have dubbed him a "wolfman," but he would certainly have earned a second look.

As he topped a rise, Sean launched into the air, then landed in a crouch atop a fallen tree. He arched his back, his face to the sky above. The frail sun was, as Artur had predicted, now blocked from view behind the mountains, and more stars were visible. Sean wanted to howl, he wanted to howl at the *moon* ... but alas, that element was sorely lacking. The moon was deep into its dark cycle, a thin sliver that was only one night away from the new moon.

Sean shared a love-hate relationship with the moon. Whatever primal urges he had in common with natural wolves prompted him to seek it out at night, to marvel at its glory. The closer it grew to the full moon, the more exciting it was for him ... and the more horrifying.

But those three nights were forever denied to him. Even if it weren't essential that he be locked away, for his own safety and the safety of others, he could never remember those nights.

Almost never anyway, but ... he chose not to think about that.

The full moon incited the animal to overwhelm the man. For Sean, the moon was like a bottle of Scotch — a little was liberating, a lot was frantic and exciting, but the whole bottle brought on black out and regret.

The moon was *freedom*.

The moon was *damnation*.

But tonight that sparse crescent offered no danger, no threat. He could soak it up for all it was worth and enjoy it. In fact, this would be the last night for the next three in which he would be physically *capable* of assuming his full wolf form, so he shouldn't waste it.

A feral man had landed upon the fallen tree, but a glorious wolf leaped back into the woods.

In the fluid impressions that flowed through his mind

while in wolf form — less than the thoughts of a man; but more than the impulses of a true animal — Sean considered the timing of the new moon in relation to this mission, and rolled his amber eyes. White nights for Alistaire, cold Alaskan weather for Trey ... didn't it just *figure* that there would be the new moon waiting for him? For seventy-two hours, he would be limited to wolfman form at night, and human form during the day.

The big difference, the element that kept this from being one more disaster, was that if *he* were limited, he knew that the werewolves he hunted would be *equally* limited for the same duration.

Sauce for the goose, sauce for the gander. The odds would remain even.

Speaking of his prey ...

Sean skidded to a halt, his nostrils flaring as he caught a scent. It took him mere seconds to localize the source, and even less time to determine that this was *not* his prey after all. This scent came not from werewolves, but from nature's own lupines — his "cousins," after a fashion.

After a brief moment of consideration, Sean moved in that direction. Why not? Since Artur appeared to be the only living *human* witness to the perpetrators he sought, perhaps some information could be gleaned from those of a more bestial nature.

Sean approached with slow caution. They were upwind, and would have little forewarning of his arrival. While he was fully confident in his ability to best their alpha male, and any other takers who might be feeling feisty, he had no desire to hurt them. He trotted without stealth, even stepping on the occasional branch with deliberate purport.

From not far ahead, he heard an alarmed bark, followed by rustling and scampering. A whine, then a short growl followed.

The pack knew he was coming. Time to make his entrance.

Sean entered the grove, then stood very still — not "timid," just equanimous — and let them have a look at him.

The lack of underbrush here meant they were all exposed, which didn't help ease the tension. There were no pups, but a pair of male adolescents lost some maturity as they cowered behind their mother. Two more adult females and an adult male paced and whined in the backs of their throat.

Only the alpha male dared to approach him. Teeth bared and neck bristling, the patriarch crept forward, ready to attack if necessary. Brave chap — as a werewolf, Sean was easily twice his size. Sean suspected that, if he did not act fast, he might be forced into an altercation after all. He glanced around until he spotted a good-sized rock sticking out of the ground.

Easing sideways, he arced around until the rock stood between him and the pack. He hiked a hind leg and sprayed the near side of the stone, then took two steps backward and lowered to his haunches.

That was all he could do; the next move would be up to them. If they didn't accept his metaphorical olive branch, he would leave rather than kill them.

The alpha, his neck still bristling but his teeth no longer bared, crept forward. Sean noticed for the first time that he had a slight limp due to a recent injury to his hind quarters.

The alpha reached the rock, and spent a fair amount of time sniffing and considering the mark until, finally, he hiked his own leg long enough to piss on his side of the tagged rock.

Sean's mark on one side, the alpha's mark on the other — the alpha had accepted the line Sean had drawn.

Now came the hard part: Communication.

While Sean's thoughts were indeed more fluid while in wolf form, the fact remained that he was still a proverbial wolf*man*, even when he walked about on all fours. He lacked the mental freedom of a true wolf, of living only for the moment, with little thought of what lies ahead and even less of what falls behind. Still, he had to try.

Remaining on his haunches, Sean lowered his head. The alpha relaxed further, and the rest of the pack followed his lead. Even the two younger males now appeared curious of this massive stranger in their midst.

Sean focused ... or rather, as contradictory as it seemed, he concentrated on being *less* focused. Ironically, it was his experience of melding with Mark Hudson which had given him better insight into this process, as it was not a far cry from self-hypnosis.

Minutes passed. One of the adults grew anxious again, but the pack as a whole was calmer — he had proven that he posed no immediate threat to them.

Finally, the lines of communication began to open. He would find the exchange difficult to relay to his partners later, but for now, the body language, the sounds, and especially the smells — always the *smells*! — began to coalesce into patterns which the still-human side of Sean's mind could interpret.

"who are you?" Sean sensed (felt? smelled?) the alpha

male asking.

(Well, not so much "asking" really, so much as ... well ... more like ...)

Sean forced himself to relax and roll with it, or he would lose the connection.

"a friend," he replied.

"you are not pack."

"no, I am not pack."

One of the younger males had crawled close enough to add his two cents. "then how are you friend?"

The alpha chuffed and swatted at the younger male, who retreated in submission. But when the alpha turned back to Sean, the look in his eyes was such that even a full-fledged human would be able to interpret it: "That was a fair question."

Sean struggled to answer. "I wish no harm. I am strong enough to be Alpha, but I submit to the Alpha. I am friend to the Alpha. I submit to the pack. I am friend to the pack."

Well, Sean thought to himself, *if that's not enough ass-kissing, I don't know what is.*

"you are different from Them."

That brought Sean up short. This communication was *so* dependent upon interpretation, and "Them" could mean just about any non-wolf out there, but ...

"what do you mean?"

"They are different from the pack, but you are different from Them. what are you?"

Sean could not allow himself to get sidetracked by trying to explain his shape-shifting nature to a wolf, if such a complicated exchange were even possible. He persisted, "what do you mean? who are 'They'?"

The alpha's only answer was a whine in the back of his throat.

Then one of the females, the mother to the two younger wolves, crept forward to join the alpha. "They are different from the pack. They smell different, They act different. They do not follow the Way."

Sean wasn't going to touch "the Way" with a twenty-foot pole, but he was excited to have stumbled upon such a concrete clue. "where are They?"

The alpha took a step back, ceding the exchange to the female, presumably his mate. "They run everywhere," she told him. "They roam the land. They attack and anger the Man. anger the Man at the pack."

Sean chose not to be offended that she conveyed "Man" as though it were a dirty word. "They anger the Man at you?"

She chuffed. "yes. They hunt the Man, the Man hunts us. hurts us."

She glanced back at the alpha, and Sean realized that his injury could easily be the result of a gunshot — he would have to smell the wound to be sure.

Sean was saddened, but not surprised. This world did not believe in werewolves ... or, to be fair, had no *real* cause to believe in them until recent years. So when a bunch of hunters seem to have been attacked by wolves ... well, it was open season on *all* wolves, not just the supernatural ones.

Just one more reason to put a stop to the killings.

"we do not like Them," the female continued. "They are not natural." Then she looked him straight in the eye, a very bold move, very challenging and dangerous on her part. "you are not like us, but you are different from Them."

"how?" Sean pressed. "how am I different from Them? why do you—?"

But then all hell broke loose.

The alpha jerked to full attention, then growled and barked. The female released her own growl and retreated to stand with her young. The other adults paced and nipped at each other in anxiety, and the young males tried desperately to disappear behind their mother.

For several seconds, Sean could only gape at them in befuddlement, wondering what in the world he had done to trigger such a reaction ...

... until he realized that *he* was not the cause.

They came from downwind, from the same direction which had allowed Sean to get so close to the pack without scaring them away. But unlike Sean, they had not gone out of their way to announce their approach. *Their* movements had been as silent as death.

Still, Sean would probably have sensed their coming if he had not been so focused on his brittle communication with the wolf pack. Not that it mattered now. They were here.

Standing tall, Sean turned to face Them.

Six

"Well ..." Trey commented as he peeked through the tiniest crack in the ajar front doorway, staring at the woods into which Sean had disappeared over an hour ago, "... that was *rude*."

It was the third time he had said it. Under other circumstances, Alistaire would have smiled at Trey's prolonged reaction — if Sean were here, and in a better state of mind, he would probably have laughed aloud.

But these circumstances were hardly conducive to Alistaire's merriment. His eyes were burning and his skin was crawling, and he felt altogether *ill* — it reminded him of the one and only time he had contracted food poisoning as a mortal, so many long years ago. In all his centuries of undead existence, he had only been forcibly awakened during the day a handful of times. After the subsequent fall of night, the whole experience usually struck him as very dreamlike in retrospect ... or perhaps "nightmarish" would be the better term — vague and fragmented and surreal, and wholly unpleasant. In that respect, the majority of the scathing discomfort he experienced failed to affect him on any meaningful level. By the time it was over, he found it difficult to recall the details of exactly what it had been like, and he was more than happy to leave it at that.

This was different, and in some ways worse. The blinding light was not as overpowering, the sting of his flesh was not as overwhelming ... and yet, because his faculties were more or less intact, he was *experiencing* these pains with greater clarity. The sensations had improved a little since the sun dipped out of sight below the mountains, but not enough. Not *nearly* enough.

He was awake ... but oh, how he wished he weren't.

"G-God," he prayed under his breath, and the lancing pain of speaking the Holy Name proved a welcome distraction from his other nisus, *"give me strength."*

Trey had closed the door (again) and locked it. He circled the cabin (again), making minor adjustments to the drawn curtains where he thought any light might be leaking through. He took a moment to warm his hands before the wood-burning stove — though both zombies and vampires were leery of fire, they had agreed that the heat would prove good for Trey's condition. Thus far, the effects had been nominal. "Don't you think ... that was rude?"

When Trey had sought his affirmation earlier, Alistaire — troubled, as he was, by his own angst — had agreed just to pacify him. Now he wondered if perhaps a more thoughtful answer was in order.

"Sean is very frustrated, Trey." Alistaire closed the lid of his coffin, then sat upon it, as approaching one of the furnished chairs would have required him to move closer to the windows.

"It was ... still rude."

"Trey, come here."

Trey must have recognized a distinct parental tone in

Alistaire's voice, as he dragged his feet more than necessary while doing as he was told. At another time, Alistaire might have requested that Trey sit beside him on the coffin, but he did not want to place Trey in the awkward position of dealing with his cold-stiffened knees. So when Trey stood in front of him, towering so high yet still seeming like a small child, Alistaire gestured for him to halt.

The gesture also prompted Alistaire to realize how severe and clawlike his own hands were in this half-night. Catering to his own nimiety, he kept his hands low and still as he spoke.

"Sean has not been his old self for quite a while, Trey," he began.

"Since we came ... to this world?" Trey ventured.

But Alistaire shook his head. *"No, his troubles began shortly* before *we crossed over. In fact, for a few months, being in this place served to* distract *him from his woes, and for that I was grateful. But our encounters with Carpenter and Hudson awakened issues Sean has long held over his sister."*

"His sister ..." Trey concentrated, then brightened as the information came to him. "... Theresa?"

"Yes, Theresa," Alistaire nodded. *"In the weeks before we rejoined on this side, he had returned to Ireland for the first time since I had known him. I believe he wanted to deal with his troubles, his fears, once and for all. But ... I do* not *believe he found the answers that he desired. I had hopes that perhaps this mission, his mission, would provide him an outlet with which he could deal with these issues. But we have gotten off to such a dubious start, I fear it may be causing more harm than good."*

Trey looked back to the door of the cabin. "Then will Sean ... be all right out there ... alone?"

Again, Alistaire's first impulse was to assure Trey, to tell him what he wanted to hear, but then he chose to answer with the truth.

"I do not know, Trey. I pray that he will."

And so the two worried men waited, and did not speak for some time.

SEVEN

The werewolves spread out, outflanking him.

The good news was that Sean was larger than any one of them; they were all bigger than the natural wolves, of course, but none of them matched Sean's sheer mass.

The bad news was that there were over a dozen of them; the largest gathering of werewolves that Sean had ever seen.

Fur white as snow, fur black as pitch, and everything in-between. Males, females, and all of them adults in their prime. Some of them crept forward, low to the ground, while others stood fully erect, their challenge unmistakable. Teeth glistening in the low light, saliva drooling from curled lips, ears flattened back against their heads — one and all, eager for the kill.

The wolf pack was right — these werewolves *were* different from him. Their smells were ... odd. Their scents were *wilder* than the other werewolves Sean had encountered over the years. He would wager a pretty pound that they spent more time as wolves than as men — they had formed a pack, they lived in this enticing environment in which Sean himself was reveling not fifteen minutes earlier ... it was no real surprise that they might have "gone native," so to speak.

None of which mattered to Sean. For whatever reason, they had decided to prey upon the local human community, and were creating unjust hardship for the local wildlife to boot. As far as Sean was concerned, they were goin' down.

Of course, this brought *another* popular phrase to mind: "Easier said than done." With Alistaire and Trey by his side, and in top form, Sean would have regarded this as a serious challenge. Alone...

Crouching to leap at an instant's notice, Sean prepared for the fight of his life.

A white werewolf, one of the biggest of the pack, emerged from the group dead center. It strode forward without caution until it stood less than ten feet away. It glanced briefly at the cowering natural wolves, then back at Sean. Its nostrils flared as it scrutinized him, then it — *he* — locked eyes with Sean.

Sean could only assume this was the werewolf alpha. And the message was clear: He knew what Sean was, and he wanted Sean's submission.

Sean let him know just what he thought of *that*. He drew a slow, deep breath ... then shook his head and snorted heavily through his snout, making sure plenty of mucus flipped through the air in the white wolf's direction. And then he punctuated the gesture with a sharp bark.

He hoped his sentiment was clear: *Fuck you.*

The werewolves went ape shit. Growling and gnashing and barking, they wanted to tear Sean to pieces. The pack of natural wolves broke and ran, which suited Sean just fine — now he would not have to worry about their becoming collateral damage.

The white wolf threw its head back and howled, louder than the din of the others. One or two joined in, but most of them quieted — they continued to stare death at Sean, but they quieted.

Sean was annoyed by this grandstanding.

So ... they admired a show of strength, did they?

The white wolf had not yet finished his melodramatic howl when Sean collided with him, his snout jabbing his smaller opponent firmly in the underside of his jaw. His howl cut short with a *yipe!* as his teeth clamped down on his tongue, and Sean's superior weight knocked him over and onto his back. Then, as the alpha rolled back to his feet, Sean gave him a good, solid bite on the tail, jerking hard and drawing plenty of blood. The white wolf *yiped!* again and scampered out of reach.

Spreading his front paws wide, his hindquarters again crouched to leap, Sean cut loose with his own howl, not directed into the twilight above, but right in their collective faces.

His new message: *Bring it on!*

The bestial cacophony resumed as the pack approached him.

Earlier, Sean had felt his human cares slipping away thanks to the serenity of running wild through the night. Now, the thrill of *battle* pounded through his heart. So he was outnumbered better than a dozen-to-one? So they would probably tear him to shreds before the sun cleared the mountains and snuffed out the scant starlight with its white night?

Sean cared about none of this. He embraced the coming fight. These bastards had been preying on humans for months — let them see what it was like to tackle prey who could bite back harder than *any* of them!

Sean snapped a deep-chested bark that echoed through the forest. He slapped and tore at the earth before him, like a mountain gorilla pounding his chest.

What are ye waiting for?! he would roar, if only his vocal chords were capable. *Afraid to start this fight, are ye? FINE!*

Sean hunkered down to leap.

The nearest werewolves, shaken but not cowed, tensed to receive him.

"Stop!"

All of them froze, including Sean. The voice had been coarse, slurred, and barely human ... but it had undeniably been the *word* "Stop," and not a bark.

The wolves parted again, just as they had given ground to the white wolf, whom Sean had assumed was their alpha — apparently, that was not the case.

A female strode toward him, and she did so on two legs. She was in wolfwoman form, her body covered with fur, her face misshapen between canine and human, and two additional pairs of vestigial breasts hanging down her abdomen beneath her larger, human pair. Her sense of authority was palatable — *this* was the pack alpha.

A female alpha, Sean marveled. *Lo and behold, feminism has invaded the world of lycanthropy.*

The wolfwoman stopped even closer to Sean than the white wolf had. She regarded him in much the same way, though since she was currently a half-wolf, he was more aware of her eyes searching him than just her snout. She ended by placing casual hands on her hips and saying in her gruff voice, "Shift. Talk to me."

After a moment's consideration, Sean decided that he had nothing to lose. He stood onto his hind legs as he shifted back into his own wolfman form.

"All right," he said, his speech thickened but understandable. "Say whatever ye have to say. I haven't got all night."

The female appeared amused by his attitude, but she chose not to address it. "You are new to this land. Why are you here?"

"I was looking for *you*, actually."

"Looking for us?"

"Aye."

"How interesting." She stepped even closer and took a brazen sniff of him, and seemed to like what she smelled. "And now that you have found us ..." She next stole an unapologetic glance between his legs, and also seemed to like what she *saw*. A shier, more conservative man, such as Alistaire, would have attempted to cover himself, but Sean had been around the block too often to let this distract him. "... what will you do?"

Sean dismissed any innuendo she might have intended and stated, "I will stop ye from killing any more people."

The odd growl and snap of teeth told Sean what the werewolf pack thought of *that*, but the female offered no reaction beyond repeating, "How interesting." She glanced over toward a brown wolf which had crept too close for her liking and barked at it; the wolf obeyed without resistance, withdrawing several paces back out of the grove.

"Ye seem to have them on a short leash," Sean observed, "if ye'll forgive the pun—"

"I heard no pun," she snapped, the first real emotion Sean had seen from her. "We are *wolves*, not dogs. Man does not leash us. *No one* leashes us."

"All right," Sean acquiesced. "It's just that I have never seen a female alpha before, wolf *or* werewolf."

The wolfwoman moved to stand near the white wolf, whose tail was still bleeding and who stared death at Sean. She reached out to give his snout an affectionate caress. "I freed them," she said, and her voice had returned to its neutral tone. "I gave them the gift to shed their trappings. I gave them *strength*."

Sean snorted. "That's one way of puttin' it. Another is, ye *infected* them."

She turned cold eyes back to him. " 'Infected them?' Ridiculous." She pulled her hand from the white wolf's snout and strode with purpose right up into Sean's space — he had to resist the urge to take a step back. "Why would you protect the humans? You are superior to them in every way; you walk in both worlds as you choose. You are strong, the strongest I have seen." She stretched her neck to one side, letting her hair flow to expose a stretch of muscular, furry neck. An amorous keening seeped from the back of her throat. "Why not join—?"

"Don't bother, lass." And now he did take a step back, but it was dismissive rather than intimidated. "This is the part where ye try to 'seduce' me into changing my poor, misguided ways and embracing the wolf within me, am I right?"

She said nothing; Sean took that for an assent.

"Better werewolves have tried to sway me over to 'the Dark Side,' lass, including females with a far more appealing scent. So let me make this short 'n sweet for ye..." Sean raised his voice to address the entire pack. "As far as my partners and I are concerned, slaughtering human beings is an act of *war*. We will not allow you to continue."

"How dare—?" the alpha began.

But Sean cut her off once more. "Ye've been livin' as wolves. I can tell. But all ye've done is bring hell down on the *natural* wolves. Ye think to shed yer human flesh and live as 'one with the wild,' is that it? Ye're all nothing but full-of-shite *hypocrites*, every one of ye."

"It is the *humans* who have declared war on *us*!" the alpha retorted. "*They* endanger the 'natural' wolves. The humans! With their guns, calling themselves 'hunters' while they hide behind—"

"When *some* folks feel that way, they go 'n join Greenpeace. They don't massacre men with *families*." The alpha drew another breath, but this time Sean stopped her before she could even get started. "I'm not interested in hearin' any more of yer chatter. I'm done. Ye wanted me to shift so I could talk to ye, fine. I've said all I have to say but this ..."

Sean made a point of looking each and every werewolf in the eye as he declared, "I will kill *each* and *every one* of ye Godless bastards before I'm through. I will rip you apart and leave ye to rot as carrion. And even if *I* fall this night, I'll take enough of you sons-o'-bitches with me that my partners will have no trouble finishing what I start."

The alpha, the entire pack, were stunned. The nerve, the *gall* of this lone werewolf dumbfounded them.

The alpha recovered first. "You ... expect us to believe that you could defeat all of us? Or that you have 'partners' in this thickheaded errand of yours?"

"Take another smell o' me, lass," Sean replied. "Take a good, hard *whiff*, and try to pay attention to more than my musk." He raised his voice again. "Ye'll find traces of both vampire and zombie. And I assure ye, I don't *eat* the undead."

The wolfwoman guffawed. "Vampires aren't real ..."

"Don't be daft. We're *werewolves*, ye idiot. Make the leap." He shook his head. "That's it. I'm done." And he fell onto all fours as he returned to full-wolf form.

The alpha female, too, shifted into wolf form. Taking him up on his challenge, she sniffed at him anew.

Despite his willful dismissal of her interest in him ... he admitted to himself that in wolf form she was a magnificent creature. The man in him was always uncomfortable with how the wolf in him responded to wolfen females, but he could not deny the raw attraction it often stirred within him.

If only she had not, like so many other werewolves he had encountered, chosen to embrace her curse as she had. While Sean was the only one he knew of to take an active role in hunting down the savage, depraved ones, he *had* met, on rare occasion, other lycanthropes who also caged themselves during the full moon to protect others, who chose to live as normal lives as they were able.

This female could have used her charisma and control to *prevent* this pack of monsters from killing people. The potential was there, if only she had chosen that path.

But ... c'est la vie. With the odds against him, Sean saw no choice but to kill her *first*.

With the alpha in wolf form, the pack returned to their initial postures. They circled around him, ready to dive in.

When the alpha finished her olfactive examination of him, she straightened to face him.

She glanced to the wolves on her right.

She glanced to the wolves on her left.

Sean readied himself for the pain of their many teeth and claws, determined not to allow it to prevent him from tearing the alpha's throat out. This was it — there would be no more interruptions now.

Here it comes ...

With synchronized precision, the werewolf pack turned tail as one and disappeared back into the woods. They moved as quickly, and nearly as quietly, as when they had first appeared.

Just like that, they were gone.

Sean was flabbergasted. He was so psyched up for a fight — hell, a bloody *death match*! — that he could only stand there like a fool for several seconds. By the time he finally bolted into the woods after them, after their alpha, they already had a discouraging head-start on him. He picked up the alpha's scent and hauled ass in pursuit.

Why would they flee? Despite his brave words, he knew he probably couldn't take them *all* down. They had him hopelessly outnumbered ... so *why would they flee?*

As Sean thundered through the underbrush after them, he discovered a problem — while he had been larger than any one of them, they were proving to be *faster* than he was. And they were working together, too. Their trails crisscrossed several times, throwing him for loops and causing him to double back on himself as he *tried* to keep the alpha as his target. And to compound matters, she kept *shifting* on him, which altered her scent somewhat each time. She would be in wolf form, then wolfwoman form, and back again.

Finally, after a frustrating half-hour of pursuit, Sean accepted the fact that he was not going to catch her, or *any* of them, tonight. The sun had finally cleared the mountains, returning the night to a pale approximation of daylight. Already he was finding it difficult to maintain his wolf form — the moon was slipping from sight into its three-night hiding. If he wanted to return to the cabin with the speed of all-fours, he would have to do so very soon.

Thwarted and angry, Sean howled, loud and long. Wherever they were, they would be able to hear him. *I'm coming for ye,* he wanted them to know, *ye've just been granted a brief recess. See ye in three nights!*

Of course, just because their shape-shifting would be limited didn't mean they couldn't still be *dangerous*. Each night, he would shift into wolfman form and patrol the area as best he could. But as different as they seemed — in ways he still could not quite nail down — they were werewolves, and he was betting they would postpone the hunt until they could return to their most dangerous physique.

Growling, Sean oriented himself and set off for the cabin ...

*   *   *

High in the trees, the werewolf pack watched their large adversary retreat. They were in human form or half-wolf forms, clinging to the bark with fingers and toes. As their scents had entwined, it had never occurred to the intruder to look straight *up*.

How naive.

When the intruder was gone from sight, the alpha pursed her lips and whistled — something that she could not do in wolf or wolfwoman form. On her cue, the pack descended back to the ground. By the time they gathered together, some of them were wolves once more.

"What do we do?" a pale, blonde man — the white wolf — asked. The bottom of his spine still bled from where the intruder had bitten him, and the smoldering hate in his eyes told her exactly what he wanted to hear.

The alpha considered the situation for a moment. The intruder had been so powerful, truly her match. Several males in the pack wanted to mate her, but *this* male was the sort she had hoped to find; the mere thought of rutting with him made her wet.

But ... he had made his position quite clear. A pity.

"Follow him," she commanded, "and kill him."

Eight

Trey jerked to attention, his stiff limbs creaking and cracking, when the front door of the cabin opened. Authentic daybreak had come, and Alistaire had returned to his coffin — Trey had placed additional blood packs in with him, because his waking schedule seemed so undependable up here in this cold, weird place. Since Sean departed without taking the key with him, Trey had felt obliged to keep the front door unlocked. Part of his regular duties, after all, was to protect Alistaire while he slept, so standing double-guard meant nothing to him.

He relaxed, however, when Sean poked his head through the crack. Upon seeing that Alistaire's coffin was shut, Sean opened the door far enough to step inside. He was wearing nothing but his jeans, but he had the rest of his clothes wadded up into a bundle and tucked under his arm.

"Hello ... Sean," Trey said in a neutral tone.

"Trey," Sean returned, setting his bundle of clothing on a dusty end table and pulling out his T-shirt. "I see ye've started a fire in the stove. Are ye feeling better now?"

Trey shrugged, then asked, "Are *you* ... feeling better now?"

Sean shot Trey a look, searching for any sign of

sarcasm on the zombie's face. When he found none, he relaxed, and even offered him a crooked smile. "Aye, Trey, I'm feelin' better. And I apologize for leaving in such a twit."

Trey approached him from his post beside Alistaire's coffin — Sean noted that his stiffened gait had not improved. "Did you see ... anything interesting? We heard ... howling."

Sean hesitated with his shirt halfway on, then broke into a warm, satisfying laugh. It was clear that Trey had *not* expected this kind of response.

"Aye," Sean answered at last, "I did." He pulled his shirt on the rest of the way. "Let's sit down and I'll tell you all about my interesting stroke of luck ..."

*   *   *

Astonishing.

She did not know whether or not it was truly a "vampire" and "zombie" she was smelling, but the presence of something unknown was undeniable. She had never smelled anything like them; unlike her supernatural brethren, these were ... unclean, and altogether *un*natural.

All the more reason to eliminate them.

She looked to the lingering sun; she yearned for night, for the moon. Their limitations were regrettable, but unavoidable.

The Intruder, as they were calling him, had chosen his side. He had challenged her pack, *threatened* her pack.

Snapping her fingers, she gestured forward.

She would not suffer his vile triumvirate to live.

* * *

"Wow," Trey said when Sean finished.

"Aye," Sean agreed. "We've got our hands full on this one, my friend." And then he stifled a yawn. What with the long hours of traveling, followed by his all-night excursion, not to mention the adrenaline crash after the forestalled battle extraordinaire, he was dead tired. He looked around the one-room cabin and saw that it offered only a single, sagging cot in one corner across from the modest cooking area — nothing he could complain about; he had informed Artur that they only needed sleeping accommodations for one.

As tired as he was now, a pile of straw would do. They would just have to wrestle Alistaire's coffin down through the floor hatch into the fruit cellar after Sean woke in a few hours.

Trey continued to sit in silence, and Sean could see the wheels grinding away behind his murky eyes. Trey was slow, *not* dumb, but he still missed Alistaire's counsel on this matter—

No. No more of that. Tired or not, he had bellyached long enough. These were the cards he held, whether the fault were his or Fate's. He had looked his enemy in the eyes, and she was, literally and figuratively, a bitch.

"All right, Trey, I'm gonna take a short nap, and then this is what we're going to do—"

One of the front windows exploded inward, the spray of glass contained only by the heavy curtains which adorned it. Sean and Trey bolted to their feet, Sean knocking his chair over backward. Whatever had crashed through the window landed with a *thump!*, the curtains wrapping around it and hiding it from view.

"Bloody hell—!"

But Sean was again cut off as a *second* window burst inward to his left, then a third, smaller window behind him over the sink in the cooking area. In all cases, the drapes which had protected Alistaire from the white night also served to block Sean's view of *what* exactly was being thrown through their windows. He knew immediately that this must be the work of the werewolf pack, but for all he knew, these could be batches of dynamite they were throwing through his windows!

Then he heard a distinctive growl behind him.

"Sean ..." Trey said, apprehension in his voice.

Sean whirled back around to face the first mound of torn drapery. The contents — a living creature, not an inanimate object — rolled out of the tattered mess and rose to its feet ... its *four* feet.

"Holy shit ..." Sean muttered, his eyes wide.

It was a *wolf*. One of *them*.

Even during this day of the new moon, they still had the ability to assume full wolf form, something far beyond Sean's own abilities.

This changed everything.

A loud *thud!* sounded from the front door as a body slammed into it. More barks and growls rolled around the room as the other wolves freed themselves from the heavy drapes. And a fourth wolf was already springing through the first broken window.

It was happening too fast! No time for a jaunty plan.

"Hit them, Trey!" Sean yelled. "*Hard!*"

As the first wolf advanced and prepared to leap at him, Sean did just that — he made a fist, hauled off, and punched the wolf in the side of its head as hard as he could. He pushed his body, striving to take at least wolfman form, but all he managed was the usual increase in body hair and slight shift in his facial features; not even as far as when he had first been running naked on his hind legs last night. He was still supernaturally strong, of course ... but then, so were they.

The first wolf rolled away with a satisfying *yelp!*, but then it was Sean's turn to grunt in pain as one of the others slammed onto his back. He tried to twist around, to throw it off, but he was too slow — it buried its front teeth deep into the meat of his right shoulder, piercing cotton and flesh and, so it felt, perhaps even bone.

Sean yelled and struggled to free himself without causing further damage, but the wolf he punched was already back up and lunging. He blocked it from reaching his face and throat, but it ended up with a scathing hold on his left forearm.

They caused him to stumble. If he did not maintain his balance, they would pull him down, and if *that* happened, Sean knew that he was a dead man.

How? How could they be in wolf form now? How?!

Then thundering footsteps pounded up behind him. Trey seized the wolf on Sean's back and jerked it away. The wolf refused to release its bite, and Sean swallowed a scream as its teeth ripped through his flesh — he felt the tendons in his shoulder *twang* like plucked guitar strings, but as near as he could tell, none of them snapped.

With a loud *crash*, the front door finally gave up the

ghost. Metal and wood chips flew as the lock splintered, the door swinging around and slamming into the wall hard enough to knock the hinges askew. More wolves tried to enter, but Trey turned and threw the wolf in his hands as hard as he could — it sailed through the open door, its head cracking against the doorframe on its way out. The wolves immediately outside were scattered like bowling pins.

In the meantime, Sean twisted and turned his left forearm until the other wolf was forced to release its hold, then he took a lesson from Trey. He grabbed it by the head rather than the body and, spinning around on his bare feet, hurled the wolf into the side of the stove, the *gong!* echoing all the way up the stove's pipe chimney. And before the wolf could collect itself, Sean raced forward and kicked it in the ribs, which prompted another *gong!* as it was pinned between his foot and the stove. Sean's only regrets were that he was barefoot and that the wolf's fur was too thick for it to suffer from the stove's heat — he smelled some singed fur, but that was all.

The Irishman turned to see how Trey was faring and ducked at the last second as the white wolf passed through the space his face had just occupied — it was so close, he felt its tattered tail whisper down his back.

Sean whipped around, but the white wolf was equally fast. It rebounded off the wall, twisted, and landed on its feet before him. It growled, hate filling its eyes.

Aye, lads, Sean thought, *I think we've got a grudge match here!*

Trey had to be doing well from the simple fact that no other wolves were breathing down Sean's neck. He and the white wolf were squared off, and the one Sean had thrown and kicked into the stove lay dazed at their feet.

For now, it was just the two of them.

Unlike last night, the white wolf did not waste time posturing. With a fierce snarl, it threw itself at Sean. Sean managed to grab its head, but as with his forearm, he paid a price — the wolf's jaws snapped shut, stabbing into the fingers of his left hand and the thumb of his right.

Grunting and snarling, Sean ignored the pain and used the grip to his advantage. Pushing and pulling in opposite directions, he fought to tear the wolf's bottom jaw right off its head. The wolf refused to retreat; its breath was hot on his face as it raked bloody trenches down Sean's chest with its front claws. It angled its weight forward and pushed with its hind legs, causing Sean to take a shaky step backward.

Somewhere in the cabin, above the barks from the other wolves and grunts from Trey, Sean heard an odd *scraping* sound, loud and deep. He did not know what it was, and he could not spare the moment to turn and find out.

Sean tried with all his might to give the white wolf the old King Kong/T-Rex treatment, but its jaw muscles were just too strong to separate or tear. He did not doubt that he was inflicting a good amount of pain, but he wasn't doing enough *damage*. This was not a stalemate, but only forestalling — he had to really hurt this wolf before it, or one of its brethren, hurt *him*.

What were his advantages? The wolf had teeth, claws, a protective fur coat, powerful hind legs that even now prompted Sean to take another backward step ... and Sean, stuck in human form, he ...

Well ... he had thumbs.

Shifting his balance, Sean kicked the white wolf in the balls as hard as he could. When the wolf grunted with the shock and pain that was universal to male mammals, Sean released its jaw with his left hand, reached forward, and jammed his thumb deep into its right eye.

The wolf whined and reared back away from him. Just before it withdrew from his reach, Sean dragged his thumbnail sideways, scratching a respectable gash across the wolf's cornea. The wolf *yiped!* louder than ever, turning in a circle and pawing at its own face.

That loud *scrape* filled the cabin again, but as Sean turned to investigate, another wolf, this one with predominantly red fur, leaped at him; they weren't giving him time to do much more than take a breath, but he was just grateful that, so far, Trey was preventing them from attacking him in mass.

The red wolf snapped at his face. Sean tried to body-block it with his elbow, but he was a fraction of a second too slow. The wolf's front teeth bit down into the meat of his right cheek; it didn't get a good enough hold to tear any flesh away, but the punctures were bloody painful! Sean's eyes watered with the sting, obscuring his vision.

Another *scrape!*, this one louder than any of the others. A second later, Trey called out, "Sean!" and his voice was filled with urgency.

Pounding his fist down onto the red wolf's snout with enough force to bounce its head right off the wood floor, Sean stole a quick glance behind him. The explanation for the scraping sounds poured ice water into his gut.

"Aw, fuck me ..."

There *was* a reason why only one or two wolves were

attacking him at a time, and it *wasn't* due to Trey's intervention.

Three wolves were keeping Trey pinned in the far corner — they were giving a good show of snapping and scratching at him, but displayed an odd reluctance to actually *bite* him. Another three wolves were on Sean's side of the cabin, including the stunned wolf lying against the stove and the white wolf, which continued to paw at its wounded eye.

The remaining wolves — in Sean's estimation, it was the rest of the pack except for the alpha — were attempting to drag Alistaire's coffin out the door ...

... and into the morning sunlight!

Sean dove forward, ready to throw himself into the bodies of fur. But the red wolf was again too fast for him, and it sank its teeth gum-deep into his right calf. He caused himself even more pain and damage as he tried to jerk his leg free, but the werewolf held on tight.

The coffin *scraped!* another foot or more toward the cabin door; a few more advances like that and it would be out on the front porch. They were using their mouths and foreheads to move it — why hadn't they turned into *wolfmen* in order to use their hands? At this point, Sean wasn't going to question his blessings.

"*Stop* them, Trey!" he yelled. "*Whatever it takes!*"

Trey nodded, took another clumsy swing at an elusive werewolf, then waded forward. The three pushed and scratched his legs, doing their best to trip him up without biting him.

The piercing pain in Sean's calf forced his attention back to the red wolf. But whereas before he had felt tension, adrenaline, bewilderment, and even fear ... now he felt burning anger. Rational or not, he swelled with a very real, searing *indignation* that these dirty beasts would dare assault Alistaire this way!

Reaching down, he curled his finger into the side of the wolf's mouth and back up into its lip. Digging in with his sharp fingernails, he pulled upward. Further and further he pulled that tender tissue as the wolf whimpered. Blood appeared at the lip's bifurcation as it began to tear at the nose, and Sean felt an added warmth to the drool in its mouth. Still he pulled.

The red wolf whimpered louder, and rolled its eyes up to meet his.

Sean snarled down at it. "Let go of my leg or I will peel your furry face right off your goddamn skull!"

Being more than just a wolf, it understood him, of course. There was only a moment's hesitation as it considered the price of failure if its alpha bitch found out it had yielded ... and then it released its bite.

Sean held onto the lip and pulled the wolf over onto its back. Then he fisted his other hand and pounded down on its exposed throat. The red wolf choked and squirmed around on its back, trying to breathe. Sean let go of its lip and turned back toward the coffin even as it *scraped!* another loud advance toward the door.

The white wolf obstructed his path, but it was more coincidence than anything else — it was still pawing away at its eye, and had stumbled into his way. Sean ignored the pain in his leg long enough to kick it aside.

Sean and Trey reached the coffin at the same time. They did not waste precious moments with a tug-of-war, but laid into their enemies. They were still outnumbered, but these wolves seemed torn between defending themselves and completing their task of dragging the vampire outside.

"Get off!" Trey bellowed, backhanding a wolf so hard it tumbled end-over-end all the way to the far wall. "Get off!" He cuffed another on his opposite side, prompting it to bite down on its own tongue as its chin clipped the side of the coffin.

Whatever reservations the wolves might have had regarding Trey, they were lost in that moment. One lunged from his right, catching his forearm; the other snapped from his left, clamping down on his thigh. They both bit hard.

The results were instantaneous: Each wolf released its hold, staggered away from the big man as they gagged and retched, their tongues rolling from their mouths with brownish ichor drooling onto the cabin floor.

Trey gaped at his wounds in a mixture of dread and rage. "No!" Trey blurted with a stamp of his foot. "No, no, *no*!" And with that, Trey submerged into one of the full-fledged tantrums that Alistaire and Sean tried so hard to avoid. Grabbing the wolf which had bitten his thigh, Trey curled it up to his face and sank his own teeth into its belly.

The wolf shrieked — it did not just "yipe" or "whine," it *shrieked*, a horrible sound which Sean had never heard uttered from a canine throat. It kicked and squirmed and cried out over and over again as it struggled to pull away from the biting zombie.

The terrible cries brought all of the wolves up short. They paced and exchanged glances, and clearly did not know what to do — whatever instructions their alpha had given them, they had not allowed for the sort of punishment they were receiving here.

Sean took advantage of the interruption to bat the remaining wolves away from the coffin. He then dragged it around sideways to the door — he didn't think he would have time to secure it across the room, and this would at least make their mission to push it outside that much more difficult.

Trey finally lost his hold on the wolf he was biting. It hit the cabin floor with an awkward bounce, scrambled onto its legs, and hauled ass out the open door without a look back, leaving a gory trail of blood in its wake. Trey had not just bitten the wolf, but had actually been *eating* into its belly; if it weren't for the healing abilities of a lycanthrope, it would be well on its way to a gruesome death.

Trey, his mouth now a sanguinary mess, growled as much as a humanoid throat could and reached for another victim. The wolves scattered before him, and another one or two escaped through the broken windows.

Sean experienced a brief moment's elation ... but victory was not theirs yet, and he paid for his distraction.

Sean cried out at the sharp pain, far worse than the rest he had endured this morning, that cut into his side. Unlike his forearm, shoulder, or calf, this attacker had nailed him in the right side of his torso — he was lucky its teeth pierced into the rib cage; lower, and this new wolf might have ripped a chunk of meat right out of his abdomen, and God only knew what organs it might have taken with it.

Gritting his teeth, Sean looked down to see that this was not a "new" wolf at all — it was the white wolf again, and he could see the pleasure in its unwounded eye.

Sean tried to strike at it, but the angle was too

bunglesome. The white wolf tugged at him, and he could feel his flesh rending.

"Trey!" he called, but the zombie was lost in his fit, too busy chasing after the much-faster wolves to hear him.

The white wolf tugged again, even harder.

Sean went down onto his right knee — if any of the other wolves joined in now, they would have a clear shot at his face. He reached out to brace himself with the top of Alistaire's coffin.

The son of a bitch pulled with all four legs now; Sean's blood flowed from the corners of its mouth. Sean heard something tearing, and he hoped it was only his T-shirt, not his flesh.

"God help me ..." he whispered through clenched teeth. He felt the coffin suddenly shift under his hand, sliding up toward him — his weight and strength, not to mention the wolf's added pounds, were toppling the coffin over onto its side. It would probably end up pinning his free arm.

This is the end, I guess, he thought. *I just wish I knew* how in the hell *they managed to take wolf form during a day of the new moon.*

But it wasn't the end. The coffin was not toppling.

It was opening.

Alistaire Bachman emerged from his coffin, into the cabin with most of the curtains missing from its windows, during true daylight. And he was *not* happy. The vampire rose up like an unholy vision, which was ironic given Alistaire's staunch religious belief. But then again, this was not the Alistaire Bachman that Sean knew and loved.

Alistaire had always insisted that, if the disturbance were great enough, he *could* be awakened during the day.

He had also expressed his desire that Sean never have to witness such an occurrence.

As Alistaire stood over him now, Sean barely recognized his friend. He had seen him with clawed fingernails, enlarged fangs, glowing white eyes, and frankly, breath smelling of the grave.

But now ...

Alistaire hissed and spat at the sunlight pouring through the open door and broken windows. He did not physically burn ... or rather, he did not literally catch *fire,* but his skin was already taking on an irritated, sunburn flush. He turned away from the door, giving Sean a full view of his hideously distorted face — his hairline had receded, he had deep wrinkles that had never before appeared on his eternally-youthful countenance, his eyebrows were nearly gone, and his ears had curved back and to a soft point, not unlike the Graf Orlok character in *Nosferatu.*

Throwing his taloned hands out to his sides, Alistaire roared at the wolves. If the wolves had frozen when Trey bit into their shrieking packmate before, they turned to stone now. The only person in the room who didn't stop and stare was Trey, but he was too busy stomping at another wolf to pay much attention to anything else.

Sean recovered first. He brought his elbow down onto the white wolf's nose as hard as he could, and the bastard finally let go. Sean tried to follow up with a backhand across its face, but his multiple injuries were catching up with him, and he missed by a wide margin. He slid down onto the floor, his back to the coffin with its open lid, as he pressed his hand to his latest, hemorrhaging wound.

Alistaire leaped from the coffin, sailing through the air

as though he were able to fly. Two wolves scrambled to get out of his way, but Alistaire's foot came down on one of their hind legs with a satisfying *crack!*, and the wolf howled. Alistaire seized it by the same, broken leg and hurled it out the nearest window, the animal crying the whole way. He turned back around and roared once more.

That did it; the pack broke ranks. Only the white wolf hesitated as he barked at his brethren, but despite his apparent displeasure at their hasty retreat, he was not far behind them when he turned to see the huge zombie bearing down on him. If Trey had been coordinated enough to dive for his prey, he might have caught the wolf as it bolted through the door, but he wasn't.

The werewolf pack's barks — which managed to sound angry, frightened, and bewildered all at once — echoed through the surrounding woods for a minute more ... and then they were gone, with only the cluttered damage to the cabin to show they had ever been there.

"Stupid wolves!" Trey stammered. He paced outside on the front porch, clearly wishing he could chase them but knowing that he would never catch them (which was, in itself, a good sign that he was calming down). "Stupid ... stupid wolves! Bit me ... stupid wolves ... *bit* me!"

Sean could guess at the thoughts crawling through his angry mind: Although Trey could sustain and recover from virtually any injury short of massive head trauma or fire, unlike Sean and Alistaire, his healing rate was, if anything, *slower* than that of a living human. While Trey would never die from blood loss or infection, a minor laceration could take days, sometimes weeks to close properly. Now that Trey's arm and leg had been bitten, it would be nearly

impossible for him to pass for normal during this mission —
even with bandages, there would be no hiding the stench
from anyone.

Sean opened his mouth to tell Trey to calm down, then
decided to let him be. He struggled to pull himself to his
feet, and was a bit startled when a pale, bestial hand reached
down to help him up.

Alistaire stood over him. His expression was blank,
but his luminescent eyes were difficult to meet. Sean
nodded his appreciation, swallowed his nerve, and allowed
Alistaire to pull him up to his feet.

The cabin swirled and tilted. Sean was one tough
werewolf, but he had taken a lot of punishment and lost a lot
of blood. He opened his mouth to comment, when he
noticed that Alistaire was staring down at his torso. Sean
followed his gaze, fearful that the white wolf might have
torn up his ribs even worse than he had realized ... but it
wasn't that simple.

Alistaire was staring at his blood.

A tickle of fear danced down Sean's spine like a little
spider. He glanced back up into the vampire's face and
cringed at the seared look of the vampire's flesh — Alistaire
looked like he just *might* burst into flames at any moment,
just like in the movies after all. "Get back in yer coffin,
Alistaire."

Alistaire did not respond. He just stood there, looking
at Sean's blood; a blackened tongue darted forth to lick his
lips. Nope, this was *not* the Alistaire that Sean knew.

Sean called out, "Trey!"

The zombie was still pouting out on the porch, still
muttering, "Stupid wolves ..."

"*Trey*!" Sean yelled louder. "Get in here, *now*!"

The zombie appeared a moment later, his bottom lip protruding. "What?"

Sean gestured to the vampire, whose gaze had not budged an inch. "Help Alistaire back into his coffin. Right now, do ye understand?"

That was enough to finally bring Trey back to his senses. He nodded and moved to Alistaire's side; fortunately, Alistaire did not resist as Trey pulled him toward his coffin, though he maintained his hungry stare at Sean's bloody wounds.

"Make sure he's still got plenty of blood packs in there with him," Sean undertoned.

Trey nodded again.

Once Alistaire's face was out of sight, Sean lowered himself into the only unbroken chair in the kitchen nook. "And let's get that coffin down into the cellar as soon as we can. I don't think they'll be back anytime soon, but I don't want to take any chances."

Trey nodded once more.

Sean knew that they had gotten lucky this morning. Their enemy had attacked in force, using abilities beyond Sean's own; Sean was torn to ribbons, Trey's wounds stank to high heaven, and who knows what lasting damage Alistaire would suffer, especially if he later remembered how he had gazed at Sean's blood.

The Triumvirate had won ... but it was a Pyrrhic victory.

Somewhere out in the woods, a single wolf howled. Sean suspected it might be the alpha female, but he was in too much pain to be sure.

Nine

But it wasn't the alpha female.

It was the white wolf. And he was pissed.

His eye hurt, his jaws hurt, his tail hurt, and he could not rid himself of the stench of that rotting thing the Intruder called a "zombie." It had all gone wrong, and the white wolf was furious about it.

As the pack hurried to meet their alpha, the white wolf began to swerve away from the group. The red wolf noticed. "we are to return to the Den."

The white wolf chuffed. He saw that the red wolf's mouth was still bleeding from what the Intruder had done to him; when he remembered that the Intruder had done all of this to *both* of them — *while in human form* — it prompted the white wolf to growl to himself.

The red wolf repeated, "we are to return to the Den when we are finished."

"we did not finish!"

Now the red wolf chuffed. "she will want to know what happened."

The white wolf knew that, and he wasn't looking forward to her reaction. He was *tired* of her reactions, her rejections, her leading the pack as though she were male — she should be his mate and tending to their children, not guiding the pack!

But the white wolf knew better than to challenge her directly. She had brought them the *power*, the freedom from their old lives and the ability to run through the wilds as they saw fit. And it had been made clear in very short order that she was the alpha, that *she* was the strongest. To drive the point home, she would choose a victim upon which she — and *only* she — was allowed to feed; it flew in the face of her Us-Against-Them bravado, but it also fortified her position of authority.

Then why did she not *join* them when they attacked the Intruder? Why had she merely told them what to do, snapping her fingers and sending them on their way like dogs? Had she known to *fear* this zombie, this vampire? Had she been willing to sacrifice the pack to save her own fur?

In the end, the white wolf veered off on his own, and the red wolf disregarded him.

He knew the alpha would be angry; she had made it clear that he was no longer to venture into the Man's territory alone, not until they had made it all their own. But she would *already* be angry that they had failed to kill the Intruder and destroy those other things, so he did not care.

Some foliage brushed the side of his face, irritating his injured eye. He knew that he would heal soon — the alpha brought not only the ability to change form, but to survive and recover from almost any harm — but for now he was hurting and aching, and spoiling for a way to vent his anger. When he walked on two legs, too many *thoughts* were like litter in his mind, always cluttering his center ... but when he ran on four legs, things were so much simpler.

He needed to hunt. He needed to *kill*.

He did not have to search long. Not far from a small river, he caught wind of what he was seeking. Laying his ears back, he snarled his pleasure and picked up speed.

He nearly missed his prey because he was watching the land (and the fact that his prey was on the side of his wounded eye did not help), but a splash brought his attention to the waterline. The man was standing about ten feet off the shore, with long rubber boots running up to his hips and a long stick — a *fishing pole*, he remembered — in one hand and a can of beer in the other. A small yellow tent was pitched a short distance from the edge of the river. He could smell the human's sweat, flatulence, and sickening cologne.

This man did not match their recent prey. The alpha had focused on those who hunted on the land, those who hunted wolves and other large animals with their despicable guns. Soon enough, *all* humans who entered their territory would be their prey, but for now, the alpha had insisted that they focus on those who posed a threat, however scant.

This man, this "fisherman," was no threat at all.

The white wolf did not care.

He crept forward, low to the ground but not quite crawling. He wove through the taller grass, his ears flattened and tail down to avoid detection — he did not fear this man, not in the least, but he preferred to avoid the cold water, and if the man saw him too early, he might try swimming across the river to escape.

The man was oblivious. He was paying more attention

to his beer than his fishing pole or the world around him. The wolf knew well how closed the senses of a human were, how empty and numb. He need not have bothered with stealth.

He rose to full stance, already judging the leap from the shallowest water onto the man's back ...

"Whoa! Dad, *look*!"

Both the wolf and the man gave a start, and together turned to the source.

A young boy had emerged from the yellow tent. His hair was tousled, and he smelled as though he had just awakened. He was still on his hands and knees from having crawled out of the tent, but one hand was pointing forward — pointing at the white wolf.

"Dad, is that a *wolf*?" the boy asked, and there was no fear in his voice, no scent of dread on his skin. He was young, and naiveté was preventing him from recognizing the danger which stood a mere twenty feet from him. "That's cool! Can I take a picture of it?"

The wolf blinked, then turned back to the man.

The man shared none of the boy's naiveté, and he knew damn well that this was a serious situation. "Hey!" the man yelled. "Get away from there!"

The wolf heard the tremor in the man's voice. It amused him.

"Get away!" the man repeated. "Scat!" The man drew back and hurled his beer can at the wolf. It missed its mark by a wide margin.

"Dad, stop!" the boy scolded, aghast at the man's actions. "It's hurt, see? Look at the blood!" The boy stood and produced a gray object from his pocket. With one hand held out as though to show he meant no harm, he stepped toward the wolf.

The man broke into action. He rushed for the shore, waving his fishing pole like a flag. He cried out, but his words all ran together without meaning. The water was slowing him down, and he splashed a lot as his legs pumped in their long rubber boots.

The object in the boy's hand made a soft *clicking* sound, which the wolf barely heard over the racket the man was making. The part of the wolf which was also a man recognized the plastic device, but its name did not come readily to mind ... not that it mattered.

The wolf crept forward, toward the boy.

The boy wore a giddy smile as he looked at the back of the plastic device — he seemed rather pleased with whatever he had just done. He returned his attention to the wolf ... and when he saw the look in the wolf's good eye, his smile faltered. Finally, he began to leak the scent of fear that the wolf enjoyed so much.

The man reached the shoreline, and his speed increased. He continued to yell and wave his fishing pole back and forth, until he was finally close enough to smash it down onto the wolf's back.

This was nothing. The man was not a shape-shifter, nor was he a vampire or zombie. The white wolf barely felt the sting through his thick fur as the pole snapped across his firm shoulders, still held in one loose piece only by the thin wire that ran through its little loops. He turned his cold gaze to the man, who stood in place like a dullard as he made a little hiccup sound in the back of his throat. He dropped the broken pole and took a step back, his left hand reaching out to pull his boy away with him.

too late, the wolf said to the man, though the man could not understand.

The wolf sprang forward, his teeth bared as he leaped straight at the man's face. The man turned away, but he was not fast enough to prevent the wolf from clamping down on him from ear to chin.

The boy screamed as the wolf's weight dragged the man down.

The wolf shook his head from side to side, and the delicious blood flowed. The man's arms wrapped around the wolf's body as though he were hugging the animal, his fingers gripping into the thick fur with very little force. The wolf could not see the man's expression from this angle, but he knew that it would be blank — he could smell and taste the man's shock.

Planting his forelegs against the man's chest, the wolf wrenched backward in a firm tug. He pulled away from the man's face, taking a good amount of skin and meat with him. His jaws still ached from his fight with the Intruder, but not enough to prevent his opening wide to tear back into the man's throat.

Only when the man was twitching in his death throes did the wolf remember the boy. With liberal amounts of blood dripping from his soaked face, he turned to regard the child.

The boy was gasping for breath, with every exhale punctuated by a short, scratchy cry. His mouth was slack, a string of drool running down onto his shirt. He smelled of even deeper shock than the man had.

If the fisherman had represented no threat, then this

young pup was barely worth the effort it would take to chew his tender meat. And, while the fisherman was not the kind of "hunter" that the alpha had chosen to pursue, this boy could still serve to spread the tale to others, to share with the world that these woods no longer belonged to the Man, but to the Wolf.

The white wolf thought about it for another second or two, then made his decision.

He leaped, his bloody fangs spread wide ... and the boy cried no more.

TEN

The pounding in his head grew stronger. Louder, even. How was that possible? Could a throbbing headache actually become audible?

"Mister Mallory?! Are you in there?!"

Slowly, grudgingly, Sean began to wake up. His side hurt, his cheek hurt, his head, his leg, his hands ... hell, his bloody *hair* hurt! And whoever was pounding on the door wasn't helping at all.

"Trey," Sean grumbled without opening his eyes, "answer that."

No answer. At least, not from Trey.

"That's it," came the somewhat familiar voice again, though it was pitched low this time. The door swung open.

Sean sat up on the cot just as Artur appeared. The cabin door had been repaired on the fly and without proper tools, and the harsh entrance was too much for its patched hinges. It broke loose again at the top, then at the bottom, then fell over flat with a loud *crash* that sent icepicks through Sean's sensitive ears.

Artur was left standing with his mouth agape, and only the doorknob in his hand. If Sean hadn't been in so much pain, it might have been funny.

"What in ... the *hell* ...?" Artur muttered as he stepped forward and took in the rest of the trashed cabin.

"Sorry about the mess," Sean said, pushing himself to his feet. He did his best to hide his limp as he walked over to the doctor, but his calf felt as though it were on fire. Normally, he would already be well on his road to recovery, but the pack had really torn him up, and the fact that these injuries came from other supernatural beings slowed the healing process — it was going to take him a while to recuperate. "We'll do what we can to repair the damage when this is over. And we'll reimburse ye for any security deposit ye might have placed."

Artur turned back to face him, his face burning with evident anger and his mouth opening to unleash a tirade ... but when he absorbed the sight of Sean before him, he swallowed whatever he had been about to say. Instead he gasped, "Good God, Mallory ... what *happened* here? What happened to *you*?"

"Let's just say that the first salvos have been fired in this little war of ours." Sean smiled to keep it lighthearted, and it hurt his cheek.

"You've seen them?" Artur asked, his voice low. "They— they *attacked* you?"

"Aye."

"But ... but you just got here *last night*!"

Sean shrugged.

The doctor stole a quick glance back at the open door. "How ... how long ago?"

"Don't know for sure. It happened first thing this morning, bright and early."

Artur relaxed, but only for a moment. "And you're still

alive. That is amazing! But ... you didn't stop them."

Sean shook his head. "No, we ... wait, how did ye know—?"

"There's been another attack. That's why I'm here. Two more people were killed this morning. A fisherman and his little boy."

The light darkened for Sean. "Bloody hell ..." He hobbled over to the unbroken chair and collapsed into it. "Ye're sure it happened this morning?"

"Yes," Artur answered. He stepped toward another chair, realized it was unusable, then just sort of shuffled in place. He also finally realized that he was still holding the homeless doorknob, and placed it on the end table. "It's the quickest we've found a victim. Rigor had not even fully set in by the time I got there. I came here as soon as I could get away, but I can't stay long." Then he looked at Sean again, and his professional training kicked in. "God, let me check you over! My bag is in my car."

"No. Thanks, but I'll—"

"Don't be ridiculous. You've bled through your dressings! And for that matter, how in the hell *did* you survive an attack when no one else has? How many wolves were there? Did you kill *any* of them—?"

"Ye know, Doctor, ye're right. I think I could use some first aid after all, if ye would be so kind." He grimaced, holding a pained hand to his side.

Artur sputtered a moment, his momentum brought up short, just as Sean had intended. He nodded, glanced around the cabin one more time, then hurried back out to his car.

In spite of the discomfort involved, Sean made a fist

and pounded it against the table. Those bastards must have gone straight from the cabin to their next kill. If only he'd been able to stop them ... but he made no serious recriminations there — he had been damn lucky to survive, and he knew it.

Then it occurred to him: Where the hell was *Trey*?

Before he could call out — perhaps the zombie had hidden down in the fruit cellar with Alistaire? — Artur reappeared. "Take your shirt off. Do you need help?"

Sean shook his head, but when the act of pulling his T-shirt over his head prompted an audible groan, Artur helped him anyway.

"This one appears to be bleeding the worst," Artur said as he carefully removed the bandages from Sean's torso. "I'll take a look here first— Good God!"

"Looks worse than it is ..."

"Pardon my language, sir, but *bullshit*. I can see your *ribs,* for God's sake! Mister Mallory, Sean, you *must* be taken to a hospital!"

"Artur, I'll be fine. Just patch me up—"

"Don't be an idiot! Why, the risk of infection alone is enough reason to ..."

Artur continued on while Sean's head spun. What could he say to the man? How could he explain that infection was not an issue for a lycanthrope without ... well, explaining that he was a lycanthrope? If only he could focus, but his head was throbbing worse than ever ...

Now Artur was actually lifting him to his feet. "Come on, let's go. You need a lot more medical attention than I can provide here. We're leaving."

"Artur—"

"Sean, if I have to sedate you, I will. Your airsick friend can just—"

"Sean ...?"

Sean and Artur froze in an awkward embrace, like two drunken dancers captured in an embarrassing photograph.

Trey stood in the open doorway, his arms full of corded firewood for the stove. He must have recognized the doctor from the previous night; otherwise he would likely have already rushed to Sean's "rescue." But that wasn't the problem.

The problem was that Trey was not wearing his sunglasses or his woolen cap; his milky eyes and necrotized skin were in full view. And worse, while Sean's blood had soaked through his bandages to partial visibility, Trey's dark ichor had drenched his own dressings to render them almost useless — if they were not changed soon, he would begin dripping pus and other gross bodily fluids onto the floor. Not to mention the rotten smell that was wafting in through the open doorway.

Artur's eyes threatened to pop right out of their sockets. His head creaked from side to side, as though to deny what he saw before him. He was both a doctor and a coroner — the man knew a *corpse* when he saw one, even one standing on its own two feet.

Sean saw they were on the verge of losing their only contact, their only ally, in this unfamiliar land, and he could think of just one way to *maybe* prevent that from happening. If he were lucky.

What the hell? he thought. *We're here because the man allowed for the* possibility *of werewolves in his proverbial backyard. What have I got to lose?*

"Artur," he said, "maybe I should explain some things..."

* * *

"No," Artur said. "I do not believe you. You must think I'm an idiot, Mallory. A moron. It's insulting. I'm leaving now."

Firm, steadfast words. Taken from a transcript, they would leave no doubt as to the doctor's position on Sean's tale of werewolves and the supernatural (even though he had avoided using the "Z" word, and had steered clear of the "V" topic altogether).

They did not, however, explain Artur's quivering voice, his shaking hands, his wide eyes studying Trey from where he stood across the room, or the scent of dread leaking from his every pore. Or the fact that he made no move from his chair to the door.

"No," Artur said again, his voice barely above a whisper this time. "I don't believe you. I *can't* believe you." He turned his eyes away from Trey to look at Sean, to *implore* Sean with tears that threatened to spill free with his next blink. "Do you understand, Mallory? I *cannot* believe this. I ... I just can't ... I *can't*."

"All right, Artur ..." Sean began.

"Arthur," the doctor said, and now his voice was below a whisper, barely audible even to Sean's sensitive hearing. His gaze had fallen to the floor.

"What's that?"

"My name is *Arthur*, not 'Artur.' Artur is what my Russian grandmother used to call me. My grandmother ..."

"Okay, Arthur," Sean said, being sure to keep his voice casual. He leaned against the table, trying to somehow favor both his side and his calf. It also said something about Arthur's state of mind that he was allowing his injured would-be-patient to stand while he sat in the only chair, his breath coming in little gulps. "Tell me ... ye said that the latest victims had been found much faster than the others. How did that happen?"

Arthur blinked at Sean for a moment as though he had no idea what the Irishman was going on about. Then, with another furtive glance at Trey, he answered, "Oh ... yes. Well, uh, you see ... this time there was a witness. Sort of."

"A witness?" Sean had been halfway to folding his arms, but now he jerked to attention. His wounds protested, but he ignored them.

"Not directly, no. So far as I know, *you* ... and your friend over there ... are the only people to have had actual contact with these wolves and lived. Besides myself, I guess. But the boy took a picture of one of them with his cell phone and sent it straight to his mother."

"I thought ye mentioned that cell phones don't work this far north."

Arthur shook his head. "Normally they don't, no. We usually have to rely on satellite phones. But with all the attacks and the inflow of state and federal officials, a cellular tower was installed on top of the police station in town." He smirked, an ugly expression for him. "They wanted to keep it as a dedicated tower for official use only, but they were so damned worried about keeping this quiet ... well, I guess that's not an issue anymore. Not now."

"Well, that's not for certain. Ye said the policeman ...

Carter was his name?"

"*Caster*, Ray Caster. Yes, he's been doing his best to keep this under wraps — that's why I turned to my blog about it in the first place. That and ..." He stole another peek at Trey, then let it drop. "But that's all over with now. The boy's mother has been screaming to high heaven over this, threatening to sue the entire *state* of Alaska if that 'dirty animal' isn't taken care of. The day's not over yet and the media's already gotten hold of this." He sighed. "It's only a matter of time before the other attacks are dragged out into the open. There's going to be some holy hell to pay."

Sean considered this for a moment. "Ye know, I'm not sure if this is good or bad for us. I mean, the more attention this gets, the more likely the, uh ... 'natures' of these beasts will finally be exposed. If ye ask me, this world o' yers could use a real kick in the arse when it comes to yer so called 'superstitions'." Sean started to continue, but he saw that overwhelmed look returning to Arthur's eyes, so he moved on. "On the other hand, it could make it that much more difficult for *us* to proceed if the constabulary is underfoot."

Arthur shrugged. "At this point, I just want this all over with. All this death ... it's enough to drive a man to drink." Then he snorted with ironic humor as he added, "You know, I *had* decided to come out here and cancel our ... contract, or whatever it is we have. I'd been letting my bourbon make too many decisions for me lately. But when I saw that little boy this morning ..."

"You shouldn't ... drink too much," Trey said. Arthur jerked as though Trey had fired a rifle rather than spoken.

Unfortunately, Trey did not absorb this as he took a small step forward. "Sean sometimes—"

"*Keep away from me!*" Arthur cried, scrambling up and around to place the chair between Trey and himself. All the panic and tension from which Sean had distracted him was back twofold. He looked like he was going to hyperventilate.

"Trey ..." Sean waved him away, and Trey retreated; his expression suggested that his feelings were hurt, but thankfully, he did not argue.

"I'm sorry," Arthur panted. "I'm just ... I'm sorry." His eyes danced in every direction but Trey's.

"Maybe we should continue our talk outside?"

Arthur nodded with vigor. "Yes, yes, let's do that, outside, yes."

Sean steered him toward the cabin door, making sure to keep his body between Arthur and Trey the whole way. Once he had maneuvered the man to the porch, he hesitated long enough to say, "Trey, see if ye can fix this door again, please."

Trey nodded.

Sean had expected to find Arthur still on the porch, but in the brief second he had spoken to Trey, the man had put an impressive distance between himself and the cabin. If he had hustled in a slightly different direction, Sean might have feared he was making a break for his car.

"You know ..." Arthur said as Sean approached. "... a few months ago I would have had you committed for the things you told me in there. Hell, just a few weeks ago I might've been ready to commit *myself* for listening to you. Now, I don't even ..." He looked down, then kicked at a rock and muttered, "*Fuck.*"

Sean kept silent for the moment, letting him finish.

"Look, Sean ... I do not believe in the supernatural, all right? I *don't*. But ... whatever is happening around here, *I* can't explain it. I can't explain these wolves' behavior, and I can't explain some of the things I've seen ..." He stared back at the cabin. "...*especially* now. But whatever is going on, you seem to have some insight into it. You have clearly had a tussle with wild animals that should have eaten you alive, and I don't know *what* to make of your friend in there. So I'm going to assume that you really can help, somehow, and I'll keep feeding you information for as long as I can."

"Believe me, Arthur, I wish I could prove it to ye, right here 'n now. But with the new moon—"

Arthur closed his eyes and held up a firm hand. "Stop! Okay? Just ... *stop.*"

"All right."

Arthur opened his eyes, saw from Sean's expression that his request was taken seriously, then relaxed a bit. He glanced at his watch, though it was such a quick, jerky motion that Sean doubted he really saw whatever time it was. "Look, I've got to get back into town. I can't have Caster wondering where I've run off to. And who knows if I'll have to sign over to a Guard doctor by the end of the day or—"

"I'm sorry, sign over to a what?"

Arthur shrugged. "A doctor with the National Guard. I have no idea how much longer I'll be on this case."

"Arthur, I think I must have missed something here ..."

"Oh. Sorry, I was just so ... anyway, yes, with this

latest attack and the mother screaming for media attention, the need for expedience is passing the need for hush. If the state police and park rangers don't take care of this very soon, as in *immediately*, the Governor is threatening to bring in the National Guard to deal with it."

"The National Guard," Sean repeated.

Arthur nodded. "Overkill, I know. Personally, I think that'll make a bigger mess of things than we already have, but you know politicians — if there's a hint that they haven't done enough, their first impulse is to do *too* much."

"But bringing in the *military*—"

"I know, I know. They'll just march in here and shoot every wolf in sight. I wouldn't be surprised if they double-use it as a training exercise."

"But they can't blame *all* wolves for this! That's ridiculous! Even if we *didn't* know what we know, surely ye understand that it's a *single pack* that is the problem?"

"I *know*, Sean. Believe me, no one *wants* it to come to that kind of fiasco — that's why it's been kept quiet up until now. Caster and the Governor don't want that because of what it'll do to our summer tourism and the region's reputation; you and I don't want that because of what it will do to the local wildlife. And you know it won't just be the other wolves that get hurt in the crossfire — they'll be shooting at anything furry, and I shudder to think of the human injuries from friendly fire ..." He drew a deep breath, then shook his head in a slow, defeated gesture. "But, Sean ... the killing has *got* to stop. One way or the other. If you want my advice, this is it: *Whatever* it is that you and your friend in there do, you had better do it very, very fast. All it will take is one more victim — hell, if this poor mother has her way, it might not even take that."

They stood in silence for a moment, Sean not knowing what to say and Arthur too exhausted, in mind and body, to go on.

Finally, Arthur muttered, "I hate this. All of it. Do what you can. I have to go." With that, he returned to his car, and was soon driving out of sight.

"No," Sean said, feeling overwhelmed and angry. But then he looked to the wilderness around him, and when he spoke again, it was not a denial — it was a promise. *"No."*

ELEVEN

"You ... did ... *what*?"

The white wolf refused to cower, refused to hunch his shoulders or step back ... but he did avert his eyes.

After the rush of killing the fisherman and his child had passed, the white wolf stalled as long as he could, dragging his feet — almost literally — before returning to the den that evening. The other wolves had gathered round upon his return, hovering near the entrance of the small cave they had claimed as their own. The white wolf tried to ignore them as he strode inward with as much confidence as he could muster.

The smell inside the den had distracted him at first. As he passed through the ingress into the inner cavern, he located the source of the odor. The alpha knelt across from him in her human form, but his attention was drawn to the figure over which she huddled: The wolf who had been bitten by that "zombie" from the cabin.

Although their kind could recover from almost any injury, the wounds the white wolf had received from the Intruder were proving sluggish to heal. This was double the case for his brethren whose belly had been partially *eaten*.

The alpha had been pressing some sort of plant into the

wound on her patient's belly, the act of which prompted a whine of pain. The white wolf did not know what the plant was, but these things held little interest for him.

"You did not return," she had said without looking at him. "Explain."

He had grunted, kept his eyes on his sick packmate.

"Shift. Talk to me."

Resigned to what would come next, he had shifted into wolfman form, but still said nothing at first.

"Now explain," she said, her back still to him.

Clenching his humanoid hands into fists, the white wolf had confessed. He told her of his frustration over their unexpected defeat at the cabin, his need to lash out, and finally his actions by the river.

That was when she whirled around to glare at him and spat the question. She repeated it now, faster, louder, "You did *what*?!"

Struggling not to shuffle his feet, he said again, "I brought down a man and his boy." To compensate for his intimidation, he puffed out his chest and tried bravado. "What of it? We have hunted *many* men since you gave us the gift. Why—?"

"A fisherman is not the same thing as a hunter," she growled, "unless you are likening yourself to a *trout*. And we have *never* brought down children!"

Steeling himself, the white wolf lifted his eyes to meet her gaze. "So what?"

The alpha stood frozen for a moment, her eyes burning and boring into him. He heard a few snorts, whines, and shuffles behind him, which only now made him realize that their exchange held an audience.

He had finally openly defied her, but he had done so in front of the whole pack. That was his biggest mistake.

The alpha came at him so fast, he had no chance of evasion. She shifted in the blink of an eye, so when he was slammed backward into the cave wall, it was a wolfwoman who pinned him against the stone, her claws digging into his shoulders.

"Your attitude is wearing thin."

Before he could respond in any way, she yanked him away from the wall, tossing him over her shoulder and throwing him onto the stone floor. He skidded several feet, coming to a stop not far from the zombie-bitten wolf. He was scrambling to gain his feet when she descended upon him. He fought back as best he could, but his efforts were in vain — even if she had not started from a dominant position atop him, she was the strongest of them all. He hated that fact, but it was true.

The alpha trapped him on his side, his arms twisted into an awkward tangle. She then bent forward and sank her teeth into his neck.

He went slack in an instant and whined his submission. But this did not satisfy her. She continued to crush him down into the stone, to clamp her jaws harder and harder, tighter and tighter. Blood ran into the fur at his neck, and he cried out.

"You are alpha!" he grunted as best he could. "I submit to you!"

But she wanted more — he knew it, and began to fear that if he did not give in to her, she might actually kill him.

Humbled and humiliated, the white wolfman released his bladder, wetting the fur of his groin and belly as it pooled beneath him.

At last, she released his neck, and not with ease. She spat the fur she wrenched out into his face, but he knew not to move or react in any way. She stood and towered over him, waiting for the slightest sign of defiance.

He remained very still.

"You are not to leave this den until I say otherwise. This is your only warning."

When he wisely said nothing, she looked around to regard the other members of her pack. They had kept a safe distance, but had not retreated — the alpha disciplining a wayward member was neither shocking nor unexpected. She gestured for the red wolf to come forward; he did so without hesitation, and shifted from wolf to wolfman without being told.

"You are my second now," she told him. "Please me, and I may choose you as my mate."

The red-furred wolfman nodded his understanding and pleasure. "Yes."

"This dog ..." she gestured to the white wolfman, and again flicked a glance in his direction to watch for rebellion; there was none. "... has escalated things. Humans will not stand for a child's death. Between this, and the Intruder and his own 'pack' ..."

Several wolves chuffed in anger to this reference; others whined in distress.

" ... we must be cautious. Remember! We are not invincible. *Yet*." She paused for dramatic effect, then said to the red wolfman, "We had a task when we first met the Intruder last night. That is more important now than before."

"I understand. I will go out alone. I will be careful, and quiet."

The alpha nodded, and gestured. Shifting, the red wolf left the cave on all fours.

Returning to her human form, the alpha sneered down at the white wolfman, making a point of eyeing the puddle of urine in which he laid. Wrinkling her nose, she said, "Clean up that mess."

The white wolfman did as he was told, and his hate was palpable.

This is the Intruder's fault. Everything was fine before he *showed up. Damn him.*

Damn him!

TWELVE

A myriad of cloying odors permeated the so-called "fruit cellar." While Sean was certain that actual fruit had indeed been stored down here from time to time, those scents were joined by the stale redolence of a dozen different animal hides, mushrooms, mold, mildew, sex (both human and animal), bodily waste (both human and animal), marijuana, model glue, and what might have been a human corpse from long, long ago.

But Sean was only aware of these things on the periphery. What had his attention was the reek of charred flesh and decay that seeped from Alistaire.

It was nearing "nighttime." The rest of the day had passed without incident, and the sun was now lower on the horizon again, its power muted by the denser barrier of atmosphere. In a few hours it would slip behind the nearest mountains and let the stars take a little peek. Sean was feeling better, though he was far from one-hundred percent, and intended to do a reconnaissance around the cabin as soon as he could push himself into wolfman form.

Despite the fact that it was even earlier than the previous evening, Alistaire seemed improved from the additional protection of the cellar. At least, as far as his lucidity and pall were concerned — he still suffered from his exposure to the morning sun during the wolves' attack. His skin was blistered and his eyes were bloodshot and irritated. Even his hair had been partially bleached, shooting through his normally deep black locks with salt-and-pepper, heavy on the salt.

He looked bad, but he smelled worse. He smelled ... *scorched.*

Sean, of course, did not comment on it.

"... so that's where we stand," he concluded, having relayed all the news he had gotten from Arthur. "Once it gets out that these killings have been going on for months, the public and media will be up in arms, and the Governor will overreact accordingly. Unless we can settle the matter first."

"I see ..." Alistaire said, and nothing else.

This unusual reticence made Sean uneasy. Trying to cover his fluster, he continued, "We can't wait for the new moon to pass. If I can meet them at night, at least I'll be able to reach half-wolf. It was warmer today, and Trey says he's feeling a bit better, too. But we still don't know what to expect from these wolves, or how they were able to take wolf form when I can't." He paused — still nothing from Alistaire. "If ye have any words of advice, I could use them."

At length, Alistaire nodded and said, *"I do have some advice. But you will not want to hear it."*

Uh-oh. "... all right. Shoot."

Alistaire first muttered, *"Es muss wohl sein,"* under his breath, then spoke up. *"I believe we should execute a strategic retreat."*

" 'A strategic—' "

"*I believe we should leave, and return to California.*"

Sean waited a second or two for a punch line, until he remembered that Alistaire rarely cracked jokes. He tried to deflate the tension with a flippant, "Ye're right, I *don't* want to hear it." When the German's face remained stolid, Sean's blood began to rise. "Alistaire, ye can*not* be serious."

"*I am.*"

For a moment, Sean was too flabbergasted and infuriated to continue. He paced toward the steps leading out of the cellar, then spun on his heel and rushed back. "Ye're giving up. *You*, of all people!"

"*I have not survived the ages by pressing forward with battles that I cannot win. I was nearly destroyed by the Brigade in England by doing so, and only G-God's grace saved me that night.*" He folded his arms. "*I chose to learn a valuable lesson from that experience, and you should do the same from this one.*"

"Oh, don't give me that—!"

"*Sean, look at us. Look at yourself. You can barely maintain your posture with the pain in your side. Whether you will admit it or not, you are seriously injured. Trey is crippled by the climate, and I am trapped in the shadows; even now, I find it difficult to focus on this very conversation.*"

"This isn't a conversation," Sean growled, "it's a lecture."

Alistaire made as if to sigh, but he did not. "*I do not intend to 'lecture' you, my friend. But you asked for my advice, did you not?*"

Sean fumed for a few seconds before admitting, "Aye, that I did. I thought ye might have something *helpful* to offer, not cowardice."

Alistaire's poker face actually slipped for a moment as he clenched his jaw in annoyance. *"You have known me for years, Sean Mallory. When have you ever had cause to question my courage, or my Faith?"*

"Never. Until now. And don't go dragging yer goddamn 'faith' into this ..." Alistaire flinched at his taking the Lord's Name in vain, but Sean ignored it. "... not when ye're willing to sacrifice these people, not to mention all the innocent wolves!"

"I am not 'sacrificing' anyone whom I have the ability to save. But we cannot be everywhere, nor can we save all the people who seek our aid. G-God did not give us that kind of power, and nor should he, else we should think ourselves higher than we truly are. As for the animals ..."

Sean barked at him, "Alistaire, I swear, if ye start in on how the animals are under 'Man's domain,' the white nights will be the *least* of yer problems."

Alistaire stiffened — Sean had *never* threatened him with physical violence, however oblique that threat might have been. In sharp, terse words, he asked, *"Sean, what is wrong with you?"*

Sean's face burned. "There's nothing wrong with *me*, but if ye could see yerself in the mirror, I'd suggest ye take a good—!"

"Enough!" Alistaire snapped. *"Where was this hostility when we retreated from the vampire haven in Hampton? Where were these accusations of 'cowardice' when we avoided the undead outbreak outside of Elkwood*

City, or when we allowed the werewolf to slip away into Hillman State Park?"

Sean deflated as Alistaire ran through the list. He grumbled, "Trey was in no shape to continue at Hillman Park ..."

"Yes. And how would you evaluate his 'shape' now? Or mine? Or yours?"

"Fine. Fine, whatever. Ye've made yer point."

"No, I do not believe I have. This is not the first time we have acknowledged overwhelming odds. We have retreated and regrouped before, and when possible, we returned. You know that."

"... aye."

"Something has happened to you. You have been ... different for some time now. Edgy, more hostile. I would like to know why."

Sean shrugged. "What can I say, Alistaire? The move to this world has been difficult for all of us ..."

Alistaire was already shaking his head. *"No, Sean. I am not buying it. Your disquiet predates our move to this world, and you know it."*

"I 'know' no such thing," Sean said, moving toward the open cellar door.

Alistaire stepped sideways to block him. *"This truly began the night you saw Mark Hudson's illustrations of your sister as a werewolf."*

"Whatever ye say, Alistaire," Sean dismissed him with another, faster move toward the cellar entrance.

But with speed inherent to a vampire, Alistaire again stood in his way before he could reach the stairs. *"I have respected your privacy in this matter. But if it is going to impair your judgement ... "*

Sean would not meet his gaze. "It won't. I'm sorry for my behavior. I'll tell Trey that we're leaving."

"I am not the 'leader' of this Triumvirate — I merely gave you my opinion. And we will consider Trey's thoughts as always, such as they are."

Sean still refused to look him in the eye. "What do ye *want* from me, Alistaire?"

"I want to know what happened in Ireland."

Sean finally looked up, revealing a glisten in his eyes. "I ... I don't want to talk about that, Alistaire. Please don't make me."

A tense silence stretched between them for nearly a minute before Alistaire sighed. *"All right. For now."*

"Thanks."

Alistaire waved it away. *"Let us consult with Trey. I believe the sun has retreated enough to allow me to leave this basement in relative comfort."*

Alistaire turned and ascended the stairs with that floating manner of his, but Sean did not immediately follow. For the moment, he could not trust himself to do anything more than just stand there and breathe.

After a time, he climbed up to join his team in the wrecked cabin above ... but his mind was two years in the past, and over four thousand miles away.

Ye won't be able to hide from this much longer.

I know.

XIII

"Why, as I live and breathe!" Samuel cried. "Sean Mallory!"

Sean was caught a bit off-guard. He had spent the last several years in the United States, the majority of that time in big cities, so he had somewhat forgotten what it was like to live in a close-knit village. In New York City or Pittsburgh, one could visit the local bars two nights in a row without seeing a single familiar face, even among the barkeep staff; hell, even Dublin's pubs could get pretty damned crowded with total strangers (a "packed house" or a "meat market," take your pick).

But the pubs here where he grew up were different. With the houses sometimes separated by kilometers of old farmland, the pub in the center of town was, in many ways, the heart of the entire community. The place not only to drink a pint or have a bite to eat, but for fellowship and comradery ... or just news and gossip.

As such, it should not have surprised Sean one bit when he was recognized the instant he set foot through the door.

"Sean, m'lad!" Samuel called as he hustled around the bar to meet him. "I haven't see ye in ... why, Lord, it's

been too many years! Come in, come in!"

"Samuel," Sean returned as the older man embraced him in a hug. "How have ye been?"

"Oh, the same! Ye know how it is, lad!" Samuel was taking Sean's duffle bag and guiding him toward one of the tables nearest the bar. Several placeable faces were now turning to regard him, and one or two even nodded in greeting, though none were showing the friendly enthusiasm of the pub's owner. There was no music playing as there almost certainly would be in an American bar, but the room was warm with chatter. Two men were playing darts in one bright corner, and another two were arm-wrestling among a small gathering of onlookers in the opposite, darker corner. The smell of lamb, the brattle of pots and utensils, and the occasional curse drifted from within the kitchen. And pints of beer were evident all around.

"And how's ... how's the wife?" Sean had a panicked moment when he realized that he could not recall her name.

"Oh, Susanna's grand, lad. She'll be glad t' know that ye're home."

I'll bet, *Sean thought. Samuel's wife had never shared her husband's affinity for the young foster children of Conroy and Abigail Finnian. The Finnians spent so much time away from the village, trading in England or abroad in Spain or the States, that Sean and his friends tended to run a bit wild for Susanna's taste. Theresa tried to act the role of mother, of course, but "boys will be boys" and all that.*

Sean's heartbeat hastened when Theresa crossed his

mind.

"*Can I get ye an ale, lad? On th' house!*"

Sean smiled, and it felt more natural now. "Far be it from me to turn down such an offer! I'll take a tall mugful of whatever ye have on tap, sir!"

"Comin' up!" Samuel beamed, and hurried around to the business side of the bar.

Sean released a slow exhale and tried to unwind, but it wasn't easy. He looked around him at the faces, both familiar and not, with so many expressions of relaxation and revelry ... and he envied them.

The circumstances behind his spontaneous return to his homeland were dubious at best. One would think that being a werewolf — and living and working with the undead — would have prepared him for anything, but that was not the case. Being called into another ... world? dimension? reality? whatever it was ... had regressed from being a fascinating excursion to a dreaded nightmare. Inhabiting the body of Mark Hudson was not without its perks; perks by the name of Lora Kilburn, for example. But seeing those drawings, those blasphemies ...

"Blasphemies," did ye say? I'd wager ye've been spending a little too much time with yer Christian friend, lad.

Whatever. The fact was that Hudson's illustrations of Theresa in various stages of ... of wolf-form had unearthed a controversy within Sean that he had labored for years to bury and forget. A controversy that had in fact been his primary reason for leaving this village, and later Ireland entirely.

Thanks to Hudson, he had to deal with this, or he

would never be able to truly move on with his life. Fortunately, since traveling here from Pittsburgh, Hudson's pull had diminished. And the fact that it was the new moon was a fortuitous, marvelous concurrence.

Bang. *"Here ye go, lad!"*

Sean had been so lost in thought that Samuel's slamming the frothy mug onto the table caused him to jump. Given his current occupation, he was lucky that he hadn't lashed out at the older man on reflex.

Instead, he labored for the happy-go-lucky persona which had always come so natural to him until recent weeks. He forced a big, callow grin onto his face, took up the mug, and pulled back a long drink, even smacking his lips in satisfaction afterward.

As he had hoped, Samuel was very pleased with his little show. "Aye, Sean, it's so good to see ye again, lad!" The barkeep slid into the chair across from him. "So, how are the States? Are ye still livin' in New York City?"

Sean shook his head. "I moved on to Pittsburgh, Pennsylvania a few years ago."

"Ah! Grand!" Samuel clapped his hands once. "First New York City, now Pittsburgh! Ye've grown into a real man o' the world!"

Sean smiled and drank more beer.

"And what do ye do for a livin' now?"

"I work in security."

Samuel raised an eyebrow. "Like a constable or something?"

Sean cocked his head in a half-nod. "Close enough."

"Ahhhh ... I see," Samuel said, though his expression suggested that he didn't, which suited Sean just fine.

Before Samuel could ask for further clarification, his thoughts were interrupted.

"Ay! Barkeep!" hollered a red-headed man from across the room, one of the onlookers from the arm-wrestling match. "Why ye sittin' down when ye got customers with dry throats?"

"Ay!" Samuel bellowed right back. "Ye can wait five minutes! Can't ye see I'm talkin' here?"

"I'm thirsty!"

"Shut it, ginger!"

"Fuck ye!"

Samuel half-stood, his grey-haired but still muscular forearms flexing as he made fists on the table. "I said shut it, *ye tosser!"*

The redhead waved at Samuel in anger, but he did indeed shut it and turn back to the arm-wrestlers, one of whom was now rubbing his sore arm and making way for a new challenger.

Sean found himself smiling over the heated exchange. Aye, I be back in Ireland, I am! *He chuckled under his breath.*

"Sorry 'bout that, Sean," Samuel said, once again jovial and relaxed. "What were we ...? Aye, the, uh, the constable job thing..." He looked as though he wanted to push for more details, but instead he just shook his head. "Well, I'm sure Conroy and Abigail will be pleased to hear it."

Sean allowed mild surprise to show on his face. "Are they in town?"

Samuel scoffed and waved a dismissive hand. "Nah, o' course not, lad. Ye remember how they are. No offense."

"Believe me, none taken."

"I understand they make a good livin', doin' what they do, but what's the point if they're never home to enjoy it, aye?"

"Aye."

"Always felt poorly for ye and Theresa ..."

Sean drank from his beer again, just a sip this time, then asked as casually as he could, "And how's Theresa been?"

Now Samuel looked a touch uncomfortable, and when he tried to cover it a moment later, his voice was a little too loud. "Oh, she's been grand, lad!"

"She still mending dresses?"

"Aye. And makin' a few of her own, I hear. That 'n tending that little plot o' land the Finnians keep. Are ye, uh, goin' to yer house from here?"

Sean shrugged. "Probably. Though it's less 'my' house these days, so I was thinkin' of staying at the inn."

"Mmm, mmm. Well, if, uh ..." He scratched at the back of his neck. "If ye wait here a bit longer, ye'll be able to talk to her first."

Sean's pulse quickened. "She's comin' in here tonight, is she?"

"Aye." Then Samuel dropped his voice a bit. "She comes in more often than not." Without waiting for Sean to reply, he raised his voice — again, a little too loud — and said, "Well, I'd better see to the ginger before he blows a gasket. And I'll top off yer drink when ye're ready — all on th' house tonight!"

Sean opened his mouth, but Samuel was already

returning to the bar. He wasn't sure what to make of Samuel's behavior but, coupled with his existing tension over seeing Theresa once again, he didn't like it.

Later, reflecting back on the evening, Sean would recall that Theresa had then appeared, almost instantly, as if on cue. In reality, a bit of time passed — Samuel experienced a brief rush as new customers came in, most of which headed straight for the bar; the arm-wrestling and darts continued; the beer in Sean's mug drained away ... Sean was just lost in thought.

But when the front door opened once more and announced the newest customers with a trill of deep-throated yet feminine laughter, Sean snapped back to attention.

He saw her before she saw him, and he was grateful for the added moments to shore up his defenses. Theresa looked fantastic for her age, as beautiful now as the last time Sean had seen her, more than a decade before, but the young lad with her — and he could tell by the way their arms were entangled that he was "with her" — was many, many moons her junior. The boy looked barely old enough to shave, and his eyes twinkled in delight and wonder that he had been so fortunate to draw the older woman's attentions.

"Samuel!" she called, waving her free arm toward the barkeep. "A bottle of Redbreast at your earliest convenience!"

"Aye, Redbreast!" the lad emphasized in what he probably thought was high wit. "I like the sound of that."

Theresa leered back at him. "Do ye now? I'm so glad to hear it." She tossed her long, dark hair and laughed at his unease. She kissed the tip of his nose, then made as though to plant a far more serious buss upon his lips.

"Robbin' the cradle, aren't ye?" Sean said.

Startled, Theresa looked his way. At first, her face was a mask of disbelief, and she blinked once with heavy lids, as though she half-expected Sean to be gone when she looked again. Once she absorbed the notion that he was, in fact, sitting there in the flesh, she smiled, but with caution.

"Why don't ye mind yer own business?" the boy challenged.

Sean offered him a very brief glance, but said nothing.

"Beagan," Theresa said to the young man, "go get our bottle. And wait for me at the bar."

Beagan bristled. "I'm not gonna let this sodden wanker talk to ye like—"

"That wasn't a suggestion."

Beagan opened his mouth, but bit his tongue as he balanced the worth of his pride against the dreamed-of pleasures of the night to come. In the end, his baser needs won out, and he settled for shooting Sean a hostile glare before doing as he was told.

With the distraction out of the way, Theresa walked toward Sean.

Theresa Mallory. His sister.

Sean hoped that she could not hear his rapid heartbeat. He hoped that she was not capable of hearing it.

She pulled out the chair opposite him, but did not sit immediately. She continued to stare at him as though he might whisk away at any instant. When he neither disappeared nor spoke, she sat down. "Hello, Sean," she said at last.

His throat felt dry and his tongue thick, but he resisted the urge to sip his beer before answering, "Hello, Theresa."

"It's been ages."

"Aye."

As her surprise at his reappearance began to pass, she gained ground. She leaned forward, resting her arms upon the table. "And what brings ye back to this lonely corner of the world?" Her tone was intrigued, but her eyes flickered with heat.

"I ... wanted to see ye again."

"Really? Just like that?" She reclined in her chair, and he steeled himself against her scrutiny. "When was the last time ye called me, Sean? Hell, when was the last time ye sent me a bloody postcard?"

He lifted his mug and nodded slowly. "It's been too long, I know."

"Yer goddamn right it's been too long." It wasn't quite a snap, but it was close. "And how long are ye stayin' ...?"

"I'm not sure. I've got at least a week ..."

"That's big of ye."

Sean stared down at the table. "I just ..." God, he had so much he wanted to say to her, so much he needed to say to her, to ask her ... but he didn't know where to begin, and this wasn't exactly the proper time or place. "I just wanted to see ye, Theresa."

Theresa continued to pierce him with her bright eyes for a few more seconds, then she sighed and relaxed a bit.

"Ah, hell. It's good t' see ye, baby brother."

She smiled, and he returned the gesture.

The sound of a bottle of Redbreast tapping on the bar a few times drew Sean's attention. "Yer date is gettin' restless."

"He'll wait as long as I want him to. And he's hardly my 'date.' He's just my entertainment for the evening." She chuckled. "Don't give me that look, Sean. Ye developed quite a reputation before ye scampered off to Dublin. Is it so impossible to believe that yer sister would want a snog from time t' time?"

"A snog ... or more?"

That *she found downright funny. "A snog, a fuck — either way, it's none of yer business."*

He nodded. "I suppose not."

"Yer damn right." She clapped her hand down on the table. "So ... will ye be stayin' with me then?"

"If that's all right."

"It is. But don't wait up for me tonight. We'll natter tomorrow."

And with a final smile and finger wave, Theresa stood and sashayed back across the room to her entertainment for the evening.

Sean stewed. This was not how he had envisioned their reunion, but then, what exactly had *he expected? And why did he have such a stick up his arse over Theresa's "recreational activities"? He'd been around the block many, many times. And as for their age difference, hadn't Sean himself been using Hudson's body to bugger a dance student half his real age?*

But she's my sister, my Theresa!

Oh, shove off! Don't ye always tell *Alistaire* to lighten up about sex? So why don't *you* try doin' the same?

"Ay! Ye're Sean Mallory, ain't ye?"

Sean looked up to see that the ginger who had been bellowing at Samuel had somehow found his way over to Sean's table. The fellow was a good deal drunk. "Aye. Do I know ye, sir?"

"Ye probably saw me around a bit. I used to work for Abbott and Quain off the southern road?"

Sean nodded, though he still didn't really remember the man.

The man waited so long to speak next, Sean almost asked him if there was a problem. Finally, the man snapped his fingers. "That's it! I remember now! I remember what was ringin' me bell."

"Is that so?"

"It is." The man giggled, and it had an unpleasant edge to it, like a man enjoying a racist joke just a little too much. "It was so bloody daft, I could never forget it."

"Why don't ye enlighten me then, so that I can get back to my beer?"

"Sure, why the fuck not?" The ginger leaned forward on the table, his breath laden with alcohol and old tobacco. In a melodramatic stage whisper, he said, "I heard ye was a werewolf." He shoved himself back upright and roared with laughter, as though it was the funniest punchline in history.

Someone won a round of arm-wrestling at that moment, so the man's words and subsequent cackle were absorbed into the ambiance. Sean found himself surprisingly relieved. "Really?" he asked, rolling his eyes for effect. "And where did ye hear such rubbish?"

"Oh! Oh, it was um ... oh, bloody hell, what was the lad's name ...?"

Sean's face darkened. "Eamon."

"Eamon! That's right! It was years and years ago, when there was some killin' or somethin' ... ah, I don't remember the details. All I remember was some fiery young lad, still wet behind the ears, comin' in here and tryin' t' drum up a huntin' party. All kinds of ballsch about ye bein' a were-wolf *and a* mon-ster. *And the best part was, some old farts actually bought into it!" He giggled until tears gleamed in his eyes. "Lad, ye must o' pissed him off somethin' fierce. What'd ye do, fuck his mother or somethin'?"*

Sean shrugged, which tickled the man even more. If the conversation continued much longer, Sean was going to have to figure out a way to direct it outside.

But the ginger was losing speed now, and his eyes were drifting back toward the arm-wrestling circle. "Ah, well, whatever ye did, ye'd think he coulda picked a better rumor t' spread about ye. Coulda called ye a knobjockey or somethin'."

"Ye'd think."

"Aye. Well, don't go sproutin' fur on us, Mister Mallory!"

"I'll try to restrain myself."

"Good, good. Well, me friends are callin' me back." They weren't, but Sean did not bother to point out the discrepancy. "Come an' join us if ye want."

"Maybe later."

"Good, good." He started to wander off, then turned

back. *"Whatever happened to that Eamon lad, anyway?"*

"He ended up on the trouble side of the 'killing or something'."

"Did he now? Oh, well. See ye around, lad."

Sean watched the redhead rejoin his group, and shook his head. The man could remember the bloody accusations of lycanthropy, but didn't remember the subsequent brouhaha when the hunters Sean killed that night turned up in pieces? Three cheers for the selective memory of an alcoholic.

It was just as Theresa once warned him: Even in the age of reason, superstitions still ran closer to the surface than most wanted to admit.

Of course, Sean was living proof that those secret beliefs were justified.

Sean drank his beer and thought about the night he was hunted by Eamon and his circle of recruits. The night Sean had first willingly used his curse to defend himself. The night Eamon had wounded him with silver and followed him back home.

The night Theresa "took care of everything" for him.

Sean glanced up from his beer to look at Theresa, who was enjoying her time with Beagan on the opposite side of the room. And he was not at all surprised to find that she was looking right back at him.

FOURTEEN

Sean knew what he needed to do. But he wasn't entirely sure how to go about doing it.

He sat at a table in the corner of another pub ... or rather, a "bar," but it amounted to the same — it was the gathering place for many in this Alaskan community. The biggest difference was that, unlike the Irish pub, there *was* music playing in the background here, but even though the music was festive, the people were not.

The various visiting police and ranger authorities had taken to the newer, larger sports bar a couple of miles further south, but that was not the crowd Sean sought. He was looking for the true locals, the men and women who maintained an intimate relationship with these lands, who knew its spirit and moods better than any touristy guide book; people who would *know* that something was wrong, that something had changed.

And hey ... if those who chose to live in such an isolated environment, with its lingering days of summer and forever nights of winter ... if those people were, perhaps, a touch more superstitious than the rest of the so-called civilized world, so much the better.

Sean had spent the previous night in wolfman form,

trying to detect any scent or trail that would lead him to the pack's main territory; since his impression was that they had gone feral, he suspected they might have a *den* rather than individual homes to which they returned. But after hours of scouring the area, he had nothing to show for it. He returned to the cabin for a nap, and then spent the *next* several hours trying it again in human form, but his efforts were once again in vain. It was frustrating, but at least he had not received any word from Arthur about new attacks.

One bright side: Shifting into half-wolf form and back again had done a world of good for his many injuries. He was still a far cry from top condition, but he no longer wondered if perhaps Arthur was correct and he *did* require medical attention.

Alistaire's pressure had also gotten him thinking about his last visit to Ireland, the night he saw Theresa again for the first time in so long. A difficult reflection, but it did spark the idea of recruiting the locals to their cause.

So now, here he sat. Normally he would shun the idea of endangering civilians, but things looked to turn worse before they got better. While his first thoughts had been about the hideous damage the National Guard would bring down upon the local wildlife as they shot everything in sight, he had broadened his scope to consider how the werewolf pack might *retaliate* against such a bold strike. After all, the military posed less of a threat to these "rogue wolves" than they could know — who knew how extreme the response would be, or how swift?

Besides, he begrudged, *I could use all the help I can get.*

"Get you anything?" the tired young waiter with

unnaturally black hair asked as he finally made his rounds to Sean's table.

"A beer, thanks. And a hamburger, rare, with everything."

"Cool accent. Where you from?"

"Ireland."

"Cool." He started to turn away, then looked back. He gestured with his chin toward the bandage on Sean's cheek. "Happened?"

"I ... well, I was bitten."

"Huh. Bummer. Back with your beer." And away he went.

Okay ... not the most stellar first contact, but then, what was I expectin'?

That was the problem — he did not know *what* to expect, or how to go about this. How exactly had Eamon handled this? How do you walk into a group of relative strangers and introduce the topic of werewolves?

Sean's order found its way, at length, to his table. He sipped at the beer and nibbled on the burger, looking around and listening to the surrounding conversations. The mood was very subdued — the tourists might have been fooled by the "isolated incident" stories, but the natives knew better. They were also aware that a stranger was in their midst, so they kept their voices low, but Sean's ears caught it all. Some talked about the little boy and his cell phone camera. Others expressed annoyance at how slow the authorities were moving to deal with the situation. A husband was even trying to convince his wife, the only woman in the place, that the whole thing was being blown out of proportion, but he was having limited success (and didn't really sound convinced himself, either).

And then, after three hours and five beers, an old man suggested that maybe there was more going on than meets the eye.

Bingo.

Moving with casual ease, Sean collected his latest beer and moseyed up to the bar.

"What the fuck is that supposed to mean?" a gruff-looking man asked, though his tone of voice was more weary than argumentative.

"How long have you lived here?" asked the old man who had seized Sean's attention, his wild, grey hair sticking out in a way that reminded Sean of Albert Einstein. "How long have we *all* lived here? I've been here my whole life. I've never even visited the lower forty-eight—"

"You got a point, Ootek?" asked the tall, slender bartender, but like the gruff man, he did not sound as annoyed as his words implied.

The old man straightened and turned to include him. Sean got a better look at his face now. He had dark skin and vaguely Asian features. Between that and the overheard name, Sean's guess was that he was an Eskimo.

"My point," Ootek said, "is this: When have you *ever* known the wolves to behave like this? Forget what the TV says, because we know better. Wolves are timid animals. My grandfather lived out among them for months at a time—"

"Ootek, I swear," the gruff man said, rubbing a hand over his stubbled cheek, "if you start spewing some Inupiat crap, I'm going to knock your front teeth out."

"I'm not talking about superstition here, I'm talking

about experience. *Our* experience." The old man nudged his own beer as though to take a drink, but in the end he just stared at it. "Wolves don't behave this way. They don't."

"Well, I guess maybe they do."

"They *don't.*"

"Ye said before," Sean interjected — he kept his voice soft, but it still caused all three men to jump, "that ye think there's something 'more' goin' on. Any idea what that might be ...?"

"Who the fuck are you?" the gruff man demanded.

The bartender grabbed a hand towel from beneath the bar and snapped it against the gruff man's exposed forearm.

"Ow! Jesus, Danny, why the—?"

"You see that beer in his hand? That means he's a paying customer, so watch your mouth." The bartender regarded Sean. "Sorry about Hill here. He works long hours and it makes him a bit of an ass."

Hill grumbled, but it smacked of agreement.

"No offense taken," Sean assured him. "But I am curious as to what Ootek here has to say."

"Whatever." Hill took his glass of something stronger than beer and walked further down the bar.

"What happened to your face, stranger?" Ootek asked, eyeing the bandage.

"I'll tell ye in a minute, after I hear what ye have to say. And the name's Sean." He smiled — it made his cheek hurt, but he did it anyway.

Ootek smiled back, and they shook hands. Danny the bartender just nodded.

"Well ..." Ootek began, "like I was saying, I was born and raised here. I've seen my share of wild animal attacks, but they're more rare than you might think. Most of them involve bears. Wolves? Almost never."

"Any idea what's changed?"

Ootek opened his mouth, but after a furtive glance toward a couple of other patrons, he reconsidered what he had to say and closed it again.

The bartender asked, "Are you one of those government guys who got dragged up here to deal with this?"

"Not exactly. I'm here in response to the threat, yes, but I'm not with the government."

The bartender rolled his eyes. "Please tell me you're not another hunter looking for a chance to bag a wolf?"

"No, not at all."

"Something's gone wrong," Ootek tried again. "Something's *changed* to make the wolves act this way."

"Something out of the ordinary ...?" Sean prompted, hoping the old man would take the first step.

Ootek nodded.

"Something ... unnatural?"

Danny the bartender was giving Sean another sideways glance, his lips shaping into a frown. Ootek just looked uncomfortable as he replied, "I, uh ... I don't know about 'unnatural,' really ..."

"Have ye considered the *possibility* that maybe — just maybe — the explanation could be ... *super*natural?"

The bartender rolled his eyes again, but for just a moment, Sean was encouraged by a gleam in Ootek's eye. Was that excitement he saw? Validation, perhaps?

But then it all went south. The man's features hardened, his jaw muscles flinching as he gritted his teeth.

"Oh, I get it. You saw my face, heard my name, and you figured the dumb old Eskimo would be superstitious and gullible enough to buy whatever it is you're selling, is that it?"

"No!" Sean replied, surprised and unprepared for the accusation.

"Listen here, you son of a bitch. I may look the part of the ignorant Inupiat, but I'm not. I even went to college in Anchorage for a couple of years, and I'd have a degree in Civil Engineering if I hadn't had to quit to take care of my mother. You think all natives are like the ones you see in the movies, is that it? You think I have a hundred different words for snow or something, and so I'm going to listen to you spew a bunch of horseshit?"

"I—"

"Tell me, when were you going to ask for my credit card number? Or did you think the dumb old Eskimo would only deal in *hides* or *fish*?"

Sean stepped back, holding his hands before him — he wasn't sure if he was showing that he wasn't a threat, or trying to ward off the old man's attack. "Look, sir, I think there's been a misunderstanding here."

"Oh, you think so?" the bartender asked, sounding amused.

"Look, I overheard ye say that ye thought something was wrong, that something *more* was goin' on than meets the eye. I—"

"So you immediately assumed the dumb Eskimo was talking about evil spirits, is that it?"

"Not—"

"That the unborn native children of the Aurora Borealis

were coming down to possess the wolves and force them to strike down the invaders of our lands?"

"Ootek, I—"

"What I was talking about, *Sean*, was a *pathogen*! Maybe a new strain of rabies, or some foreign disease that got brought in from another region. Or maybe a *toxin* of some kind. I don't know. All I know is that the wolves' behavior has changed. That's all." Holding himself almost painfully erect, Ootek seized his beer. "Now if you'll excuse me, I have to get back to my *igloo*." He stomped away and left the bar, slamming the door behind him.

Sean slowly became aware of the chuckles and snickers coming from the other patrons. His face burned with embarrassment.

"Ootek's been fighting stereotypes his whole life," Danny the bartender explained, "mostly from tourists and visitors. The only reason Hill got away with that Inupiat crack earlier was because they're friends."

"Aye. Um, 'Inupiat' is, uh—?"

"The Eskimo."

"Ah."

"Yeah. Okay, Sean, I think maybe you better take that last beer and clear out. I don't think you'll find any friendly company here tonight, and Ootek might come back once he cools off. And *if* you decide to stop by later in the week, I suggest you keep any crazy talk to yourself. You hear me?"

"Aye ..." Sean turned away from the bar, leaving the beer behind.

"You never said what happened to your face."

"No, I didn't."

Once outside, Sean indulged in a muttered deluge of

curses, most of which were directed at himself — it helped drown out the laughter that raised in volume the instant the door closed behind him.

However Eamon pulled it off back in Ireland, he must have handled it a hell of a lot better than Sean had just now. Whatever chances he'd had of local recruitment had flown right out the damn window when he managed to insult the local Eskimo, Inupiat, on his first venture into town.

And the shameful part was, Ootek wasn't entirely off the mark. Sean's hopes *had* lifted when he saw that the man was a "true" native to these lands; Sean *had* immediately assumed that he would prove more superstitious than his white neighbors.

Sean trudged away from the bar. Things could not have gone worse if—

If the werewolf pack had planned this.

Sean's pace slowed until he came to a halt. He turned and regarded the bar. Normally the windows would have been glowing by this time, but it was still so damned bright outside, all he could see in the glass was a reflection of himself standing across the road, looking very small.

Was he being paranoid, or was he onto something? No, he couldn't assume that the wolves had *wanted* him to recruit the locals ... but they might have considered the possibility, might have been prepared in case he tried it, or something like it.

Had some of them been in the bar tonight? Had they been the first to laugh at his foolhardy blunder, or could their number have *included* Hill, Danny, or even Ootek himself? None of them — *no one* in the bar — had smelled of his kindred, true ... but then, until very recently, Sean would have sworn that no werewolf could take full form during the days of the new moon.

Maybe Alistaire's right. Maybe we should retreat.

No! I refuse to surrender innocent lives to—

Those lives will be forfeit either way if ye get yerself and yer partners killed.

Sean growled deep in his throat. He would *not* give up, not yet. By God, he had faced tougher situations than this!

Sean continued on his way, but he could not shake the feeling that he was being followed.

XV

Sean felt as though he were being followed.

He knew that it was just his imagination — or rather, bad memories. Although he had continued to live in this house for several years after he first turned furry, attacked and killed Thomas, and was later hunted by Eamon ... Sean could never approach this front door without remembering that night. The night he limped home, burned and wounded by silver; the night Eamon had followed behind him to finish the job.

The funny thing was, he had not even known *that he was being followed when it happened. He had not heard Eamon's footsteps nor caught a trace of his scent until minutes later, just before he had passed out from pain and exhaustion. Until that last moment, he'd believed that he had killed Eamon with a lucky blow — an assumption he never made again, and would not have made even then if he hadn't been in such poor shape. So, no ... when he crossed the threshold of his home that night, he'd had no idea that Eamon was stalking him. His "memory" of the incident was cultivated by hindsight, purely in his mind.*

And yet, as he placed his hand upon the doorknob, he could not resist the urge to look behind him, anyway.

He half-expected to have to feel for the spare key atop the doorjamb, but this proved not to be the case; the knob turned in his hand without resistance. Sean doubted that Conroy and Abigail would appreciate Theresa's leaving their house unlocked.

Maybe they've changed, *he mused.* After all, their legal obligations to keep Theresa sheltered ended many, many years ago, but they let her stay. Maybe they're not as indifferent as they used to be.

But he doubted it. He suspected they viewed Theresa as free help these days, and nothing more. He was sure they weren't "mean" about it — they never had been. That's just the way they were.

Easing into the house, Sean maneuvered into his old room before turning on any lights. It had changed a little bit — the Finnians had added a simple treadmill, which did not appear to have received much use of late; he was also not at all surprised to find that his KISS poster had been taken down (he hadn't really cared for their music, but the poster had been one of his few stereotypical acts of adolescent rebellion). Otherwise, it was pretty much the same, though he did not remember the bed being quite so small.

Closing the door behind him, he set his duffle bag down on the bed and sat beside it.

Now what?

Sean had remained in the pub longer than he had intended, hoping that Theresa would call it an evening so they could leave together. But eventually he got it through his thick skull that, like it or not, Theresa was enjoying herself, enjoying having the young tosser fawning over her in his clumsy hopes of seeing her home. Samuel had done his best to keep Sean distracted and comfortable, and Sean showed his appreciation by pretending that his efforts were successful. But in the end, he decided it would be best for all if he left and waited for Theresa to come home.

So he waited.

And waited.

Hours went by, enough that Sean was sure the pub had already closed. Though he had never been much of a reader, he had regretted not bringing along a book for the plane flight over to Ireland. This waiting was even worse, but since he no longer felt comfortable enough with the house to camp out in front of the telly, he just sat, and eventually reclined onto the bed. And waited.

Finally, Sean heard movement outside the house. He started to sit up, then froze when he heard the mumbling of Beagan's voice.

Ye've gotta be shittin' me ...

Nope, the front door opened, and now Sean could hear both of them, speaking in low voices and giggling. Theresa made a brief shushing sound, but she must have known it was a pointless gesture with his *hearing.*

Exactly. She knew he would be able to hear her, hear them. *She knew that Sean would be here, and yet she brought the boy home anyway.*

Why would she do that? *he stewed.* If she must be with him tonight, why bring him here instead of taking him somewhere else? Why, damn it?!

Sean heard them stumble into Theresa's room, and the festivities began.

This was going to be one long fucking night ...

* * *

And it was. Sean never slept, because they didn't. When Beagan finally dragged his young ass out of there just after sunrise, Sean huffed to his feet.

"Mornin', Sean," Theresa said from the front door when he emerged from his room. To his relief, she wore a robe. But nothing else. "Oh, sorry, I forgot. Ye're American now." She closed the door, then theatrically cleared her throat. "Top o' the mornin' to ye, Sean!"

"Very funny."

"I thought so." She moved toward the kitchen. "Do ye want some breakfast?"

Her nonchalance infuriated him. "Theresa, what the bloody hell was that—?!"

She whipped her head around, her hair flowing after, to glare at him. "I'm sorry, Sean, were ye about to ask me something? Maybe demand an explanation to which ye are not entitled? Maybe even comment that I smell like I've been fucking? Because if that's what ye're plannin' to do, then ye can take yer shit and get yer arse right on out of here. I'm sure ye can get a room at the inn. Is that what ye're plannin', Sean? Is that what ye want?"

Sean glared back at her, his jaw muscles flexing.

"Take yer time. I'm puttin' some bacon on the stove." And with that, she padded on her bare feet into the kitchen, leaving him standing and stewing.

Sean counted to ten (counted up rather than down, so as not to stir up any Hudson-related hypnotic reactions). Damned if she wasn't right. He'd known she had a man with her last night; he could have stayed at the inn if he'd wanted to avoid getting an earful. He didn't like it, of course ... but Theresa was forty years old. Whom she took to her bed was her business, not his.

He told himself that, but that didn't mean he wanted to hear it. When he joined her in the kitchen, he was only half as calm as he had hoped. Where, oh where, was the happy-go-lucky Sean Mallory these days? Damn Mark Hudson and his experiments.

But, to be fair, it had been a very long time since Sean had felt relaxed around Theresa. Not since—

The kitchen smelled of bacon and sausage. She saw him enter from the corner of her eye, and with a gesture asked if he wanted her to add some sausage links for him as well — her expression showed that it was still up to him, she really didn't give a damn either way. He nodded his affirmation and thanks, and sat down at the kitchen table to wait.

As the minutes went by, Sean was pleasantly surprised to find that he was relaxing a bit after all. Theresa's making breakfast for him again, here in this house, this kitchen ... it invoked memories going back to before his curse had awakened, before the tension began. When she brought their plates to the table, he sensed that she was unwinding, too.

"Milk? Juice?" she asked.

"Juice, thanks."

She retrieved the orange juice from the refrigerator, and sat across the table from him. She poured into two glasses, then dug into her breakfast without another word.

They ate together. After a few minutes, Theresa began, "So ..."

Sean waited.

"How have ye been? Are ye still in New York?"

"Um, no. I've relocated to Pittsburgh."

Theresa nodded, and when she spoke next, there was distaste in her voice. "Are ye still living with that ... man?"

"Aye."

Theresa shuddered. "How ye can sleep at night knowing there's a vampire *under the same roof is beyond me."*

"I've told ye, Theresa. Alistaire is different."

"So ye've said."

"And we've taken in a new charge, as well."

She looked up from her meal. "Another vampire? Or someone like you*?"*

"Neither, actually. Trey is a zombie."

Theresa nearly dropped her fork. "Yer jokin'."

Sean shook his head. "I take it ye didn't know they were real, too?"

"I did not. Why in the world—?"

"He's like us. Alistaire and me, that is. He's not like the others of his kind. He resists, he fights, he does good."

Theresa made no comment, but returned to her breakfast. Sean did the same.

Finally, the bacon and sausage were eaten, the juice drank. Theresa moved to gather the plates, but Sean stopped her. "I've got it," he said.

Theresa laughed, and it was warm and good to hear. "My! Maybe that vampire really is a good influence after all!"

Sean smiled. "Piss off." He took the plates and

glasses to the sink and began to wash them.

"Sean ...?" Theresa asked from behind him.

"Aye?"

"Why are ye here?"

Sean did not answer right away. He finished the dishes, set them aside to dry. He could feel her waiting, but she did not rush him. At last he turned to face her, reclining against the counter and striving to remain calm.

"Something strange has been happening in the States..."

Theresa smirked. "Sean, ye're a werewolf, and ye live with a vampire and now a zombie — all ye're missin' is a Frenchman. And now ye say that something 'strange' is happening?"

Sean offered a small grin in response to her tease, but pushed on. "It's rather ... complicated. I'd be lyin' if I said that I understood it, really. But that's not the issue at the moment." He swallowed, forced his breathing to remain steady. "These experiences I've been havin' have raised some old questions for me, things I've tried to ignore for a very long time."

Theresa straightened in her chair, her back now stiff. But she said nothing more, made him take it all the way without any help.

"Theresa, when I changed, ye told me that our father's curse only passes along to the men in our family. That ye were not cursed like me."

Theresa said nothing. She did not move, she didn't even blink.

"Theresa ... did ye lie to me?"

Still nothing, damn her.

"*Theresa. Are ... are ye a werewolf?*"

She stood without answering, turned to leave the kitchen.

Sean wanted to follow her, to grab her by the arm, force her to answer him. Instead, he relied on his words, his voice. "Theresa. Are. You. A. Werewolf?"

She stopped in the doorway. For several seconds, she stood there without moving forward or back, without turning or responding.

He waited, his fingers gripping the underside of the counter so tight it was a wonder he didn't tear right through the wood.

Finally, finally *... Theresa turned to look at him. There were tears glistening in her eyes, but they did not spill onto her cheeks. "Are ye askin' if I am 'cursed' like yerself? The answer is no."*

Sean cocked his head, noticing the fine distinction she was making. He opened his mouth to demand more, to insist on a clarification, but she cut him off.

"No, Sean, when the moon is full in the night sky, I do not lose control, turn into a wolf, and run into the night looking for prey. Our father did that to you, *not to me."*

His throat was so dry it was hard to speak. "Theresa—"

"I'm tired, Sean," she said, and her face showed it to be true. "I'm goin' to bed. We'll talk more later."

Sean wanted to say more, to ask more ... but instead he nodded. He, too, was very tired.

So he was quite surprised when Theresa pivoted back once more and said, "Let me ask you *a question, Sean."*

He blinked. "All right."

"Why is it so important to ye?"

That caught him completely flatfooted. "Wha— Are ye serious? I mean ... I ... for fuck's sake, Theresa, how could it not *be important?"*

"Every muscle in yer body was hard as rock when ye asked me, every tendon in yer neck was standin' out as ye waited for my answer. If — if — I were cursed, I woulda been doin' this longer than ye. Hell, I'm the one who *taught ye all about lockin' yerself up. I'm* the one who *looked after ye until ye got everything figured out."*

Sean's heart was racing, his head pounding. "Theresa ..."

"Is it somethin specific *ye're worried about, Sean? Was there somethin'* special *that drove ye from yer home, yer friends, from* me*?"*

Heaving for breath, very near the panic that sent him running from Neil Carpenter and Alex Monroe when he saw Hudson's illustrations, Sean gasped, "Theresa, please—!"

"Would this have anythin' to do with Eamon and his huntin' party? Or maybe—?"

"Enough!"

Theresa nodded, her expression victorious but not in the least joyous. "I see."

Sean, bent forward over his roiling guts, could not look her in the eye.

"I'm going to bed."

Sean said nothing, hiding his eyes.

And she was gone.

Damn her.

Sixteen

Damn him! raged the white wolf. Damn the Intruder!

The first time the alpha left the den, he made a run for it. He knew the consequences of his actions, but he did not care. Her display of "dominance," her choice to abase him in front of the pack, had not convinced him of her strength. To him, this signified that she was *weak* — not of body, of course, but of spirit (or so he told himself).

Despite her proclamations and her promises, the white wolf had come to believe that the alpha *feared* the Man. She had always warned that Man was not to be underestimated, that he could strike back at them in many ways, and she had insisted that there was a difference between "fearing" an opponent and "*respecting*" them. But now the white wolf had decided that these words were nothing more than a rock behind which she cowered, even as she lorded over her own pack with an iron fist.

The white wolf was not without fear. He feared that stinking zombie, and he sure as hell feared that ... that *thing* that had emerged from the coffin in the cabin. But he did *not* fear the Man, with his soft flesh and his runty claws and his puny teeth — he knew now that the wolf was his *true* form, the body he was always *meant* to wear. Take away a man's guns, and he was nothing compared to a wolf.

And he *hated* the Intruder. Oh, how he hated him.

The Intruder's appearance prompted the sudden change in the alpha, her unfair reaction to his killing the humans by the river, her new, cowardly posture — to think that she had belittled him for doing what *she* had taught him to do, even putting that sniveling red wolf before him!

This would not stand.

So the white wolf had decided to mix business with pleasure. He would hunt the Intruder on his own. He would not make the same mistake they had before, attacking openly and relying too heavily on their superior numbers. He would *stalk* the Intruder and bring him down. Then he would drag the carcass back to the den for all to see, to demonstrate that *he* had accomplished what the alpha had been too afraid to attempt.

The alpha was powerful, as she had proven again last night. She was more powerful than the white wolf ... but she was not as strong as *all* of the wolves. She had given them their strength, but that did not warrant their absolute servitude — if he could win over the others, *together* they could defeat her ... but first he needed to inspire them.

Then she would either mate with him, or she would die.

So now he watched from the trees as the Intruder trudged away from the town, up the road back toward his cabin. For some reason, the fool had not driven into town, but had walked; he had failed to consider what could happen on the long walk back. The wolf would wait until he was away from the town, but also still too far from the cabin to summon help from his monstrous companions.

He glanced away from the Intruder toward the sky. The evening was cloudy, overcast. The paling sun was hidden, making it darker than it had been of late.

So much the better; the wolf would stay downwind so that the Intruder could not smell him, step with caution so that he could not hear him, and the dark would help prevent his seeing him.

Poor Intruder. Poor Sean.

If the white wolf had been capable of chuckling in this form, he would have. Oh, yes, he had learned the Intruder's name. While he had not been present in the bar when the incident occurred, two men had emerged not long afterward, and their words had carried to his sensitive ears. They had laughed and bantered about Sean's having made a fool of himself in public.

Poor Sean.

But the wolf could not chuckle; instead, he licked his snout and pressed onward.

Sean shuffled along the road, his hands in his jeans pockets, his feet dragging, and his head hung low. He smelled of beer, but the wolf would not assume that he was drunk — it took far stronger alcohol to truly affect their kind. The Intruder was probably brooding over his embarrassment in the bar.

The wolf would have loved to know *what* Sean had done that had made him appear so ridiculous to the crowd; perhaps the Intruder would *thank* him for ending his misery. It was unfortunate that he would never know what hit him — the wolf intended to stick to his plan of striking fast and lethal; he had learned his lesson of trying to best the Intruder in open combat.

The wolf continued to trail after him, and he eased his way closer to the road. He salivated in anticipation of tasting Sean's blood.

But then something changed. Sean's pace slackened. He slowed ... and came to a stop.

The wolf flattened himself to the ground, keeping his ears and tail low. Had he made some sound, perhaps given himself away by panting with mounting excitement? No, he was sure he hadn't.

Plus, Sean was not looking around, in suspicion or otherwise. He had just come to a stop, his hands in his pockets, his eyes downcast. He just stood there in the road.

The wolf remained absolutely still.

After several long seconds, Sean pulled his hands from his pockets. He laced his fingers, cracked his knuckles. He scratched the side of his face, then pulled off the bandage. He continued standing where he was, looking at the underside of the bandage and then folding it and shoving it into his back pocket.

Then Sean did turn his way — the wolf tensed but did not flinch. A moment later, it was clear that Sean was not scanning the trees for a stalker, but was checking both directions of the road, perhaps for cars. Sean stretched his arms now, then unzipped and removed his jacket.

What the hell is he doing?

Next came his T-shirt (the wolf was gratified to see the torso wound he himself had inflicted), which Sean folded neatly with his jacket over his forearm. Then he actually sat down in the road and removed his sneakers and socks. He stuffed his socks into his shoes, tied the laces together, and then looped them over his forearm as well.

Now, wearing nothing but his jeans, Sean strolled along his way.

The wolf waited a moment before following. This behavior was bizarre — he did not like it. He, too, was less affected by chilly air than regular humans when in his man-form, but still ... why had Sean done this?

In spite of his aims and bravado, the wolf truly did not want to chance another face-to-face duel with the Intruder — he wanted to kill Sean, and reap the rewards from doing so ... but his own wounds had not yet healed, a reminder of the punishment Sean could inflict.

Sean was pulling away from him, nearing a bend in the road. What should he do? He nearly whined in frustration before catching himself. What should he *do*?

Up the road, Sean's voice drifted back to him. It sounded as though he were humming a song — his tone was relaxed, carefree, completely unsuspecting.

The white wolf followed him.

Things proceeded as planned for the next few minutes. The wolf made up for his lost distance, and gained some ground. Sean continued up the road, behaving as though he had not a care in the world. Once an old pickup truck drove by — the wolf bounded behind some undergrowth, but Sean gave the driver a friendly wave, heedless of the dumbfounded reaction his half-naked state provoked.

The wolf was thinking of the terrain ahead, planning the best spot to catch Sean and bring him down, when something new happened: Sean cut to his left and stepped into the woods along the side of the road.

The wolf hesitated, but not as long this time. He followed.

Sean was looking back and forth casually, as though he were searching for something. His eyes were upcast, not looking down at the ground. His pace remained casual and unhurried.

The wolf struggled not to lose patience. He remained mindful of his step, and forced himself to freeze whenever Sean's gaze swung around in his direction; even so, he still managed to draw closer to his prey. His excitement was growing again.

I will tear out his throat, I will taste his blood!

Then Sean passed out of view behind a large, thick tree ... and did not reappear on the opposite side.

The wolf tensed. Had Sean continued on at another angle, blocked from view? Or ... was Sean *waiting* for him?

A trickling sound drifted to his ears, followed by the *braaack* of an unabashed belch. A second later, he smelled Sean's urine, its scent heavy with beer. The humming returned as well.

He would not find a better opportunity than this. It was time to strike!

He moved forward, faster, bolder. The wind caressed the fur of his face, his claws dug into the earth as he lowered his bearing in expectation.

Sean belched again.

Now! Now!

The wolf burst into full speed. In seconds, he crossed the line of the large tree, then bounded to the side, toward his prey, throwing all his weight behind it, his teeth bared and aimed for Sean's throat.

But Sean was not there.

The wolf landed without grace, spinning back around

as quickly as he could. The Intruder had vanished! But the wolf could *smell* him! Smell his ...

Sean's clothes were there on the ground, as was a small puddle of his urine. But Sean himself was nowhere to be seen.

The wolf spun in all directions, casting about and finding nothing. His heart raced even as his mind raged, confusion and fury competing for his attention. How was this possible?! Where had he gone, damn it?! It made no—

A flicker of movement, not from around him, but from *above*!

The wolf turned his gaze upward a moment before the silhouette landed on his back. The irony of the situation flittered through one corner of his mind — this was how the pack had eluded Sean that first night, by taking to the trees.

But the wolf had other concerns as Sean's impact knocked his hindquarters flat. He struggled to twist and shake him off. It did not work.

Sean's breath was hot as he whispered into the wolf's ear, even as one hand closed around his snout and the other forearm pressed against his throat.

"Got ye, motherfucker."

The wolf panicked, fought to free himself. Maybe if he could shape-shift ...

The world grew darker before his eyes. Even werewolves needed to breathe.

Sean twisted his merciless grip around to one side, then as the wolf pushed against him, he whipped the wolf's head back the other direction. The angle was sharp, but the white-hot pain that shot through the wolf's neck was sharper.

I hate you, he wanted to say.

And then the darkness took him.

*   *   *

"Hey! Evening, Doc Petrov!" Danny the bartender said as he turned and saw him mousing up to the bar. "Haven't seen you much lately, Arthur. Where you been keeping yourself?"

"Busy," Arthur replied.

Danny's countenance darkened. "The wolves?"

Arthur nodded.

"Goddamn it. Everything comes back to the wolves these days, doesn't it?"

Arthur released a quiet snort. "That it does."

"The usual?"

"Please."

Danny stepped away to retrieve the bourbon, and Arthur breathed a sigh of relief. He had been worried that his doddering nerves would be obvious to everyone he encountered. But maybe not.

With the exception of meeting Sean at the airport, this was Arthur's first outing after work hours since the wolf had followed him through town. The things he had learned, had *seen*, since then were enough to turn him into an agoraphobe, but he was determined not to let that happen. So, here he was at the local watering hole, among familiar faces and friends. Not a "werewolf" in sight.

As far as you know, *Artur ...*

Please shut up, Grandma.

Danny returned with his bourbon. As he pushed the

glass forward, he leaned in and spoke in a low voice, "Any news on them bringing the National Guard up here?"

Arthur replied with a sour expression.

"Shit ..." Danny groaned. "This place is going to be a madhouse."

"I know."

"All because the rangers can't find a few wolves, because that cop can't find his dick with both hands ..."

Arthur shook his head. "Caster doesn't want this anymore than we do."

Danny guffawed. "He's just worried about his own ass."

"True, but the result is the same. He's doing his damnedest to get this taken care of before the weekend warriors arrive on our doorstep."

"Hey! Artie!"

Arthur grunted under his breath. He was particularly hoping that Hill wouldn't be here tonight — the man was far too much of a curmudgeon for Arthur's taste, not to mention the fact that he hated being called "Artie." "Hello, Hill. How are you tonight?"

"Been better," the man grumbled gleefully. "The bump on my elbow is itchin' again. Do you think you could take a look at it?"

"Maybe in a bit."

"Leave the man alone, Hill. He's here to relax, not give out free samples."

Hill gave Danny the finger. "Did I hear you guys talkin' about the National Guard?"

Danny sighed. "Unfortunately."

Hill asked Arthur, "Any word on how soon they're

gettin' here?"

Arthur shrugged. "Next week, maybe sooner if we find another body. I just heard they might be sending a squa—"

"Fuck, that long? Can't they move any faster'n that?"

Arthur gave him an incredulous look. "You don't actually *want* them up here, do you?"

Hill slapped his hand on the bar, making an obnoxious *pop* that hurt Arthur's ears. "Fuck if I don't. I'm sick of havin' to drag my rifle with me every time I go out to check the lines. I got enough problems without having to worry about a wolf takin' a bite out of my ass." He snorted. "I shoulda figured you'd agree with Danny. You'd have to be a fellow veteran to understand."

Danny rolled his eyes. "Hill, you served in the Air National Guard for a whole four months before they booted your ass."

"They – did – *not*! I was discharged on medical grounds."

(Further down the bar, Arthur heard some eavesdropper snicker, "Probably *mental* ground." Fortunately, Hill missed the remark.)

Hill waved a dismissive hand in their faces. "Whatever. You two just think they'll be a bunch of dumb jarhead wannabees up here trompin' on the pretty flowers."

Arthur said, "I have nothing against the armed forces. But you have to admit that they're not known for their subtlety."

"Fuck subtlety! We need help up here, and the fuzz ain't done shit."

"I'm not saying we don't need help," Danny chimed in. "I just think they should bring in more park rangers from

Montana or Colorado, maybe even borrow some Canadian Mounties. People who know how to deal with *wildlife*, not rioters."

Arthur wondered what they would say if they knew the kind of help *he* had brought in; he shuddered to think of it himself. "We don't mean any offense, Hill."

Hill guffawed. "You wanna talk about 'offense'? Danny, did you tell him about the guy who pissed off Ootek earlier?"

"No, Hill, I hadn't brought it up."

Hill either missed, or more likely ignored, Danny's leave-it-alone tone of voice. "You shoulda been here for that, Artie. Ootek tore the guy a new one right in front of everyone. It was even better than when that old bitch asked him about igloos a coupla summers ago."

"What's he talking about?" Arthur asked Danny.

Danny shrugged. "Pretty much just that. Some guy treated Ootek like he was the 'local Injun' and Ootek let him have it. It was pretty unpleasant, so of course, Hill ate it up."

"You bet I did." He turned to Arthur once more. "You shoulda heard the guy. Talkin' about the supernatural and shit, with this fruity Scottish accent ..."

Arthur felt a chill in his guts.

"He wasn't Scottish," Danny said, "he was Irish."

"Nah he wasn't! He was *Scottish*. He sounded just like a Leprechaun."

"Leprechauns are *Irish*, you idiot."

Arthur wanted to ask, *Did he mention my name?*

"Whatever," Hill shrugged. "Same difference, anyway. The guy said he was up here lookin' into the wolves, thought they might be 'supernatural' or whatever. Tried to get Ootek in on it." He barked a laugh, spittle peppering both of them. "Bad call!" He slapped the counter again. "Give me one more whiskey, Danny, and then I'm outta here."

Danny served up the drink. "Don't forget to take your rifle with you," he said with a smirk.

"I left it in my truck. I knew you'd throw a fit if I brought it in here. Besides, ain't no wolves gonna come this far into town ..."

"Don't count on that," Arthur said under his breath, his nerves firing high once again.

"... and even if they did, I'll tell you what *I* would do. I would just kick them right in their furry little balls—"

A *thump* sounded from the front door, loud enough to get everyone's attention. Arthur turned to look, but the door remained closed. The decorative curtain and the relatively-dark evening outside made it impossible to see who was there.

"Door's open!" Hill yelled, then laughed alone at his own joke.

A dragging, scraping sound followed, then another *thump*.

"For God's sake, can someone please open the door for them?" Danny called to those sitting closest.

No one moved, and Arthur could understand why. There was something unnerving, almost ominous about that thumping. Just a few months ago, no one would have given it a second thought, but lately ...

A third *thump*, followed by a muffled male voice saying something that Arthur could not make out.

"Oh, for fuck's sake," Hill grumbled to himself and the room at large. He marched across the bar to the door. "You pussies. A coupla wolves eat some big city boys and you all freak ou—"

Hill was reaching for the door handle when a fourth and final *THUMP!*, harder and louder than all the rest, rattled the door right in its frame. Behind the curtain, it sounded like the glass cracked, letting in what might — *might* — have been a growl.

Hill lost some of his piss-and-vinegar then, and took a step back. "Uh, Danny, maybe we should call—"

The door broke inward, followed immediately by a flash of white fur.

Everyone else yelped in surprise; Arthur screamed in terror.

"Delivery for all ye skeptics! Who'd like to sign for it?"

No one said anything right away. They were far too busy trying to make sense of the bizarre scene before them. Arthur, at least, was familiar with the players involved.

Sean Mallory stood in the doorway, big as life and stripped to the waist. His wounds were still evident, but they had nevertheless healed to an impossible degree since Arthur had treated him.

And in Sean's arms, twisting and twitching but in a stupor, was the big white wolf that had chased Arthur through town and, more recently, been photographed by a little boy's cell phone.

Sean took three big steps forward and dropped the wolf onto the nearest table. The two men who had been using it shoved their chairs back so hard, one fell over backward and the other had to catch himself from spilling out sideways.

"All right," the half-naked Irishman said. "I tried to bring this up all nice 'n subtle earlier, but Ootek blew up and none of ye would've listened to me after that." He pointed at the wolf, which was panting soft whimpers and squirming around, but seemed unable to coordinate itself. "So when this bugger came sniffing up my backside, I decided maybe a little *proof* would get yer attention."

"Jesus Christ," Danny said in awe. He turned to Arthur. "That's, I mean ... is that one of them, Doc?"

Trembling, Arthur nodded.

One man, the man who had snickered behind Hill's back earlier, tried to speak up, but all he managed was, "What did— did, I, uh ... wow ..."

"Wait, wait ..." Hill said, a tremor betraying the authority he forced into his voice. "Are you telling us that this big fucker, this is one of *the* wolves that's been killing people?"

"Aye."

Hill took a small step forward. "Did you drug it or something—?"

The wolf kicked hard, its biggest movement yet. Everyone scrambled away, Hill especially.

"I didn't drug it. I broke its neck. But werewolves — aye, that's right, I said *werewolves*, and ye'd better get used to it real quick — are a tough bunch. Takes more than a broken neck to put them down for good."

The men were all exchanging glances, waiting for *someone* to call bullshit on this; the only woman in the crowd would not take her eyes off the animal before them.

"Should ..." Danny began, then had to swallow and try

again. "Should we call the police? Or, I don't know, animal control?"

"Tell ye what, lad: Let me show ye the next step in my little demonstration, and then we can all sit down together and decide what to do next." He looked over to Hill. "Could ye close the door, please?"

Hill nodded and went to the door, but instead of closing it, he ran outside. Several men grumbled over this, but since no one could really blame him, they said nothing aloud.

Sean sighed. "Right. Well, I'd like as many witnesses to this as possible, but I don't know how much time we have left. Took me a while to carry this bag o' fur back here." Then he asked Danny, "Do you have a large towel? Or maybe a spare table cloth? This next part is going to get a bit messy."

"Uh, what exactly are you planning to do ...?"

Sean stood tall and firm. "I am goin' to *kill* this werewolf, gentlemen and lady. And then ye all are going to see something that will squelch whatever denials ye might have left."

No one spoke. No one felt capable of interrupting such an outlandish show. And surely that's what it was, right? A show, one of the most eccentric jokes of all time? A bare-chested, barefooted Irishman, explaining he was going to kill a *were*wolf, apparently with his bare hands? No wonder Ootek had blown up at the crazy bastard ...

... and yet no one made any effort to bring a halt to the proceedings.

Arthur stared hard at the wolf, unable to look elsewhere, unable to even breathe properly. Were its eyes meeting his? He thought they were. And was it *grinning* at him, like it had the night it chased him? Yes, he thought it might be. If only he could take a moment, maybe step outside and get some fresh air ... but he could *not* turn his back on the thing.

Sean was saying something else, but heavy footsteps and a sharp *cha-click!* from the front door drowned him out. They turned to find Hill standing there, his rifle aimed at the wolf.

"Don't worry, guys!" Hill called out, his voice full of bluster. "I got it! I'll take care of it! I'll blow its head off!"

Sean held his hand up, suggesting that he wanted Hill to take it easy ... but then he hesitated. After a moment, he stepped aside. "Ye know, I think this'll help make my case, too." He gestured at the wolf, a have-at-it motion. "By all means, take yer shot."

"Now wait a minute ..." Danny protested.

Sean raised his voice to the whole crowd. "When ye see that bullets do not do one damn bit o' good, ye'll have to accept what I'm—"

The white wolf jerked to life. Its head remained at an odd, painful angle, but it struggled to its feet, its bark echoing off the walls of the bar. Everyone else fell over themselves to back away, but Sean just looked annoyed, and reached out with a confident hand to seize the wolf by the scruff of its neck.

The wolf barked again. Hill panicked — many of them did, but Hill was the one wielding a rifle. He fired, missed the wolf ...

... and caught Sean in his left shoulder. Sean grunted, the force of the shot knocking him off balance. He stumbled back and fell on his ass.

The wolf spun toward the source of the gunfire, its teeth bared. Angled neck or no, it tensed to leap at Hill, who dropped his rifle with a cry and turned to run.

A second gunshot, not as loud but still piercing within the confined space, rang out. The wolf yelped, looking almost surprised, and a second later, collapsed. It fell back onto the table, then slid off onto the floor.

Sean rose, wiping the blood from his wounded shoulder — the muscle and skin were already knitting themselves back together, a welcome return to his normal recuperative power after so many slow-healing werewolf bites of late. He glanced around with apprehension, but thanks to the chaos, no one appeared to have *seen* the bullet hit him. And he also located the source of the second gunshot.

Arthur Petrov stood still as a statue, both white-knuckled hands holding his pistol in a death grip. His eyes were open too wide, and he was starting to hyperventilate — Sean hoped he wasn't going into shock.

"Jesus, Doc," Danny said as he rose from where he had crouched behind the bar. He clutched an old baseball bat, cradling it close for comfort. "When did *you* start carrying a gun?"

Arthur did not answer. He continued to gasp for breath.

Sean reached down and hauled the wolf back up onto the table. This prompted a short scream from the bar's female patron. One man was also huddled in the furthest corner, muttering "Goddamn, goddamn, goddamn," over and over, and another man took this moment to follow

Hill's example and run through the still-open door. Danny hefted his bat as though to strike the wolf if it tried to get up again — the fact that he still stood a dozen feet away behind his bar did not seem to register with him.

Everyone else was silent and still.

The wolf was panting, its breaths coming even shorter and faster than Arthur's. Its eyes were glassy, its tongue hung loose — blood flowed from its flank.

"Nice try," Sean said to the wolf in a low voice, "but I'm not fallin' for it. Shrug it off, show'em that yer not really hurt, and I'll make it quick. Keep play-actin', and I'll crush yer balls before I rip yer throat out."

The wolf's eyes rolled back, showing nothing but white. Sean put his hand over the bullet wound, intending to pinch it to provoke a reaction ... and then jerked his hand away with a startled hiss. He gaped at his tingling fingers, then down at the wound, then up at Arthur.

"I'll be damned," he said as realization dawned on him, but he stopped there. He *wanted* to ask where Arthur had managed to get his hands on silver bullets in the modern age of this world ... but he instead kept his word to keep Arthur's ties to his Triumvirate as quiet as possible. Suffice it to say that Arthur had believed his story after all — at least enough to take certain measures.

So instead, Sean settled for a minuscule nod. This unspoken exchange was lost on Arthur; for the moment, the doctor's mind had taken a holiday. This was understandable, given the circumstances — Sean was just grateful that it had been *Hill*, not Arthur, who accidentally shot him!

The wolf keened deep in its throat and began to

shudder. The bar patrons had retreated as far as they could until now, clinging to the walls and, in some cases, hiding behind and under tables. But with the animal clearly near death, some of them were drawing closer.

"Okay ..." Sean said carefully, trying to figure out the best way to recover from his proclamations that bullets would *not* hurt this animal — it would have been a hell of a lot easier if he could tell them about the silver, maybe even have someone dig it out and show it around. Instead, he tried, "Looks like we've done enough damage after all, lads. The broken neck, the, uh, pierced lungs ... this wolf is a goner for sure. But ye haven't seen anythin' yet. Keep yer eyes open!"

Any second now, Sean thought. *Any second now he'll die and revert. And if some of these people recognize his human face, so much the better.*

The wolf coughed and rattled, causing a spurt of blood, which in turn prompted one man to cover his mouth to avoid vomiting. If it went on *too* much longer, Sean might have to...

The wolf bent its forepaw, resting it against Sean's forearm where he leaned on the table. The paw warped ever so slightly, distorted toward the shape of a human hand. Sean glanced up, but the people were still too far back to see it clearly.

No matter. Here it comes ...

The wolf lolled its head toward him, its eyes focusing one last time on Sean's face. Its jaws — which looked like they might be shortening — moved, and it made a rumble in its throat. The sound was more growl than anything else, but Sean thought it *might* have contained the words "hate you."

Then the wolf relaxed. Its paw fell away from Sean's arm ...

... and it was still a paw.

Sean looked at its face, studied it. But it was still very much the face of an animal.

The wolf was dead. And it remained a wolf.

"Did Arthur kill it?" Hill called from where he peeked around the corner of the front door. Two new strangers, a man and a woman from outside the bar, joined him, their faces slack in bewilderment.

Sean stood up, staring down at the wolf with his own brand of bafflement. Werewolves that could change during the days of the new moon, and that *remained* in that form after death? How ...?

"Look, stranger ... er, Sean, right?" Danny said, finally creeping his way around the bar. "Whatever you did to catch this animal, we appreciate it. We really do. But ... well, I don't think any more talk of 'werewolves' and 'the supernatural' are going to do anybody any good." He indicated the wolf. "You see that, right?" When Sean did not reply, he turned back to the crowd. "I'm going to call the police, I guess. Arthur, do you know Ray Caster's number by heart? Arthur?"

But Arthur was still out to lunch, so Danny returned to his side of the bar, picked up his phone, and settled for dialing 911.

Sean glared down at the white wolf, resisting the urge to punch it in frustration. He had thought his fiasco with Ootek had hurt his credibility, but that didn't hold a candle to *this* debacle!

In the immortal words from *48 Hours*: Sean's big move just turned out to be shit.

He had one more option, a change within himself that he had not registered until now: Between the overcast sky and the later hour, the sunlight was repressed just enough that he felt he could maybe push into his wolfman form a little early tonight, if he tried hard enough.

Aye, that would prove that werewolves are real, all right. And then who *would be the* only *proven werewolf around here, lad?*

Sean grunted. He didn't need Alistaire's counsel to recognize *that* was a bad idea.

The commotion grew as more people showed up. Sean needed to retreat before the police arrived and took the half-naked wolf-slayer in for questioning. He should retrieve his clothing and get back to the cabin.

For all the good that would do. What the hell was he supposed to do next?

Face it, lad: You're lost.

The crowd pressed around the wolf's body, and Sean slipped away.

XVII

The following night, sometime after midnight, Theresa slipped out of the house. She had fed Sean a steady supply of beer after dinner, presumably as an olive branch — even though a tense silence remained between them. Never having gotten more than a two-hour nap, the International flight coupled with the all-nighter, followed by a healthy helping of barley and hops ... Sean was out like a light by ten o'clock that evening. Once Theresa was confident that he was down for the night, she turned out all the lights, closed her bedroom door, and then exited through the kitchen, which was the farthest door from his bedroom.

Sean kept his breathing slow and steady for another minute, just to be sure she wouldn't double-back to check on him, then made his own exit through the bedroom window.

Theresa tip-toed across the lawn to the small barn on the south side of the property and entered without turning on a light. Sean crept low, following as close as he dared — until he could confirm otherwise, he was treating his sister as though her senses matched his own.

A minute later, Theresa reemerged pushing a rundown

Moped, which struck Sean with both nostalgia and amusement; he could not believe she still had the old thing. She glanced toward the house once, then pushed her small motor bike toward the road. Once she reached what she must have considered a "safe" distance from the house, she climbed onboard, started the engine, and puttered away from town.

Sean glanced up at the moonless sky and grunted. If he were able to shift into wolf form right now, he would be able to keep up with her without a problem. Still, Mopeds weren't exactly known for their speed, and Theresa's was ancient to boot; as a wolfman, he would still be limited to two legs rather than four, but he had found long ago that the swell in his leg muscles gave an extra kick to his running speed, not to mention his endurance.

He stripped out of his clothes, shifted into wolfman form, and took off parallel to the road.

Over an hour passed. Theresa rolled along her way; Sean tailed her on foot. He couldn't imagine where she was going at this time of night. He had considered that she might just be planning to see her little friend Beagan, but she had made it abundantly clear that she wouldn't bother hiding that fact from him. Besides, that would have taken her into their local village, not away from it. Where was she going?

Finally, Sean saw some lights ahead, and Theresa turned off the main road toward them. As they drew nearer, he saw that it was a large lorry park, what in America would have been called a truck stop. Drivers of all sorts would come through here, to refuel or enjoy the pub; one or two might even be heading for Sean's own town, but most would be making their way between the bigger cities.

Theresa pulled her Moped around to the air pump. Sean stopped a fair distance away, keeping well away from the light. Was she just checking her tires before moving on again? Maybe he was wasting his time here.

While his sister fussed with the tires, Sean began to remember a bit about this particular lorry park. It was a little rough, with fistfights breaking out weekly or better, but it was more known for its seediness — the kind of place a young lad could seek out to lose his virginity. If Theresa moved on, then it didn't matter. But if she stuck around ...

Sure enough, when his sister finished, instead of climbing on, she pushed her ride around to the closed café across from the pub. She set the kick stand, then turned and reclined against the seat.

Was she waiting for someone? Sean wondered if he had discounted little Beagan too soon. But why would they meet all the way out here?

Sean wished he had brought some clothing along with him, so that he could get closer without causing all hell to break loose if he were seen — either as a wolfman or a naked man. Even with his ears, he wouldn't be able to hear well from this distance if she spoke to anyone, and if she went into the pub itself, how long would he huddle out here before—?

The pub door opened and a dirty, bearded young man was shoved outside so hard he fell to one knee. A huge bugger in a black T-shirt stuck his head outside just long enough to say, "... and stay out!" or something to that effect. The door was slammed, after which the young man, probably a drifter and a piss artist, attempted to regain some dignity with an obscene gesture. He stood and brushed off his pants, though they were so filthy it made little difference.

The drifter collected himself and started to walk away before spotting Theresa. She said something. He glanced around, as though to see if she were addressing someone else. This made Theresa laugh, and she crooked her finger for him to come closer. He complied.

Sean emitted a low growl deep in his throat.

The drifter reached the Moped, and they chatted up. He made some wild motions, giving Sean the impression that he was conveying his version of whatever had happened in the pub.

Theresa hung on his every word. It was nauseating.

After several long minutes, she took the drifter's hand, pocketed the keys to her Moped, and led him away. Not toward the pub, not toward the closed café or even the public restrooms, she just led him straight out into the grassy field behind the lorry park, headed not far from where Sean crouched.

Sean shook his head in disgust. Had she come all this way just to lay some bum? Had she sunk so low in her tastes, so indiscriminate? Seeing her with Beagan again would have been less repulsive.

Sean almost left then and there ... but he had followed her all this way, hadn't he? In for a penny, in for a pound. Stooping even lower to the ground, lower than he could have in human form without pitching forward, he slunk sideways through the tall grass to both follow them and maintain his distance.

Theresa continued along, pulling the dirty drifter by the hand and ignoring his occasional question or comment.   He tried to appear nonchalant, but his excitement drifted downwind. And why shouldn't he be excited?   Theresa was handing him one of the most popular adolescent fantasies on a platter. Under other, very different circumstances, Sean might have envied him.

But soon they were so far out that the lorry park had returned to little more than a glow on the night's horizon. And Sean again began to worry that Theresa had something more than just sex on her mind.

A minute later, Theresa slowed, then stopped. She turned to face the drifter, stepping in so close that Sean expected her to kiss him. Instead, she whispered something which made him giggle before fighting to regain his cool. She stepped back a few paces, facing him.   When he reached out toward her, it prompted another quick step backward — the young man lowered his hand in obedience. When she was satisfied that he was going to remain still, she lifted her hands and unbuttoned her shirt. She wore no brassiere.

Sean averted his eyes as she dropped her shirt to the grass. He again considered leaving, but the situation was just odd enough to force him to stay. He tried focusing on the drifter, tried not to look at his sister as she stepped out of her jeans.

Theresa stood naked before him, them. The night was moonless, but the skies were clear and the stars threw her into a beautiful contrast, defined as much by her silhouette as by the contours of her body.

The drifter drooled; Sean grunted.

Theresa stiffened, then whipped her head in Sean's direction. He froze like a statue, thankfully low to the ground amidst the tall grass. Theresa's eyes scanned the field — had she heard him grunt? Something had gotten her attention. But even if his fears were correct, he was downwind. He did not move a muscle, drew only shallow breaths.

After a few seconds, Theresa decided it was nothing, and returned her attention to the dirty young man. Tossing back her hair, she held her arms out to him, drawing him in. As he stepped into her embrace, he asked something that Sean did not catch, but he heard Theresa's reply of, "Yes ..." and he did not like the gruff edge to her voice. She brought her hands around to the drifter's front, ran them down his chest to his belt, prompting a groan, then back up again ...

... and locked them around his throat. The drifter spat a surprised choking sound, but could get nothing else out. He grabbed at Theresa's wrists but could not move them so much as an inch.

Sean was running before his brain had time to register it all. And the instant before he reached them, his heart lamented to smell fur.

Theresa sensed his coming, but too late. He knocked her away from the drifter hard enough to send her to the ground; the drifter, in turn, collapsed to his knees, holding his throat and coughing.

Theresa rolled over to all fours, her fur darker than his but her eyes a whiter shade of amber. She bared her fangs at him, growling in anger and frustration. Seeing her in her wolfwoman form for the first time made him want to cry — she looked just *like the drawings in Mark Hudson's sketchbook.   This made* him *angry and frustrated, and confused: Had art imitated life, or the other way around?*

"Ye should not have followed me, Sean," she grumbled in a thick voice.   "And ye should not have interfered."

"Ye know what I do.   Did ye really *expect me to just sit 'n watch?!"*

"I expect ye to mind yer own business and go yer own way.   Like ye've been doing for years now."

They were growling at each other when the drifter finally came back to his senses.   "Holy shite! *Wha' th' fook is goin' on?!!"*

"Kids and Scotsmen," Sean mused with sarcasm. "Nice tastes, Theresa." He reached sideways and whacked the drifter on the back of the head, knocking him unconscious — Sean may have spared his life, but the last thing he needed was a ruckus drawing other innocent bystanders into this.

Theresa watched the man crumple back to the ground, her white-amber eyes transfixed on him.   "Ye scratched his scalp.   He's bleedin'.   Do ye smell it?"

"I smell it."

She looked back to her brother.   "But I won't try to tempt ye with it.   Because I respect yer life, even though I don't always agree with it."   She regarded the drifter once more.   "Is it too much to ask that ye return the courtesy?"

"Yes, Theresa, it is.   And ye know it."

She growled.   "What now?"

He didn't know.   They stood across from one another,

each waiting for the other to make the next move. Could he really fight his own sister, perhaps kill *her? Surely even Alistaire would not expect that of him. But what could he do? Let her continue to prey on stragglers and strangers?*

"Ye killed Eamon that night, in yer wolf form. Ye mauled him, ate *part of him."*

"Aye," she admitted without hesitation. "The only reason I didn't tell ye at the time was because ye were too young and confused as it was, in too much pain to handle anythin' more. The knowledge that yer sweet sister was a 'beast' would have been too much for ye to bear."

"Why didn't ye tell me later, then?"

She cocked her head to the side, an unnerving "Theresa gesture" coming from this wolfwoman. "Do ye really not know, Sean?"

He stared at her, swallowed hard. His heart raced.

Her scent ... it's familiar ...

Don't be daft. *Of course*, it's familiar, ye idiot. She's yer sister!

No, it's not that. It's familiar in *this* form. I ... I think—

DON'T GO THERE!

He looked down at the ground.

"Ye didn't want *to know, Sean. I know ye didn't. Especially not after the eclipse."*

He almost looked at her. "What ... what eclipse ...?"

She stepped forward, her voice softer. "Do ye truly not remember, Sean?"

"Ye don't ... that is ..." Sean stammered, desperate to change the subject. "Ye don't lose control during the full moon, do ye?"

"No," she answered, closer. "I never lied to ye. I am not cursed in the way ye are, the way Dad was. I don't know if maybe it's because I'm female, or if I'm unique in some other way. But no, I don't lose control like ye and other werewolves."

He half-grunted, half-spat. "That makes it worse, *ye know. That means ye don't* have *to do things like this!"*

"That's a lie, *Sean, and ye know it. Ye may be strong enough to resist the call away from the full moon, but ye know that the urge to hunt, to feed on these helpless cattle,* never *goes away. But that's not the issue here, is it?"*

She stepped closer still, forcing Sean to retreat. But he couldn't go far — he had to protect the drifter, he had to!

"The issue is what happens to other werewolves, to you, *during an eclipse of the full moon, the red moon. Have they had one in your part of America since ye left, Sean?"*

He didn't answer.

"Have they?" she demanded.

"... just once," he answered, very low.

"And what happens during the red moon, Sean?"

Sean turned away, toward the drifter. He reached down to pick the young man up, but Theresa seized him by the arm. "Tell me!"

"No!" he snapped, jerking his arm free. She was close, too close — he had to get away from her, away from her scent!

a flash of memory, fuzzy and dreamlike ... something at night, out on the moors, under the red moon ... something about a dog, and a child ...

Theresa placed her hand on his arm again, and this time her touch was gentle. She said, "Sean ..."

It was enough, it was too much.

Sean shoved her away with all his might, then scooped the drifter up into his arms. And then he was running, running toward the lorry park, toward the light. He never slowed, but arced around so that he would approach from the back of the pub. The drifter stirred in his arms, groaning and reaching up for his wounded head, his eyelids fluttering, but it didn't matter. Sean flexed his legs and leaped, landing atop the roof of the single-storey pub, and dropped the drifter — how he would get down was his problem; Sean had other worries.

Sean heard her half-wolf howl, and it only spurred him further. With another leap he was back on the ground, and he was running again, away from the lorry park, away from her, away from memories he did not want.

He was running and running, and did not know if he would ever be able to stop.

EIGHTEEN

" ... and I ran all the way back here," Sean said. "I'm tellin' ye, Alistaire, at this point, I'm not sure *what* to think. A silver bullet put it down ... but then, how do I *know* it was the silver that did it? Maybe *any* bullet would have been enough." Sean shook his head. "They take wolf form when they shouldn't be able to, they stay in wolf form when they die ... they're the strangest bunch of werewolves I've ever encountered."

Alistaire nodded. The overcast night, coupled with the sun's passing behind the mountains, had him looking and behaving more like himself than any time since they had arrived here. *"What do you think, Trey?"*

Trey straightened, pleased as always to be included in their discussions. "Maybe ... maybe they're not ... werewolves at all. They're ... smaller than Sean is. Maybe they're ... just regular wolves? Big, *mean* wolves?"

Sean covered a small grin. "That's a good idea, Trey, but I've smelled them, and seen them change form. They're definitely werewolves." He folded his arms. "I don't know. I hate to sound like the bigot that Ootek already thinks I am, but maybe it has something to do with the *region*, ye know? Like the weretigers I heard about from India? Maybe it really is an Eskimo thing."

"Who's ... Oo-tek again?" Trey asked Alistaire in his version of a whisper.

"The man who scolded Sean in the bar," Alistaire reminded him, which prompted a nod of recognition. *"Anything is possible, Sean, especially in this world. As we have seen more than once, the rules with which we are familiar do not always apply here."*

"Aye, true." He shook his head again. "I really screwed up the notion of bringing in the locals on this. Any ideas on what to try next? Do I just go back to patrolin' the area at night?" He thumped a frustrated fist against his thigh. "If only *I* wasn't held back by the new moon! I don't know which would have been worse: Arriving when we did, or during the full moon."

"Or during ... an e-clipse?"

Sean's heart skipped a beat. "What did ye say?" he asked, trying to sound calm. From the corner of his eye, he saw Alistaire turn to regard him.

"I was reading ... 'bout e-clipses. As a were-wolf ... I bet moon e-clipses ... really mess you up."

Although Trey had not really been asking a question — he was just spouting a random thought that had entered his mind, as he often did — Alistaire waited for a response. Sean knew that it was his own tension prompting Alistaire's curiosity.

Sean tightened his walls and kept his tone as casual as he could. "Aye, they do, uh, feel weird, that's true." He waved it away with a smile that felt a little forced even to himself. "But then, if ye think about it, none of it makes sense. The sun limits me, but moonlight is just reflected *sunlight,* so if ye take that into consideration, then it should be the *new* moon which drives me wild, since that would make for the biggest absence of sunlight." He chuckled, trying not to overdo it. "I guess it's right up there with why Alistaire's *clothes* don't cast a reflection, or why yer body doesn't decompose all the way. That's why they call us 'supernatural' — we don't follow any laws of science or logic, now do we?"

Trey gave a slow shake of his head, his eyes wide with all that Sean had just given him to process. Alistaire merely stared, his intense gaze making Sean feel naked and a fraud.

Sean was saved from any further comments by the sound of a car pulling up in front of their cabin. He stepped toward the front door and opened it a crack (a tricky business with the busted hinges). The only person who should be driving out here ...

Sure enough, Arthur Petrov emerged from his car. He cast about with sharp jerks of his head, trying to watch every shadow at once. It had begun to drizzle, but he appeared oblivious to it. Sean tensed when he saw that Arthur was brandishing his handgun — especially knowing how it was loaded.

After satisfying himself that the coast was clear, Arthur broke into an ungainly run toward the cabin. Upon seeing that Sean was peering out at him, he waved the Irishman back. "Let me in! Let me in!"

Sean eased the door open just in time. Arthur burst in, whirled, and reached past Sean to slam it shut, which only served to knock it askew. Sean pulled it back, adjusted it, and closed it himself. "Ye're looking better, Arthur," he commented.

But Arthur did not reply.

Sean turned to find the man frozen, only his eyes moving as they darted between Trey and Alistaire, who — despite looking better by comparison — still did not look quite ... right.

"Wh-who ... who's this?" Arthur asked, his gun arm tensing but not quite raising.

"This is my other partner, Alistaire."

Alistaire nodded, remaining silent.

"Is ... is he, uh ...?"

"No, he's different from me, or Trey. But, um ..." He placed a careful hand on Arthur's shoulder. "I think ye might prefer not to know any more about us than ye already do."

"Yes ..." Arthur agreed, staring at Trey again now. "Yes, you're probably right."

"Why are ye here, Arthur?"

Arthur stared at Trey and Alistaire a moment longer, then replied, "In town, it's all ... all hell is breaking loose. The wolf you brought in, the one I, uh, shot ... Caster went ballistic. And I still haven't decided if it was *good* ballistic or bad. I think maybe you and your friends should get out of here, Sean. They were asking all sorts of questions about you, who you were, where the hell you came from. Danny's telling them one thing, Hill's telling them another ..." He pushed up his glasses and pinched the bridge of his nose, his eyes closed. "The only reason I got away was because of the chaos. Danny's bar looks like a circus." He lowered his hand, but now his face scrunched in disgust. "Christ, what is that smell?!"

The smell, Sean knew, was Trey's wounds, the stench

of which had saturated the cabin since Arthur's last visit. He began, "Why don't we—?"

But Arthur plowed right over him. "The townspeople are all excited now. They're sure we can hunt the wolves down, take care of them on our own without the National Guard showing up in force and creating a fiasco. Hill's trying to rally everyone up, and Caster isn't exactly trying to stop him. They're calling local rangers out of their beds, off-duty police officers. They think that if that white wolf was close by, then the others probably are, too."

"They could be right about that," Sean agreed.

"But *they* don't know what they're *dealing* with! I couldn't tell them that I had silver bullets in my gun, I don't know how I'm going to explain it when they figure that out."

"Where *did* ye get the silver bullets?"

Arthur dismissed that with a shake of his head. "I got them online, ordered them the same night I first chatted with you. I was so drunk I didn't remember doing it until after they arrived." He glanced down at his revolver and chuckled without humor. "I didn't know if they would work or blow up in my hand. Silver bullets. Fuck!" He made as if to hurl the gun away, but didn't. "There are no laws about registering handguns here in Alaska. Otherwise, Castor probably would have arrested me. Hell, he might do it anyway, I don't know, I'm not a cop. I just, I— this is all coming apart. Sean, you need to get out of here."

Sean glanced at Alistaire, who offered only a small shrug. He was keeping very still, mindful of the effect he could have on Arthur — Trey, thankfully, was doing the same. "If ye really want us to leave ..."

"Sean, you *can't* leave!" Arthur pleaded in direct contradiction to his previous statement. "They don't know what they're up against! They think you're addle-headed or a junkie, that you're a one-with-nature hippie or something, that you caught the wolf somehow through delusional dumb luck. They're going to go out there with regular guns ... they ..."

"Arthur, what do ye want—?"

"*I - don't - know!*" he bellowed, then slumped back against the wall next to the front door and struggled not to cry. Sean stood in silence, giving the man a moment to gather himself. When he did, he said, "Caster told me that the Governor has *already* sent out a National Guard squad — *one* squad, just for show — to evaluate the situation. So they'll be here, probably tonight, they're late already, and the rangers and the townspeople are going to be running around, and the police ... Jesus, they'll all probably kill each other before the wolves have a chance."

A *Pop!...crack!* resounded through the night. Faint, full of reverberation, but in spite of the echo, impossible to miss or misinterpret: It was a gunshot.

They all stiffened, exchanging apprehensive looks but not yet jumping to conclusions. If that were the *only* shot they heard, then maybe—

Pop!...crack! again. *Pop!...crack!*

"Where's that ... comin' from?" Trey asked.

Both Sean and Alistaire cocked their heads to one side. *Pop!...crack!* Alistaire replied, "*I am uncertain. It sounds a fair distance away, but it has been many years since I have lived in terrain like this.*"

Rat-tat-tat! Rat-tat-tat-tat!

"Is that a ... ma-chine gun?" Trey asked.

"I think ..." Arthur said, then licked his lips before finishing. *Rat-tat-tat!* "I think it's coming *from town*." He pleaded with his eyes, begging one of them, any of them, to tell him he was wrong.

Pop!crack!Pop!crack!Pop!Pop!crack!crack!Pop!crack! Rat-tat-tat-tat-tat-tat!

And then, through it all, came the howling of wolves.

The Triumvirate moved.

*   *   *

Raymond Caster was not happy. He felt as though he were living in a movie that had been set to fast-forward, but somehow *he* was still moving at regular speed. And things got worse when the National Guard squad showed up.

In they rolled, in their big armored mini-tank or troop transport, or whatever the fuck it was called. They just rolled right in like they owned the place, like it *wasn't* past midnight — if the whole town wasn't already awake and running around because of the wolf shooting, this loud metal fucker would have done the job.

And to top the whole thing off, it was just starting to drizzle — too light to carry an umbrella without everyone thinking he was a pussy, but just enough to fuck up his hair and send cold little trickles down the back of his collar. Just fucking wonderful.

The armored transport rolled to a stop, and a second later, the back door lowered. A young soldier emerged and looked around, clearly startled to find so much activity at this time of night. A few citizens were gawking now, and he raised his voice. "Who's in charge, please?" His voice was pleasant and polite, which pissed Castor off even more.

"Over here!" Castor called, waving his hand high before that idiot Hill could make the claim.

The soldier said a word or two to the troops behind him, then stepped down. Castor could see that they were a dozen men and women at most; if these were *all* that arrived, the situation might be salvageable, but he could only guess as to how many more squads, units, or garrisons would be sent if this reconnaissance team did not report results, very, very soon.

The soldier in charge pushed his way through the crowd, offering only noncommital responses to the questions he was asked along the way. Castor made no effort to meet him in the middle.

Finally, the soldier stood before him, and appeared unsure as to whether or not he should salute a civilian. He finally settled for a sharp nod of his head. "Lieutenant Tracy McGehee, Alaska National Guard, reporting, sir. And you are ...?"

"Deputy Chief Ray Caster, State P.D." He did not offer his hand.

"I hear you have a wolf problem, Chief."

"Nothing we couldn't have handled on our own."

"Yes, sir," the soldier agreed, then waited patiently. He could afford to wait, since the light rain was running off his helmet.

Caster swore under his breath — he would have *preferred* if the soldier had been an asshole. "All right, look, we're in the middle of something right now. Someone shot and killed one of the wolves earlier tonight ..." He looked around. Where the fuck did Petrov go, anyway? He was here just a minute ago, wasn't he? "...so we think they're in the area. You guys are here to evaluate the situation, right?"

"Yes, sir. Evaluate and assist."

Caster rolled his eyes. "Fine. You want to back us up against a bunch of wild animals, be my guest. You're sure as hell not getting any sleep before I do."

But the soldier again let the dig roll right off his back. "Yes, sir." He turned and marched back to the transport.

Everything continued to move too fast after that, with Caster doing his best to guide the general flow of events. Someone had seen this Scottish hippie guy heading north-east after his run-in with the Eskimo. Although Caster was well aware that this meant little in regards to where the guy caught the wolf — and Caster was looking forward to asking him just how the fuck he managed *that*! — but it was a place to start.

Personally, Caster did not believe they would find anything tonight; he was pretty sure that all the activity would have scared the wolves away, especially that big loud tank-thing.

After all, they were just a bunch of dumb animals.

So, in no time at all, a big cluster-fuck of off-duty policemen, excited civilians, and a squad from the National Guard were spreading out north-east. The people who were staying behind, those who weren't smart enough to go back to bed, stuck around Danny's bar.

Caster planned to take them out into the immediate woods, let them poke around for a couple of hours and figure out that the wolves were gone, let them get cold and sleepy all on their own, and then act like he was "grudgingly" calling it a night. If he could keep them from shooting each other, and save a little political face while he was at it, he would consider this night a marginal success.

And then he could find out where the fuck Petrov went off to when he *should* have been starting a post-mortem on that big white wolf that *he* shot, and chew his ass out! It was a big fucker, and it sure *looked* like the wolf in that kid's cell phone picture, but didn't Petrov need to measure its teeth or inspect the contents of its belly or something to be sure? So where the—?!

A loud rumble brought his attention around. Fuck, did they really need to bring that transport along? As soon as they cleared the town limits, it would have trouble squeezing through the narrow roads, and moving through the trees would be next to impossible — that thing might do well out on the tundra, but not here in the thicker woods. Not to mention what the heavy thing would do to the dirt roads, especially now that they were damp. He fell back, waved it down.

The transport lurched to a stop before it could get too far past Danny's bar, and Lieutenant McGehee rolled back a door on the side. "Yes, Chief Caster?"

"Do you really need to bring this thing along?" Caster demanded.

"Standard procedure, sir."

Caster was again irritated by the young man's reasonable and *not*-tired voice. "It's big, it's noisy, and it's going to tear the fuck out of our—"

"I'm sorry, sir. This serves as our command post, and we're required to—"

" *'Command post'*?! It's just a bunch of fucking *wolves*! And with the racket this thing makes, you're going to scare them off before we get within a mile of them!" He turned away, disgusted — *this* is why he told the Governor that bringing in the National Guard was a waste of time. They didn't need the military up here making things worse, they needed ...

And that was the problem: He didn't know *what* they needed.

*   *   *

Two hundred yards ahead, the lead soldier, Private Mike Searing, and his accompanying group of armed civilians had reached a cluster of trees when the Private registered the lack of noise and realized that the transport had stopped. He gestured for the civilians to halt, and they did. He smiled over how grievously some of them were taking this mission, how they had fallen into a movie-influenced perception of what it meant to be a "serious soldier" out searching for the enemy. They were a sleepy-looking group of middle-aged men, but they were earnest ... and, so far, hadn't given him any flack about his comparative youth.

"We aren't stopping *already*, are we, Private Searing?" asked one of the men (Jack, was it? Jake?).

Mike shook his head while shrugging. All he knew was that they had gone right into this so-called mission without a pit stop, and he needed to take a piss. He leaned back against the nearest tree and thumbed his transceiver.

"Searing to Corporal Elliott."

It took a moment for the Corporal to reply. Then she said, *"Elliott, here. Go ahead, Mike."*

"What's the hold up?"

He heard her snort into her microphone. *"Not sure yet. That state cop is whining to the Lieutenant again."*

Mike chuckled his own reply. "I'll bet he thinks he sounds all take-charge, too."

"He thinks *so. He sure as hell isn't impressing McGehee, I can tell you that."* He heard her stifle a yawn. *"I wish they'd wrap it up either way, Mike, because I could sure use some shut-eye."*

Mike opened his mouth, ready to tell her that he was tired but needed a restroom even more, ready to keep the conversation going, to maybe figure out the right words to flirt with a superior without getting his ass in trouble.

But sadly, Mike never got a chance to do any of that.

A dark shape loomed over him, emerging from the branches above. Before he could get a fix on whatever the hell it was, he felt two hands wrap around his throat ... and what felt like *claws* digging into his skin?

He managed to roll his eyes far enough to look up at his attacker. For a moment, just a fleeting moment, it looked like one of the creatures from the *Alien* movies — he saw nothing but teeth, teeth, and more teeth.

Then the teeth lunged forward, the mouth closing right onto his face. He felt something ripping and something very wet, and then concerns about having to urinate, flirting with Elliott, and how in the world a wolf could climb a tree all went away ...

*   *   *

Caster had just about had his fill of McGehee's bullshit. He was wet, cold, and so fucking tired. And this snot-nosed Army-wannabe was determined to argue with his every order.

"Look!" Caster snapped, cutting off yet another of the Lieutenant's reasonable comebacks. "I don't care about your normal procedures! You are here to *assist* us, and I am in charge, and I am telling you—"

"Um, Chief Caster ...?"

"*What?!*" Now even his own men were interrupting him!

The police officer, in civilian attire except for his police cap and his badge hastily pinned to his heavy jacket, was pointing across the street. "Stone's found something strange. I think you need to look at this right now, before we go any further."

Caster fumed for a moment, trying to rein in his temper; McGehee waited. From somewhere inside the transport, Caster heard a woman say, "What was that, Mike? I didn't copy. Say again?"

Without speaking, or waiting to see if McGehee would follow, Caster stormed across the street to where Stone was waiting next to a parked vehicle. It was a station wagon, the driver's door was ajar ... and the inside of the driver's side window was splattered with blood.

Stone showed relief at seeing Caster. "Chief, I just happened to spot this, and I didn't want to touch or disturb *anything* until you'd seen it, not with you being so close and all."

Caster reached for his flashlight, his fingers numb with cold, and a growing sense of nightmarish dread. Surely this didn't—

Pop-crack!

Caster spun on his heel and demanded, "Where did that come from?! Where?!"

McGehee, who had indeed followed at a respectful distance, was already speaking into his microphone and trotting back to the transport. "Sound off! Does anyone have a location on that gunshot?"

Caster deflated inside. *Fuck, one of 'ems already shot another one. Goddamn it.*

To hell with it. Let McGehee be first on the scene, let *him* take responsibility for this cluster-fuck, let the National Guard take over the whole damned thing. He didn't care anymore.

Pop-crack! Pop-crack!

Two more gunshots, somewhere just up the street. Low-powered rifles from the sound of it, so it was definitely civilians.

Caster realized that he was holding his flashlight in his hand, and at first he could not remember for the life of him why he had pulled it out. Why had he needed ...?

The station wagon, that's right. The blood on the inside of the window.

Castor turned back to the vehicle, clicked on the flashlight, and with a single finger, pulled the ajar door further open. He expected to find a wounded person inside, though exactly *how* the person would be wounded was anyone's guess.

He did *not* expect to find himself facing a very large, reddish-furred wolf, its jaw dripping gore from its latest bite of the driver's throat.

"*Fuck!*" Caster shoved away from the car with so much force, he tripped himself. And it saved his life.

As he fell onto his back with an explosion of breath and a banged elbow, the red wolf leaped from within the station wagon, sailed over his head, and struck Stone full in the chest. Stone discharged the handgun he'd been holding, but the shot went up into the sky. The wolf took him down, tearing his nose and right eye from his face. Stone screamed like a little girl, and Caster did not hold it against him.

The wolf took another bite, but before Caster could react in any way, the night tore open with the brattle of an automatic weapon. Caster covered his ringing ears, not even aware that he had cried out. The wolf was struck several times, the force of the impacts knocking it back — first up onto its hind legs, and then all the way over onto its back. Stone twitched a few times, but Caster could already see that it was too late for the man, a fellow officer with whom Caster had worked for four years. Damn it.

McGehee stepped forward, tendrils of smoke drifting from the barrel of his machine gun. "Chief Caster! Are you all right, sir?"

Caster sat up, and did not resist McGehee's helpful hand while doing so. "I ... I'm fine. Thanks, Lieutenant. Now what the ... fu ..." Caster's jaw lowered as his eyes widened. "You *gotta* be fucking *kidding* ..."

The red wolf was getting up.

"Shit," McGehee muttered, bringing his weapon to bear once more. He barely managed to fire a few more shots into the wolf before it gained its feet, but even with those — one of which struck the wolf in the head, damn it, the *head*! —

the wolf went down but was *not* out, and was already struggling to get up once more.

Caster got to his own feet, and this time he did not need help.

More shots rang out, most from up the street but some from other directions.

"Lieutenant," Caster said, his pistol now in his hand as he and the guardsman backed away from the wounded, but somehow still living, wolf, "I suggest we get back to that armored transport of yours. It can make all the racket you want."

It was only in those very few, very long seconds as the two men rushed back to the transport that Caster had a chance to think about what had just happened, if "think" was the appropriate term: Stone was dead, and a wolf — a big wolf, a wolf that would not die even when shot with a motherfucking machine gun! — had killed him. He simply could not *process* that information; his mind was not built that way.

And it got worse. As they ran across the street, with gunshots and screams echoing through the night all around them, Caster caught glimpses of things that made even *less* sense. Wolves tearing through the town streets, dragging people down and mauling them, was bad enough ... but Caster also saw what looked like some sort of *mutant* wolves as well, wolves that ran almost upright on their hinds legs, with hands on arms instead of paws on forelegs, wolves that moved less like wolves and more like *men*.

It's just stress, he berated himself. *That fucked up wolf, probably rabid or something, freaked you out, so you're seeing things that aren't there. Get your head on straight, for fuck's sake!*

A "mutant" wolf loped (*sprinted*) up to a car that's engine was just rolling over, pawed at (*opened*) the door, and grabbed (*how do you explain away* that *one?*) the woman and dragged her out onto the street before biting into her throat, ripping it out with a fine arterial spray.

If he had felt that the world was fast-forwarding past him before, it was like he was the only one trapped on pause now.

They reached the transport, and the woman who had been on the radio before reopened the side door for them. Caster could hear the squawking coming from the headphones around her neck. McGehee barked, "Report!"

"Situation ... unclear, sir," she replied, her sidearm in her hand and her eyes darting back and forth, watching for any immediate danger — Caster wondered if she would just close the door on them if a wolf showed up right this instant.

"That's not good enough!" McGehee put a hand behind Caster's back and pushed him forward, toward the safety of the transport, leaving Caster torn between machismo and self-preservation. "I need to know what's going on, Corporal!"

"Yes, sir! I understand, sir. But ..." She floundered, her shoulders sagging. "Tracy, the wolves are *attacking* the town! Martin reported that firearms don't have— don't *seem* to have much effect. That's not ... I ..." As Caster relented to McGehee's insistent hand, as he reached up to the side and pulled himself in, the woman flared without warning. She grabbed Caster by the shoulder and shoved the policeman against the doorframe, her gun almost-but-not-quite pointed in his face. "What the fuck is going on?! What didn't you people tell us?! What's going *on*?!"

"Corporal Elliott!" McGehee snapped, furious and appalled. "Stand down!" He grabbed her shoulder, so that they had a nice little shoulder-grabbing chain going. "Right *now*!"

"This is bullshit, Lieutenant!" she replied, pleading. "Animals don't act like this! This is all wrong! There's something he's not telling us!"

"I'm not going to say it again, Corporal!"

"I *don't* know what the fuck is going on," Caster said, now the calmest of the trio. "All I know is we've had a few more wolf attacks than usual lately. The pressure got turned on, the shit rolled downhill, and I got stuck in the middle of this."

Then they all three shared a communal chill as the night was filled with a cacophony of wolf howls. It came from all sides, and for a moment, drowned out all other sounds, even the gunshots.

"I don't know what's going on," Caster repeated, though he wasn't certain they could hear him. "One of these damn things was shot, shot and killed *dead*, a couple of hours ago." He shook his head. "We haven't seen *anything* like *this*."

The Corporal let go of Caster's shoulder, her eyes returning from angry to fearful. Caster crawled into the transport, then reached back to offer McGehee his hand. McGehee nodded his thanks, grabbing the policeman's wrist and heaving himself up and forward into the—

A hand snaked down from above, catching McGehee full in the face. The hand, shaped like a human's but covered in fur, dug its claws into the underside of his jawline. Blood squirted, its heat splattering Caster where their wrists were locked. McGehee, his struggles disoriented and inefficient, was lifted toward the roof of the transport. Caster attempted to hold onto him, but the blood proved more slippery than its stickiness suggested.

"Tracy!" Elliott screamed, pushing forward to help. Now it was Caster's turn to grab her shoulder and shove her back. He reached out to slide the door closed — just as he had feared the Corporal would do to *him* a minute ago — before it was too late.

McGehee's unmoving body was thrown away, thrown so hard it struck the side of Danny's bar with an audible *crack!* When the transport door was mere inches from closing, that same furry, now-bloody hand reached down and grabbed it. Caster had momentum and leverage on his side, but it didn't matter. After a brief deadlock, the door began to slide back open.

To her credit, and for all the good it did, Elliott acted. She shoved her sidearm forward, firing a pair of shots at the furry forearm. Only one struck their target, and if it caused any serious harm or pain, no indication was given — the only thing accomplished was that Caster was pretty damned sure he would never hear out of his left ear ever again.

A wolf head — a normal one, not one of those fucking mutant things — appeared at the bottom of the doorway and snapped at Caster. He finally accepted defeat and let go of the door, scrambled back, and leveled his pistol at the entrance; Elliott did the same.

The door slid open all the way, and the furry hand was withdrawn. The transport creaked as their adversary shifted its weight on the roof, then with unnatural yet beautiful grace, it swung down and into the transport.

All Caster saw was dark, flowing hair, tits, fur, and blood-coated fangs. The last part was enough for him. He fired.

The bullet struck the furry woman-thing between her heart and her left shoulder. Whether it was because of her mutant (or whatever) nature or because his pistol could not compete with the power of an automatic weapon, it did not matter — the furry woman flinched, and that was all; unlike the red wolf, she did not go down ... hell, she barely even bled.

Speaking of the red wolf, it appeared in the entrance on the right side of the door, so that the furry woman was flanked by two wolves now. The red wolf still bore obvious wounds, especially the one in its head, but as far as Caster could tell from its behavior, the damage was just cosmetic now.

They all remained still for a moment — Caster and Corporal Elliott on one side, their guns still aimed and ready; the two wolves and the furry woman on the other.

"Humans," the female said, drawing a gasp from Elliott. "You killed one of my pack tonight." At least, that's what Caster *thought* she said — she was difficult to understand with those teeth and that misshapen jaw of hers. But the intent in her eyes was unmistakable. "You brought this on yourselves."

She gestured, and the two wolves leaped.

Caster fired, over and over; Elliott followed suit. Not that it mattered.

A minute later, as the policeman and soldier

disappeared into the bellies of her packmates, the alpha again stood atop the humans' transport; its engine still ran, but no soldiers remained to operate it. There were still many humans nearby — she could smell them, hear them ... but not for long.

She did not know *how* they had managed to kill her white wolf, but it did not matter; nor did it matter that she had been very near to killing the rebellious bastard herself. He had belonged to her, and his death demanded vengeance.

This was not how she had envisioned their first major ascension, but it would have to do. Now that they had begun, there was no turning back. They would kill every man, woman, and child in this town. And now that the soldiers and most of the policemen had been neutralized, there remained only one obstacle before them.

A howl sounded through the night, and it did not belong to one of hers. She smiled.

"Come to me, my warrior. I'm waiting for you."

XIX

"Come on out here, Sean!" Theresa called. "I know ye're in there, and I know what ye're planning!"

Thanks to Sean's little stunt, Theresa had been forced to return home on foot. Once the drifter had started screaming bloody murder from the pub roof, the area had become far too active for her to retrieve her Moped. It was a mild inconvenience, as she could run just as fast as Sean in her wolfwoman form. She had indulged Sean's precious little scruples long enough; it was time he faced facts and bloody got over it!

She reached the house in little more than the hour she had traveled away from it; the only reason Sean had beaten her here was that he had gotten his unexpected head-start, and he had run like hell was biting at his heels. That just irritated Theresa further.

Now she stood outside her home, her clothes in a disheveled pile under her arm, which she promptly threw to the ground. She remained in wolfwoman form, and felt very unapologetic about it.

All the lights were out in the house, but she was not fooled.

"Ye're runnin' away again, aren't ye, Sean?" she

called, her hands on her naked hips. "Ye're in there, packing yer bag and already planning yer route back to the airport in Dublin. But ye're not leaving until we talk about this. And if ye don't think I'll use force to keep ye here, try me."

After a moment of silence, the front door opened. Sean deterred there, in human form, dressed, and, as she expected, his duffle bag in one hand. She could feel the force, the judgement of his gaze, and she was not intimidated.

Sean had *hoped to slip away without having this confrontation, he truly had. What was to be gained by this? Nothing she could say would "convince" him to just let her keep hunting humans ... and yet he could not bear the thought of killing her. His solution had been to flee, to remove himself from the equation. He would tell Alistaire what he had discovered and let* him *decide how to handle it — if Alistaire chose to travel with Trey to Ireland, Sean would neither assist nor dissuade him.*

But now here Theresa was, faster than he had hoped and feared. She stood there. Angry. Beautiful.

He averted his eyes. He did not like looking at her human breasts, let alone the vestigial breasts she gained below them when she was half-wolf. "If ye wanna talk to me, shift back and put yer bloody clothes on."

"They're not bloody," she returned with a humorless smirk. "I always hunt naked."

"Cute. Now get dressed."

"Fuck yerself," she replied, and did not move.

"Fine." He dropped the duffle bag and stepped off the dark porch. "Ye want to have it out, let's have it out."

He kicked off his shoes, dropped his shirt on top of them, and shifted into wolfman form. "I'll kick yer ass and be on my way. Ye can lick yer wounds while I'm flyin' back to the States."

Theresa did nothing, said nothing.

Sean growled at her, but his heart wasn't in it. After a moment, he dismissed her with a wave and turned back to his clothes. "Forget it. This is ridi—"

Theresa ran at him, but Sean had half-expected as much. He spun back around, prepared to meet her head on, but at the last moment, she leaped, sailing over his head. But rather than carrying past him, she reached down, dug her claws into his shoulders, and pulled herself down onto his back.

Sean grunted against the pain. He was impressed by her agility, but not stunned by any means. He prepared to twist and throw her to the ground so that—

Theresa latched on, craned her head forward, and bit him on the side of his neck.

It wasn't an aggressive bite; it barely broke the skin. It was more like ...

Sean bucked hard enough to throw Theresa off and dashed forward several paces before turning around. "What the fuck was that?!"

Theresa wiped the small amount of blood from her lips. "Oh, calm down, Sean."

"'Calm down'?!"

"Ye said ye wanted to fight, didn't ye? Ye were going to 'kick my ass', all American like, before leaving?"

Sean sputtered, but could come up with no reply.

"We don't have to fight, Sean. Ye can leave and

return to yer life, and leave me to mine." She scowled. *"But before ye go, you will do me the courtesy of admitting why ye left."*

"I— I just ... ye can't ..." he sputtered some more.

Theresa rolled her eyes. "Fine. Ye're right, forget it. If the whole thing disgusts ye so much *that ye cannot even say it, then leave. Go. And don't ever come back, ye bastard." Amidst the anger, she actually sounded* hurt.

Sean rallied. "Well, of course *I find it disgusting, Theresa! Ye're* killing people*! Ye know I'm not like that, ye know the stand I've taken! How did ye expect—?!"*

"That's not what I'm talking about, and ye know it."

Aye, Sean, ye know it.

Sean shook his head, both to his sister and himself. "Well ... then, ye mean about ye're bein' a werewolf? I, I ... well, ye lied to me about it, lied for years. And yer my sister, of course I wouldn't want ye to be—"

"That's not what I'm talking about!"

"Then what the hell are *ye talking about, damn it?!"*

"I'm talking about the eclipse*!"*

Dizzy and nauseous, Sean made one final attempt to avoid the subject he had been avoiding for twenty years. "Ye ... ye said something before about an eclipse. I don't know what—"

Crying out in a very human show of frustration, Theresa stormed right up to him. He only managed one step backward before she reached him. She took his furry face in both hands — for an instant, he was afraid she was going to kiss him with her misshapen mouth! — and forced him to look her in the eye.

"The eclipse, Sean. The red moon*."*

The red moon ...

*   *   *

Since his first shift, Sean's existence had been defined by the moon. Even though he had chosen to resist his bestial nature, he could not escape the moon's influence, its power. The cycle of the moon dictated his habits, his actions.

The new moon freed and limited him; the full moon horrified and unleashed him.

And then there was the red moon. The red moon changed the rules. Sean could not speak for all werewolves, but a full lunar eclipse affected him in ways that were profound yet difficult to articulate.

During the regular full moon, Sean lost all control. As a double-edged blessing, he was robbed of all human restraint and *of all memory. He never remembered anything that occurred during the full moon. No echoes, no deja vu ... no recollections whatsoever.*

Except for during an eclipse of the full moon, during the red moon.

It would be overstating matters to suggest that Sean gained any real "control" during the red moon. Far from it — whatever supernatural laws gave the moon its power over werewolves had not provided that particular loophole.

However ... during the red moon, Sean found that some *semblance of his human mind remained intact. But that awareness was relegated to the role of* observer, *much like one experiences in a dream, or a nightmare — even though he could recall, in a fragmented and shadowy manor, the events that took place during the eclipse, it was as though he were a passenger in his own body, recalling the sights and smells in bits and pieces.*

One month not long after his seventeenth birthday, Sean escaped during the full moon. His foster parents were away (as usual, but thankfully), and even Theresa had been forced to travel south for the night to deliver some contracts for the Finnians. As a result, Sean had been left alone to lock himself in the soundproofed cellar ... and somewhere along the way, he must have missed some step. The manacles had to be very tight, so as to remain on his forearms and shins when they shifted into wolf legs — were it not for his wolf's sheer mass, they would not have worked at all. Maybe he didn't tighten one of them enough, or something. They were never able to figure out what exactly had gone wrong.

Regardless, sometime after night fell and the full moon rose in the sky, Sean was loose on the moors.

Later still, an eclipse began.

Sean's first memory — literally his first-ever memory as a wolf during the full moon — was of bringing down some stray dog. It must have wandered away from home, and now it would never return. Sean chased it down and killed it. He ate some of its haunches, but that was all; he had been more drawn to the hunt than the kill. And the part of his mind that was flickering with dim humanity breathed some relief ... and reveled in the naked exhilaration of the wolf. Then he lost awareness again.

When his mind returned, the eclipse was very close to completion and the moon was looking quite red. The wolf stared at the moon in abstract confusion, but somewhere inside, Sean figured out what must be happening. Theresa had never mentioned the effects of an eclipse, and it had never occurred to him to ask. Then the wolf lost interest, and he was running, running.

Somewhere in the night, he heard a sharp bark that brought him to a halt. Another dog? No, this had sounded ... different. He caught the barest scent on the wind, and pursued.

But as he searched for the source of the intriguing bark, another *scent captured his attention: Prey. He switched to hunting mode without missing a step.*

He located his prey in no time. A young human, a girl, was wandering the moors, much as the dog had been. In fact, she was calling some word over and over, and she carried a colorful length of fabric with her — it had probably been her *dog that Sean had brought down.*

The wolf salivated and thrilled at this opportunity; the human inside recoiled, but could do nothing but watch.

Keeping downwind — the animal not understanding that this was unnecessary when stalking humans — Sean snaked his way toward her. She was young and very scared, as whatever senses she did *have at her disposal had warned her of some danger. Not that it would help her.*

When he was less than twenty feet from her, Sean again caught the first *scent he'd been tracking. But where—?*

Something landed on his back, knocking him forward onto his belly. He felt teeth sink into the side of his neck.

"submit!" he was told, through means his human side could not grasp. "she is my prey! submit!"

Sean bucked hard and threw his attacker off. The teeth ripped away from his throat, taking fur but little blood with them — the bite had not been meant to truly harm him, and he did not understand that either.

Spinning, he faced his opponent. It was another wolf, a female, the first he had ever seen. Her fur was a shade darker than his own. She licked his blood from her chops as they circled one another.

The human girl screamed, but it was broken and frail. She was frozen in her tracks, and would likely remain so while this was settled.

"she is mine!" the female demanded.

"no," he replied, feeling his way through this bizarre communication that the wolf understood far better than his human side. "I will take her."

The female snarled at him, but did not quite growl. Her circling slowed, and he matched her. "you cannot take her," she warned. "I will not submit!"

Sean's reply was to dive forward, claws at ready and teeth bared. The female was fast, but still he slammed into her hindquarters. As she spun around out of control, he hit her again in a near-human tackle, using his superior size and weight to drive her into the ground.

Now it was Sean who had the dominant position, his teeth latched onto her neck. "Submit!"

"No!"

"SUBMIT!"

After another moment of struggling, the female calmed. She whined her compliance.

Sean kept his teeth on her neck a bit longer. His eyes rolled around to the human girl, who had broken her trance just enough to begin backing away from them. Her pace was pitiful.

The female wolf whined again. Sean growled, pinched his teeth to make sure they broke through the fur and skin, then released her. He gave a brief, dominant howl of excitation, and then tore after the child.

No! the human inside cried, *but the wolf was deaf to his plea.*

In less time than it took to count, he had her. He knocked her to the ground, in a manner not unlike he had used against the female wolf. Her tears silenced as the wind left her body. Her blood was hot; he could smell it, and he would taste it.

A sudden, sharp pain brought a yipe! *of surprise from him. He twisted to find the female wolf, her teeth sank into the thigh of his left hindleg. She snarled at him and twisted her head to deepen and widen the wounds.*

But ... she had submitted! On some instinctual level, he knew that this broke the rules, that this was ... "cheating?" A concept that baffled his wolf side but that his human side understood just fine.

The human girl was forgotten again as Sean turned on the female wolf in earnest. They rolled over the ground, barking and biting at one another, teeth and fur and blood flying in fury. He bit her cheek, she clawed his ear; he ripped her tail, she tore his paw. She refused to back off— hell, she was determined to put him *in his place!— and he was outraged by her defiance.*

Outraged ... and excited.

Without warning or announcement, the fight changed. Sean felt a pull to her that he had never experienced before. It was very different from his human attraction to girls; it was far more primal than that, almost depraved.

She reacted the same. Her bites became less aggressive, more needful. Without open submission, she twisted and turned until her body was in position.

"Take me!" she insisted.

He took her.

The human girl ran away, and neither of them noticed or cared.

*   *   *

"Fuck!" Sean yelled, knocking Theresa's hands from his face and shoving her away. He turned and bent over, the urge to vomit strong but elusive.

"Sean ..." she said, her voice soft.

He afforded her a sideways glance, and found that she had reverted to human form. He then realized that, somewhere along the path down memory lane, he had done the same.

"Stay away from me," he said, his voice trembling. He held up a hand against her, but it, too, was trembling and ineffectual.

"Sean ... ye weren't yerself. It was the red moon, but it was still a full moon. Ye had no control over yer actions, no influence over yer behavior. Am I right?"

He didn't answer, he couldn't. He couldn't speak. He was too full of revulsion, and he wished he could vomit and get it over with, something, anything to relieve this dirty nausea.

She continued, "If it weren't for the eclipse, ye would

never have known it happened."

"That doesn't make it right."

"Ye're a male wolf, and ye encountered a female for the first time—"

"Stop it!"

"Sean, ye didn't know *what ye were* doing*!"*

Sean half-growled, half-howled. Without a conscious thought, he shifted into wolfman and raked his claws at her throat.

Theresa shifted just as fast, bending back and away from him. His claws tagged her, but the cuts were superficial.

She was angry again. "But ye didn't want *to know, did ye?!" Just as they had that night over twenty years ago, they began to circle one another. "Ye woke up back home the next morning, but ye didn't ask how, did ye? Ye never asked me about my injuries the next day, never questioned any of it! No, ye just pushed it away, and pushed* me *away, pushed away the slightest notion, the barest fucking hint that I might even* be *a werewolf. And then ye left!"*

Sean growled. "What we did was wicked, an abomination!"

She spat. "That's just yer religious friend talkin'!"

"Shite! Ye cannot really believe that!" She thrust forward, raking her claws across his chest before he could dodge. He counter-swung at her, but missed. His frustration was twofold as he continued, "Because you aren't affected by the full moon, are ye?! That means that you knew *what we were doin'! Didn't ye?!"*

"No!" she lunged again, but he evaded her. He

lashed out as she passed him, and this time she did not dodge him; his claws sliced across her shoulder blades. She roared, and it transformed into her yelling, "No, ye bloody bastard! The red moon is the opposite *for me! An eclipse is the one time that I* do *lose control!"*

He slowed, stopped. Was it true? Could he believe her after she had lied all this time?

But then, had she really "lied" when he had never asked the question?

Her half-wolf face was still twisted with rage, but there were also tears running down her furry cheeks. "Am I so disgusting to ye, Sean, that the mere thought *of being with me would send ye running across oceans to get away from me?"*

"Theresa," he said, struggling to hide some of the repulsion in his voice, "you - are - my - sister. *"*

She barked a harsh, dreadful sound, much like a cough, a laugh, and a sob. "I can't *be with anyone else, Sean! No one can replace ye — believe me, I've tried. Ye're ... ye're my alpha." Her voice softened again. "I'm a wolf, and ye're my alpha, Sean." She reached out to him, her hand and body and eyes pleading along with her voice. "Please ..."*

Thoughts of his own many lovers, of his own constant longing to fill a need ... to replace something or someone ... danced through his mind. But none of that made any difference; he could not allow *it.*

Sean struggled to remain stolid as he shook his head. "No. Never. Never *again."*

Terrible emotions warred across Theresa's face. But the final look in her eye was one that Sean knew from numerous battles: Murder.

With a howl that lacked all humanity, Theresa threw herself at him.

And she kept coming, and coming.

Sean, all desire to fight drained out of him, did his best to fend her off, but she just would not stop. He begged her to stop, begged her to end this, but it was as though she had surrendered to her animal in every way.

She wanted to kill him, and she would not be denied.

Eventually, after suffering repeated slashes, gashes, and bites, Sean defended himself. Theresa may have been the older, more experienced werewolf, but Sean had spent many years fighting by Alistaire's side, fighting vampires, werewolves, and other supernatural creatures. Like it or not, he was a hardened veteran, and a professional killer.

In the end, he had Theresa pinned to the ground, her good arm (he had broken the other) held in one hand and his knee against her throat. She bent at the waist, trying to claw at him with her feet, but he was too far forward for her to do much more than kick away tufts of fur.

"It's over, Theresa," he panted. Blood from a scalp wound ran into his eye and he blinked it away.

She glared at him, her white-amber eyes burning. "No," she said, her first words since their true fight began.

"If I have to, I'll hold ye here until sunrise, Theresa. And then—"

"And then ye'll leave."

"... aye."

"And I will keep hunting people," she taunted. "The people ye and yer freak friends protect. I will kill one every night, maybe more."

"Theresa—"

"I will kill and kill, and maybe I'll even infect a few. And they will spread, spread us like the disease we are. And then ye will have *to come back home, won't ye?"*

"Theresa—!"

"I'll do it, Sean! I'll do it all!" Her brow furrowed even as her eyes widened, and it gave her a disturbed, maniacal look. *"The only way to stop me is to kill me."*

He gaped at her, shook his head.

"Kill me, Sean. Because if ye don't, I'll do it all and more!"

"No."

She thrashed anew. "Kill me, ye bastard! Do it! Kill me!"

"Theresa—!"

She arched her back, her eyes wilder than ever. "If ye won't be *with me, then* kill me*!"*

She brought her broken arm around and clawed at his face. She twisted and convulsed, and Sean knew he was in danger of losing hold of her.

*"*KILL ME!*"*

With a cry of anguish, Sean lashed out. His claws, as extended as he could push them during the new moon, tore through her throat so deep, his middle finger scraped across her neck bone.

Theresa coughed and sputtered, yet she still did not stop. He could no longer tell if her wild eyes were envisioning his death or her own.

Tears streaming down his face, Sean slashed and slashed until her head separated from her body. And then he held her and cried until the sun came up.

*   *   *

Smoke was already billowing from the windows. Sean had started the fire down in the basement, where he had placed Theresa's remains alongside his old full moon restraints. He hadn't expected the fire to spread so quickly ... but then, he'd poured so much petrol down and around there, he shouldn't have been surprised.

Sean felt hollow as he watched the Finnian house set ablaze. He knew that he needed to get away as quickly as possible — enough people knew that he was in town that the constabulary would want to speak with him sooner rather than later, if not just arrest him outright on suspicion of arson, and murder.

In retrospect, he supposed he could have just taken Theresa elsewhere and buried her. The Finnians and others might have assumed that her wayward brother had convinced her to return to America with him, and written the whole thing off as uncharacteristic and irresponsible judgement on Theresa's part. But given the fugue in which he had been operating this morning, it was no wonder that he wasn't thinking on his feet as well as he should.

He picked up his duffle bag, took a few steps toward the road ... and stopped.

"I can't do this," he said aloud. Running back to America, warning Alistaire that they should relocate in case he could be traced there ... he was tired, so tired. He wanted, needed a break from everything, from life. Now that he remembered the atrocity that had occurred with his sister, he would have to deal with it, all of it, if he wanted to lead any sort of normal life.

That brought a bitter guffaw from him. Normal? As if that even remotely applied to the life he led.

But maybe he had an out: Mark Hudson.

He was loathe to run away yet again, but ... if he could take some time to gather himself together, maybe he could make some sense of it all, at least enough to return as a productive member of their Triumvirate.

He had imagined that this bridging between the worlds (if that's what it really was) could not go on forever, and sooner or later he and Alistaire would return to business as usual. But on the "other side," he knew that Mark Hudson had retreated to his mother's home after the encounter with the two loan sharks, or whatever they had been — all he really recalled at the moment was Neil Carpenter's amusing labels "Flat Top" and "Square Shoulders."

Maybe he could spend some time in that *world, for however long it lasted or until he could get his shite together, whichever ended first.*

Yes, that was it. He would retreat into Mark Hudson.

Turning to look back at the burning house, Sean surveyed his Irish home for what was probably the last time.

And then he closed his eyes ... and began counting down from one hundred.

TWENTY

Crouched upon an overlooking hilltop, Sean surveyed the Alaskan town. It was *swarming* with werewolves — far more than he had seen in the woods, far more than had attacked them in the cabin.

"This does not bode well," Alistaire commented.

Sean howled again, hoping that his challenge would distract the wolves from their prey long enough for more people to reach at least temporary safety. Then he glanced at his vampire partner, and up at the sky. The clouds remained, but the drizzle had stopped, leaving the night all-too bright. "Ye shouldn't be out here, Alistaire."

Alistaire shrugged, but his wincing eyes betrayed his pain. *"The sun is behind the mountains, the sky is overcast ... I will endure."*

"For how long?"

"As long as it takes. Arthur said there were fifteen hundred people down there right now." He looked at his partner. *"This has the makings of either a slaughter, or the largest lycanthropy infestation we've ever encountered. Or both."*

"What are ... we waiting for?" Trey asked from Sean's other side.

"Well said," Sean replied. "Let's go."

* * *

In the town below, the red wolf rejoined the alpha near the armored transport. He shifted into wolfman form and said, "Hundreds of them are running into the school and the blizzard shelter on the west side. A few dozen are boarding up in the church." He smiled, the expression gruesome around the still-healing gunshot wound in his furry cheek. "Many tried to drive away. We caught them at the south road. The new wolves are doing well."

"We have given them power," the alpha remarked, sounding disinterested. "Freedom. Their old lives mean nothing now."

The red wolfman followed her gaze up into the surrounding mountains. "No one has seen him yet. But the cabin is empty."

"We do not need to *see* him. We are wolves."

"Yes," he said, dropping to all fours as he shifted back into wolf form.

Another foreign howl echoed through the night, the source still unclear but much closer.

The alpha nodded. "He is here. *They* are here."

Without warning, the red wolf dashed away as a human female broke cover at the far end of the block. The smell of so many prey and so much blood was tempting for all of them, but the alpha must demonstrate greater discipline tonight. The white wolf had died earlier because he failed to follow her orders; the word now was that he had been killed, not by Sean the Intruder, but by a *bullet*, which was absurd — where would one of these humans have located a silver bullet?

Regardless of the white wolf's standing, a serious blow had been struck against her pack; with the exception of the failed assassination of Sean and his partisans at their cabin, this was the first real setback she had suffered since gathering her numbers together.

This could not be tolerated. And after tonight, it would be clear to all.

This land belonged to the *wolf*.

*   *   *

Down the street, Kathryn, the woman who had run from cover, pushed herself hard to reach the perceived safety of her Jeep. She *had* to get home to her children, she *had* to!

Kathryn regretted beyond words leaving the house earlier tonight. Bonnie had called to gossip that they'd killed one of the rogue wolves, that they were certain they could kill all of them tonight, and that they were looking for support at the bar before they pushed off. Kathryn, who had been eyeing Danny for some time, had made sure her two boys were asleep in their beds, debated it for a few minutes, then sneaked out of the house. She would stay for an hour, no longer. But then the National Guard squad had shown up, and then ...

Kathryn caught movement from the corner of her eye, and screamed when she saw the red wolf running toward her. The funny thing was, she felt some small relief that it was "just" a wolf, and not one of those other monstrosities she had seen attacking people, but ... that wouldn't make her any less dead if it caught her. And then who would protect her babies?

She ran harder.

Using her remote control to unlock the Jeep's door, she dove forward, yanked it open—

As she was pulling herself inside, the red wolf hit the outside of the door. It slammed closed on her right forearm and the inside of her right knee, fracturing both. She gasped, wanting to scream but the pain was too overwhelming. She stumbled back, then slid down the side of the Jeep to the ground.

The red wolf circled around in front of her, licking its chops and drooling. Dried trails of blood exposed where it had been shot in the shoulder, chest, and head ... but that made no sense. If it had been hit so many times — especially in the head! — it should be dead, not preparing to turn her poor boys into orphans!

You never should have left them alone! she chastised herself.

The wolf stepped closer.

In futile defiance, Kathryn threw her keys at it. They bounced off its snout. If she hadn't known better, she would have sworn it rolled its eyes at her.

The wolf stepped closer, opening its jaws.

Kathryn closed her eyes and whispered, "Anthony." Which was a bit of a surprise, because she rarely thought of her late husband anymore.

The wolf's breath caressed her face ...

She heard a ripping sound and felt a splash of hot, sticky wetness all over her face, and she realized that this was her own blood. She cried, thankful that she felt no pain, but dreading what came next. She would be with Anthony again soon, but what would happen to her babies?

But then she heard another ripping sound, and this one didn't sound as close and she felt no more blood. Moaning, she forced herself to pry her eyes open.

The red wolf's body lay about ten feet away now, its chest cavity split wide along with its throat. Its blood was everywhere, including all over her.

Standing over the wolf was a sick-looking man whom she had never before seen. His face was haggard, his fingers distended like talons; his right hand in particular was a gory mess, and he was staring down at the blood in what seemed like an unhealthy fascination.

Kathryn wasn't sure if she should be relieved or not.

The man finally turned to look at her, and she wished he hadn't. His eyes were ... wrong. *"Are you all right?"* he asked, and his voice was as unsettling as his eyes.

"Yes ..." she answered. She grimaced as the pain in her arm and knee crept back into her awareness.

"I suggest you be on your way, ma'am." He reached down with his cleaner hand to assist her, and she almost refused.

But she had to get home, so she allowed him to help her up and into her Jeep. It hurt like hell to turn the key in the ignition, but she got the Jeep started and reached out to close the door. At the last moment, she said, "Thank you," then accelerated down the street.

Alistaire watched her until she rounded the corner, then hunched over, supporting himself with his hands on his knees. He wanted to save as many lives as possible, but he could not stand this not-quite-night for much longer. Usually, werewolves were little threat to him — with the exception of especially powerful ones, like Sean, werewolves simply could not match the sheer power of a vampire his age.

But tonight ... God, the sky was so bright to his burning eyes! ... the red wolf was only the second wolf he had dispatched, and he had *almost* not been fast enough to slash its neck and rend its heart in two before it had bitten back at him. The next time he might not be so fortunate, and in his current state, he was uncertain as to the outcome of open combat with one of these beasts, smaller werewolves though they were.

With a deep breath and a brief prayer, Alistaire pushed himself up and hurried toward the next disturbance ...

*   *   *

Trey came across two wolves tearing their way into a small home a couple of miles from the bar. The windows on this house were small and placed very high, probably in anticipation of large snow drifts, so the wolves were up on the front porch and clawing their way through the door. They had already made short work of the screen door, and the wooden door behind it did not look as though it would stand much longer. As Trey approached, one of the wolves shifted into wolfman form, as it stood to claw at the upper portion of the door, while his four-legged partner continued thrashing the lower portion.

Trey could hear children crying inside — quite a few of them, by the sound of it. One adult, a man, was trying to console them, but his voice was saturated with fatalism.

Moving as quickly as he could on his stiffened knees, Trey advanced upon the two wolves. One of them, the wolfman, was too preoccupied with clawing at the door, but the full wolf smelled him coming before he could reach them.

Dang it! he thought. *Stupid wolves!*

Trey did not recognize this particular wolf, but it clearly could *smell* that something was dreadfully wrong with this "human," and it retreated a few steps even as it growled at him. The wolfman finally smelled him or reacted to its companion's rumbles. It showed none of its partner's caution, but threw itself at Trey with abandon.

Trey met the wolfman head-on. He outweighed the beast, but his stiff joints betrayed him — the werewolf knocked him sideways against the house, and that was all that prevented him from falling to the ground. The wolfman barked at the wolf, and then the two were attacking him together.

Trey's forearms and hands were soon clawed open and leaking. As in the cabin, the werewolves seemed reluctant to actually bite him, but they were doing plenty of damage as it was.

"Stupid wolves!" Trey yelled in frustration. He finally managed to get a grip on the wolfman's head, and he wasted no time in ripping its elongated ear off.

The wolfman howled. As it put a shocked hand to the side of its head, Trey took the opportunity to punch it in the face as hard as he could. Its jaw sank inward and sideways, its lower canines breaking into pieces. Before it could react or respond to that, Trey grabbed its head again, this time in both hands, and shook it. He shook it and shook it, back and forth and side to side. Soon he heard several very satisfying *snaps!* and *cracks!* from inside its neck and he threw it to the ground, then stomped on its mangled face for good measure.

The werewolf that had remained in wolf form had lost much of its verve. It whined and retreated from Trey a few steps, then howled.

Calling for backup? Trey wouldn't give the stupid wolf a chance for that!

Trey jumped at the wolf, and this time his body cooperated. The wolf was just ending its howl when he seized its left hindleg in an iron grip and burrowed his fingers deep into the thick fur on its back. The wolf squirmed and twisted, managing to claw him a few more times with its free hind leg as Trey picked the wolf up. He lifted it high, then slammed it back down onto the edge of the front porch. The concrete step creased into the wolf's side, breaking ribs and gouging organs. The wolf whined in pain, and Trey repeated the process to get it to shut up.

After the second blow, the wolf was barely conscious. Its tongue lulled from its mouth, its eyes rolled back in its head. Drool hung from its jowls, and it was tinged with blood; it was bleeding from somewhere on its torso as well.

Trey started to let go, but the blood snared his attention.

He was normally ambivalent to the stuff, but something about this werewolf's blood called out to him. It felt ... different.

His brain did not process fast enough for him to make the connection that, just days before, he had bitten into the belly of another werewolf. Bitten into it, chewed on its meat, had its blood everywhere — in his mouth and down his throat. His thoughts were no longer sharp enough to realize that the attraction he felt now harkened back to that encounter, which had affected him more than he realized.

Given time, he could put it together, as he so often did. But the night was intense and his *own* blood, such as it was, was running hot; his veins pumped with his version of adrenaline, he bore days' worth of frustration over his stiff joints and his stinking, slow-healing wounds, not to mention the *new* wounds he had just sustained, which would also take miserably long to heal.

In short, his body had needs ... and his guard was down.

Sliding both hands under the wolf's back, he scooped it up, bringing its thinner-furred belly toward his face.

Wait! a part of him warned at the last second. *Alistaire and Sean wouldn't like this!*

It did not matter. Trey brought the still-living wolf's belly to his mouth, and he began to feed ...

*   *   *

Where the hell did all these new werewolves come from?! Sean thought as he killed another wolf — his fourth for the night, and another which he had never before seen. *I thought their bloody pack was large with just the first dozen!*

Since Arthur — whom the Triumvirate had instructed to drive the hell out of here as fast as he could go! — had not mentioned any reports of additional missing people,

Sean could only assume that these were *very* new recruits, people the alpha or others had infected within the last twenty-four hours.

The problem was, Sean had very little personal experience with the spread of lycanthropy. He ... and Theresa ... had inherited the curse from their father. He knew that the curse *could* be spread via a bite, but so few werewolf victims survived an attack, he had never been able to collect much information on the process — certainly none of their shape-shifting opponents over the years had been very forthcoming. A new vampire took about three days to rise from death, but how long did a new werewolf take? Days? Apparently not. Hours? Unless the alpha had deliberately hidden her numbers...

Sean shook his head, and used his nose and ears to locate his next target. It didn't really matter right now how so many new werewolves had appeared. All that mattered was taking out as many of them as he could, saving as many people as possible. The rest he could work out later.

At least they weren't ganging up on him this time. One-on-one, he could beat any of them, with the possible exception of—

Another howl broke the night, and he knew without a doubt who it was: The alpha was calling him out.

Suits me just fine, ye bitch.

Sean circled around town toward the call ...

* * *

The lowest stained-glass window of the church was nothing more than shambles and shards at this point, but it looked like the occupants had pushed an organ or some other large piece of furniture over to cover the breach. One werewolf, in wolfman form, was trying to claw his way through the gap, and each time he was greeted with flames from a brass candle-lighter set on high — if the wielder wasn't careful, they could set their own haven on fire. A full wolf was clawing at the front door, and a wolfwoman was on the roof, searching for another way in.

Alistaire would start with the one on the roof.

The wolfwoman sensed his coming before he could reach her, but did not know what to make of the ivory mist swirling across the rooftop. This allowed Alistaire the extra moments — longer than he would normally require — to coalesce as he descended upon her.

But he was still too slow.

The wolfwoman ducked under him and struck upward, her claws catching him from sternum to under his chin, exactly the kind of wound he needed to avoid right now.

Unleashing his own ferocious side, Alistaire engaged her. She was clearly confused and unnerved by his unknown nature, but that did not prevent her from fighting back. They bit and slashed at one another, and Alistaire knew that this was taking too long, that each second he wasted fighting this one werewolf gave the others that much more time to get inside the church.

The wolfwoman pushed against him, and he lost his footing on the uneven roof. He staggered, the wolfwoman biting at his defending arm, and when he fell back against something solid, his shoulder screamed in a new but very familiar pain.

Struggling not to cry out, Alistaire glanced up at the

rooftop cross she had pinned him against. As ever, the Lord was testing him, the icon by which he had lived for over half a millennium rejecting him by his very nature.

I accept your trial, G-God, he prayed. This did not, however, prevent him from pushing himself away from the searing pain as soon as possible. The abrupt movement sent the two of them rolling down the angled roof to fall over the edge together.

The wolfwoman twisted through the air as best she could, ensuring that when they struck the ground, Alistaire would suffer the brunt of the impact. Indeed, this might have afforded her the opportunity to inflict further, perhaps critical damage upon him ... which was why he made sure to shift back into mist the instant before they struck the ground. The wolfwoman *yiped!* as both of her wrists broke.

A pair of howls preceded the other two wolves as they advanced, but their numbers mattered little now. His dominance restored and his Faith bolstered, Alistaire faced all three and delivered upon them the wrath of God ...

*   *   *

The man inside the house with the children was Ootek. Which was funny, since Ootek himself did not have children, and had never wanted them. And yet, here he was, trying to calm screaming, crying kids as wolves from hell tried to break through the front door. And it wasn't even *his* front door!

Ootek had been walking back to his mother's house after stopping to check on their hardware store, something he always did at least twice each day. He had still been fuming over that foreigner's insults when he'd seen the first pedestrians going the opposite direction. Then a few more, and then more. When he started inquiring as to what was going on, he got third- and fourth-hand versions of events, but the meat of the story was always the same: Some crazy Scottish or Irish guy had turned up at Danny's bar with one of the attacking wolves. Details got fuzzy after that — the wolf was alive or dead; the wolf was shot or beheaded; the wolf was snow white or jet black — but none of that mattered. Ootek had followed the foot-traffic back toward the bar, both curious about and irritated by Sean's sudden celebrity.

But when he had gotten close enough, he took one look at the chaos surrounding the bar and decided it wouldn't be worth the headache. He turned back around and headed for home once more, stopping only long enough to ogle the National Guard transport as it rolled past him.

After that, events accelerated and became a bit of a blur. He remembered hearing what sounded like a gunshot, dismissing it as something else, then hearing more of them. Then more still, and not long after that, wolf howls. And then more of those.

He had already quickened his pace when the sounds of bedlam began to spread out. It was no longer just behind him, but coming from the sides. He'd walked even faster, just short of jogging.

Ahead of him, he had seen a child, a girl about ten years old standing at the edge of a front yard. Not far behind her, two younger boys clung to each other. And behind them, two even smaller children, one barely old enough to stand, waited in the open doorway of the house on that property.

"S-sir?" the girl had asked. "What's going on? Do you know?"

"No, ma'am, I'm afraid I don't," he'd admitted, flinching at the sound of another gunshot, this one closer than any of the others. "What's your name?"

The girl had hesitated, then answered, "Lisa."

"You're Bonnie Lang's daughter, aren't you?"

"Yes, sir."

Ootek had glanced at the two boys, who stared back at him wide-eyed. As if sensing his question, Lisa told him, "They're Tim and Kiefer. They're Kathryn Connolly's boys from across the street. My mom called their mom, and they went to see about the stuff going on at the bar." She'd straightened, still nervous but swelling with pride. "When I started hearing all those noises, I went across the street and got them. I didn't think they should be alone."

"That was a very smart thing to do, Lisa," Ootek said. He had looked back down the street, toward the source of that latest gunshot, and something had caught his eye. Something was running toward them. It might have been a dog, but he didn't think so. "Lisa, I think we should all go inside your house. Right now."

"Um ... I don't know what my mom would think about that, sir. What's your name again?"

"Ootek." Now something new had joined the first, but he had not been able to make sense of it. It had looked like another wolf, *felt* like another wolf ... and yet it had been running upright, on two legs. But in the time it had taken Ootek to register these contradictions, the second creature had fallen to all fours, and then it was just two regular wolves running toward them. Running at full speed.

Thoughts of the Irishman had flickered through Ootek's mind, but he pushed them away. He had also decided the time for delicacy was past.

"In the house, Lisa!" he'd ordered, pushing her toward the two boys, and then all three of them ahead of himself. "In the house, right now!"

All five children, including Lisa, had cowered from him as he got them inside and slammed the front door. He glanced around the living room and was relieved the see the high windows — he could only hope the entire house followed this design. Then he was pushing the sofa toward the door.

"Lisa," he'd said, "make sure all the other windows and doors are closed and locked!"

Just a few seconds after he had gotten the sofa into place, the door rattled on its frame — he could hear the screen door being torn to ribbons. This had frightened all of the younger children into instant tears, but spurred Lisa into action as she dashed off to follow his instructions.

"Good girl," he'd panted as he added his weight to the makeshift blockade.

The next several minutes were the biggest blur of all — scratching and growling and howling at the door, the occasional but thankfully brief noises from other parts of the house. The two wolves were determined and strong, absurdly strong, and Ootek began to question if his barrier would hold much longer. The children, including Lisa, were all crying, and he did his best to console them.

The fleeting notion that he might owe Sean the Irishman an apology shot through Ootek's mind, but he afforded it no more attention than he had before. He also steadfastly ignored how out of breath he was — children were depending upon him; he did not have time to deal with his aging body.

Then, finally, the attacks on the door stopped. The commotion outside was still present, but changed. It sounded as though the wolves were fighting something. Each other? If they were only so lucky. At one point, he *thought* he heard a deep voice yell "stupid wolves," and he did not know *what* to make of that.

Finally, the madness died down, though Ootek could still sense as much as hear something going on out there. Carefully climbing up onto the sofa, he peered through the spyglass in the front door, but one of the wolves had scratched the glass at some point — he could not make anything out in detail.

He did, however, see what appeared to be a man after all. The large fellow was on his knees and hunched over ... one of the wolves? Ootek had not heard any gunshots — not from right outside, anyway — but some of the rumors *had* insisted that the Irishman killed one of the wolves with his bare hands.

Was this Sean outside right now? If only he could see better!

Ootek pressed his ear against the door, but could hear nothing distinct, especially since the children were still crying up a storm. He called out, "Hello?" in a low voice, then louder, "Hello? Who's there?"

He checked the spyglass again, but its poor image was only enough to show that the figure was not responding. He glanced at the windows, but while their height had been a lifesaver before, it was a deterrent now. He could probably find a chair or something in the kitchen ...

Leave it alone, he told himself. *The wolves are gone for now, and the kids are scared out of their wits. Count your blessings, sit down, and take a few deep breaths before you drop dead of a heart attack.*

Sound advice. He wasn't sure why he didn't follow it.

He dragged the sofa back from the front door, just enough so that he could step over it. He prepared to open the door, then turned back to the kids, to Lisa. "Be ready to close this door again if I tell you to. Even if I'm still outside."

"Ootack ...?" she asked; he forgave her, since most adults couldn't get his name right on the first try.

Worried that she would just get upset if he waited any longer (or that he would lose his nerve), Ootek opened the door a couple of inches. All he could see was one of the wolves, and it did appear to be dead, its head a messy ruin.

Opening the door further, he poked his face out just far enough to see with one eye.

A man was, indeed, on his knees a few yards from house. And he was hunched over another wolf ... holding it in his arms? Ootek could not make sense of it.

At that moment, a Jeep screeched to a halt at the house right across the street — it pulled into the driveway so fast, it failed to stop before two of its four wheels ended up on the front lawn. A woman emerged; she had a severe limp, but she still managed to get inside the house in record time.

Ootek realized that this was likely Kathryn Connolly, the mother of the two neighbor boys, and he almost called out ... but something stopped him. He instead returned his attention to the kneeling man before him, who had looked up briefly when the Jeep's tired squealed but was already back to doing whatever he was doing.

Ootek decided to address him first. "H-hello ...?" he said, his tongue dry.

The man raised his head, then looked over his shoulder. Ootek gasped. The lower half of the man's face was covered in blood and gore; his shirt and hands were nearly as bad.

Was he ... was he *eating* the wolf?

The man's eyes widened, and now Ootek could see how cloudy and empty they were, like a dead man's eyes — maybe he *looked* like a man, but there was nothing human in those eyes. He opened his mouth wider, snarling, further baring his bloody teeth. He released a low, horrible moan, a rumble that sounded very savage, very threatening ... and very hungry.

Ootek decided that Bonnie Lang must have her neighbor Kathryn's phone number around here somewhere, and that would just have to do.

He closed the door ...

*   *   *

Sean ended up by the remains of Private Searing and his group of civilians. He checked for pulses as a vague formality, but his senses already told him that they were all very dead. He caught the scent of the werewolf who had attacked them, and found it familiar — not one of the new ones, then.

Moving with caution, he made his way along the street

toward the National Guard transport; its engine was still running but it had not been moved. The whole area reeked of blood, of death, and it was narrowing the usual scope of his olfactory. More bodies, some partially eaten but all of them mauled, lay in sad heaps around the bar. This had been the hub of activity when the killing started, and everything had spread out from here.

The alpha was close. Even through the interference, he could smell her.

He kept among the trees for cover as long as he was able, but he knew that sooner or later he would have to expose himself in order to check out the transport — it was painfully obvious as a potential ambush, but he could not dismiss it, either.

He opted for sooner.

He crouched low, preparing to sprint fast and hard, to hurl himself into the transport before any aggressors could react—

He caught a scent at the last moment, the same one he had detected by the first Guardsman's body. It saved him from receiving serious wounds across his back — he twisted around and grabbed his attacker, a wolfman, by the wrists. The wolfman spat and snarled in frustration, trying to both free himself and press his attack.

"Let ... me ... go!" he growled, his words muffled more than usual around his blunted snout.

Sean answered with a swift kick to the wolfman's stomach, raking his toe claws deep for good measure.

The wolfman stumbled back, floundering to keep his footing while pressing a hand to his bleeding belly. Sean did not recognize him by sight, and yet he *knew* his scent.

Did these shape-shifters change that drastically between wolf and half-wolf, fur patterns and all ...

... or was this someone from the town, someone whom Sean had met in human form and who had since been turned? If so, how had he been turned so bloody *fast*?

Why not ask a few questions and find out?

Why not, indeed. Sean seized the wolfman by the wrists again and drove him backward against the base of a tree. He brought his face to within inches of his opponent's, growling and showing plenty of fang before saying, "We are going to have a little talk, lad." He dug both thumbnails deep into the wolfman's wrists, threatening to sever the tendons with the slightest increase in pressure.

The wolfman whined, then began to shift into full wolf form. Sean adjusted his grip—

He received no warning this time before his lower back was slashed open right above the kidneys. Biting down on a howl of pain, he backhanded the shifting wolfman before him, then twisted around to face his new attacker.

It was another wolfman, a wolf*woman* in this case, and she was pissed! Sean had not managed a full turn before she was on him again, fighting literally tooth and nail as she tried with all her might to tear him to ribbons.

As Sean defended himself, he registered that, although he did not recognize her by sight, he again recognized her scent — just like he had with the other one. Had he encountered *both* of them in the bar? There had only been the one woman, the one with her husband—

The female werewolf pressed her attack on and on with enough intensity to keep Sean focused only on his defense. All he needed was one good swipe, one good punch, and his superior strength would end this, but he couldn't get an opening. It also sounded as though his first opponent was gaining his four feet, which meant they were moments away from pinning him between them. He could not let that happen.

Sean crouched as though to leap at the wolfwoman, but instead he jumped straight up into the air, deliberately entangling himself in the limbs of the surrounding trees until he could solidify his position.

But he underestimated the wolfwoman's frenzy. Before he could orient himself, she was in the trees with him, and he was back on the retreat. He had improved his situation only by maintaining a single opponent, but in other ways he had made matters worse — in addition to avoiding her attack, he now had to avoid falling, a concern this bitch did not seem to share.

Then she surprised him further by maundering, "I remember you." He barely understood her — her words were particularly thick, much like the other wolf below them.

"I'm happy for ye," Sean returned, ducking under a swipe of her claws. "Care to tell me how I made yer acquaintance?"

She threw herself at him with total disregard for gravity. Sean managed to save them both from a head-first fall, but his only thanks was a reopening of the wound on his right cheek as she bit his face.

"You said you were a friend!" she spat, spraying his own blood into his eyes.

Sean tried to process this, but too many things were happening at once, not the least of which was the snapping of the branches below them.

They fell, striking the ground hard. Sean's breath exploded from his lungs as a rock or tree root dug between his ribs. At least the female was equally stunned, rolling away from him as she struggled to catch her own breath.

But then the first werewolf, now in full-wolf form, was on him, standing on his chest and snapping at his face. And another, third wolf, clamped its teeth down on his right calf, reopening yet another wound. Then he heard a bark from another direction, and knew that a fourth wolf was coming.

"Alistaire! Trey!" he called as he held the wolf lunging at his face at bay and kicked at the other wolf with his free leg. "If ye guys are close, I could use some bloody backup here!"

"Those *things* are not here."

The two attacking wolves did not exactly stop, but their intensity died to almost nothing. The fourth wolf arrived and the wolfwoman was on her woozy feet, but neither of them joined the fray.

Sean lifted his head and spotted the alpha. She was in human form and gazing down at him in clear disdain. She said, "Those *things* are killing my wolves somewhere else. They will not save you, my warrior."

"Good for them," he returned. "Even if ye kill me now, they'll finish ye off in no time."

She smirked. "Then you have not reconsidered my offer?" One hand drifted up to a nipple.

Sean rolled his eyes theatrically. "I told ye before, I've been tempted by *far* better. Let's not waste each other's time." He kicked hard and freed his leg.

The alpha turned to ice. "Kill him."

But her melodramatic entrance had given him the breather he needed.

Sean reached up and over his head to the incoming new wolf, seized it by the snout, and swung it around like a sack of meat to knock the one off his chest. That one went flying into the wolfwoman, and Sean finished by hurling his wolf-club into the one that had bitten his leg.

The entire reversal took all of three seconds. The alpha backed off a step, her eyes burning with a mixture of hot emotions, as Sean stood to face her. She shifted into wolfwoman form and warned, "More are coming."

"They won't get here fast enough to save ye," he returned, advancing on her.

The wolfwoman recovered first and, shifting into full wolf, leaped between Sean and her alpha. Ears flat, teeth bared, haunches ready to move, she unleashed an enormous howl, clearly telling him that if he wanted the alpha, he would have to go through her first.

But Sean was no longer approaching the alpha; he was no longer even looking at her. He was staring at the female wolf who now defended her. Seeing her in wolf form, he realized that he *did* recognize her. He *had* met her before, but it had not been in human form.

He stared at her, then up at the alpha.

It all came together. It explained everything: Their ability to take wolf form during the days of the full moon; their remaining in wolf form upon death; their inherent, feral nature; *everything*.

Trey almost had it figured out, was almost right, but because Sean thought that *he* was the expert, he hadn't given it due consideration.

Somehow, lycanthropy had spread to the animals.

These were not people who turn into wolves ...

... they were wolves who turn into people.

The female wolf before him growled again. The female who had been a *natural* wolf when they had last met, helping her mate communicate with him. Sure enough, a closer look at the wolf who had been on his chest before and was just now getting up confirmed it — it was the former alpha of their own pack, their family unit. The werewolves had found them, and infected them. They were both larger now, just as Sean was very muscular, very sturdy in human form, but it was definitely them.

In fact, he realized that because of their inverse reaction to the new moon, he had yet to *see* one of these special werewolves in their full-human forms. Just as *he* made for an enormous wolf, *they* would probably make tremendous humans, a bunch of Mr. and Ms. Universes.

Except that he *had* seen one of them in human form: The alpha.

He once again fixed his gaze upon her as another piece fell into place.

"*You* are like *me*, aren't ye?" he said, his voice a mixture of wonder and loathing. He took a step forward, sending the female wolf into another barking frenzy, but he ignored her, focused only on the alpha. "That's why ye didn't join them when they attacked the cabin, why ye're not taking wolf form even now." He scowled. "Ye sick bitch. Aren't we freakish enough as it is? Ye have deliberately spread the infection to the wolves!"

The alpha opened her mouth as if to speak, perhaps to explain or defend herself, or even to tempt him further. But he wasn't interested.

Sean leaped from where he stood, without taking any steps for momentum. It surprised the female wolf, as well as the other males who had recovered enough to start outflanking him. Best of all, it surprised the alpha.

He slammed into her, tackled her to the ground. He knew that he would not have time to deal with her properly just now, not with so many of her pack to help her, and he had no intention of performing a kamikaze tonight. But he needed to get this close, just for a moment.

He buried his face in the nape of her neck — she flinched away, expecting him to bite — and he inhaled deeply, taking her musk all the way in. She was struggling in earnest now, but he lowered his head and did the same thing near her armpit. Finally, as he allowed the alpha to squirm away from him, as the first teeth dug into the back of his own writhing thigh, he inhaled of her womanhood.

He shoved her away then, twisting around to kick the head of the biting wolf, and bounding to his feet to face them all.

And he would. He hated to do it — he doubted that any of these wolves had asked for this — but they were werewolves now, shape-shifters. The Triumvirate had been concerned about lycanthropy spreading through the human population, but the stakes were even higher than that. To Sean's knowledge, *no one* had ever infected an animal before ... and he was going to end this experiment before it could spread further.

With Sean's having gotten far too close for comfort, the alpha retreated. But it did not matter. He had her strongest, most personal scents now; there would be no more confusing or hiding her trail from him.

Now, he could track her all the way to hell.

* * *

The alpha paced her den, unable to sit still for even a moment. The toe claws of her wolfwoman feet clicked on the stone floor as she strode back and forth, back and forth.

Should she flee? Abandon her den? She had called this little cave her home for so long now, she hated to leave it. She'd had such plans for her kind, for her pack ... but now her pack was dead or dying, and she knew that Sean would be coming for her soon.

She agonized over the decision, and as it turned out, she agonized too long. A shadow swelled to fill the entrance, a silhouette plunging the cave into near darkness.

She stopped her pacing, turned to face him. "Hello, Sean."

Sean said nothing at first, merely stood at the entrance, sniffing to see if any more of her pack were here in the small cave to defend her. What he found was a strong reek of sickness. He had forgotten about the wolf Trey had bitten at the cabin. Maybe these unique werewolves could not match his own enhanced immune system?

Regardless, he did not see the sick wolf here, or any of the others ... but then, he was not in top form at the moment.

Sean was exhausted, *beyond* exhausted. He bled from so many bites and cuts and scratches, he was feeling lightheaded. To make matters worse, his left heel was freshly torn up from one of a large number of foot-sized pitfalls surrounding the entrance to the den — he had been so out of it, he had stepped right into it, and he was lucky the damage hadn't been worse.

He knew that he should hold off on this confrontation, or at least have brought backup of his own. But the brightening night had sent Alistaire back to ground, and they had not been able to locate Trey, whom they could only hope was all right.

No. Sean could not risk the alpha's fleeing to other parts of Alaska or Canada and starting this mess all over again. He had complained to Alistaire that they spent too much time fighting vampires and not enough time fighting werewolves. Well, he had struck the mother load with *this* mission, and he wasn't going to stop until it was completed.

But he also realized that he was really fucked up right now, so when he had escorted Alistaire back to the cabin, he'd picked up a little insurance policy. It would feel a little ... "distasteful" ... if he had to use it, but he wasn't taking any chances.

He was stopping this here and now.

He took a step into the cave, trying to hide how much the side wall was supporting him. "It's over," he said.

The alpha noticed that he was in human form, and now wore jeans. She shifted herself into her own human form, and stood proud not to hide her body with clothing. "So. You killed my pack, my children."

"They weren't yer children. Just yer victims."

She placed her hands on her hips. "Is this where *you* preach to *me*, Sean? Pathetic."

"I have no interest in preaching to ye." He stopped, leaned against the cave wall for support and folded his arms in a weak attempt to appear relaxed and unconcerned. He needed a breather before moving in for the kill. "Why bother? Ye started this nightmare. God only knows why, who ye are or where ye're from—"

The alpha snorted in derision. "It doesn't matter where I'm 'from.' I lived here long before I was changed. Felt closer to animals than I *ever* have to people. People are the real predators." She swelled with pride. "One night, during meditation, I found the answers. And I was changed ..."

Sean nodded to himself. She continued on, talking about how her senses increased a hundredfold even as her silver earrings had seared her ears, but he had heard enough. She was a loner, probably abused, and sounded a little "new agey" ... and now she said that the change came during her meditation.

Meditation, which was often so similar to *self-hypnosis*.

Who knew if the woman, if the *mind* speaking right now was truly from here, or from *his* world? Or maybe a perfect merging between the two? Sean doubted that even she knew. Regardless, lycanthropy had found a woman who hated people and loved animals.

It made a sad kind of sense. But he still had to make sure it didn't go any further.

"... and then we would take back the land," she was saying. "The land that belonged to the *wolves*. Before Man. Before his guns—"

"Yes, yes, fine. People suck. I get it." He pushed off from the wall, and was distressed to find that he was too dizzy to make it. He turned and reclined against it, again trying to make it look casual and deliberate. He felt the object dig into the small of his back, and he was increasingly relieved to have brought it. "It was more than just 'luck' that I found ye on my very first night here, wasn't it? Ye were there for the *wolves*, on some twisted recruitment drive — *I* was just in the right place at the right time. Am I right?"

She ground her teeth and said nothing, stewing that he had interrupted her monologue.

He regarded her for a moment, then said, "I'll bet ye don't lose control during the full moon, do ye? I knew someone like ye once. That's how ye were able to keep yer wolves furry, and under yer thumb, even then. I'll bet they were still chompin' at the bit, though, with that big, terrible moon in the sky. Made ye drunk with power, didn't it?"

But it was the alpha's turn to ignore *him*. She cocked her head to one side, studied him. She might or might not have bought his carefree act before, but he could see the confidence growing in her eyes now. She looked him over, taking in the many wounds he sported.

"Why do you fear me, Sean? Why do you fear yourself?"

Sean sighed. "Look, I've told ye—"

"You're not interested. Yes, I know. What does that say about you, Sean? You hold the *power*, all the strongest traits of the wolf."

"I prefer to embrace the best traits of wolf *and* man," he corrected. "And as soon as ye began killing innocent people—"

"They were *hunters*! Men with *guns*!"

"What about the fisherman and his little boy?"

She stiffened. "I did not order that."

"No, yer wayward white wolf did. But would he have done that if ye hadn't perverted him with this 'power' of yers ...?"

Despite her human form, she growled at him.

Sean stood away from the wall, and this time he made it. He placed his hands on his hips. "Ye know what I think? I think ye're just a sad, lonely woman, who's been so rejected, so *damaged* by other people that she would rather whore herself to wolves than face her human pain."

She shifted into wolfwoman. "I will *kill you!*"

He held his left arm out to his side, but kept his right arm where it was. And he also remained human. "Ye want me? Come and get me."

The alpha took a step backward — had she detected Sean's trap? But no, she was placing one heel against the far cave wall, gaining leverage for when she leaped at him...

Sean very nearly died then and there. His focus on the alpha, along with his many injuries and strained senses, prevented his detecting the sick wolf until it was already within striking distance. He never figured out where it had been hiding — in some unseen fissure? within the pile of branches and leaves? — but it was in his face now, standing on its hind legs as it clawed and bit at him. Its breath was fetid, and though it appeared to be on the slow road to recovery after all, it still had a long way to go.

Given Sean's current condition, the wolf's malady was a blessing. Sean dug his still-human fingers into its throat and crushed its esophagus.

And then the alpha was sailing through the air right at him. Sean seized Arthur's gun from the waistband at the back of his jeans, brought it between them at the last instant, and fired a silver bullet directly into her chest.

The alpha's momentum still managed to knock them both to the ground, right next to the gagging, dying wolf, but she was not fighting when she landed on top of him. The proximity of the silver was stinging Sean's own chest, just as it had been irritating the small of his back .... but as he looked into the shocked pain and deep sorrow of her eyes, he felt compelled to hold her close. He didn't want this — he *never* wanted this — but he knew it had to be done.

"Silver ...?" she asked.

He nodded.

She shifted back into human form, her blood running out of her wound and onto his chest. She blinked back tears and said, "Was I ... so disgusting to you, my warrior? That you would use *silver* ... before even *considering* ... being my mate?"

The words, so similar to those spoken by his sister two years ago, chilled him. And finally — *finally* — he was able to say the words he so wished he had spoken back then.

"Ye never disgusted me. *I* disgusted me ... because I *did* want ye. But I believed it to be wrong."

She blinked again, but this time the tears escaped. "You ... wanted me?"

"Aye."

"My wolf ... was so beautiful, wasn't she?"

"Aye. Yer wolf, and yer *true* self."

She chuckled at that, and something rattled inside, almost making her cough. Her eyelids were getting heavier, too. "Liar. I was always ... too butch."

Sean just shook his head.

She smiled, a small smile filled with appreciation and release.

And then she died.

EPILOGUE

"Please don't take this the wrong way," Arthur said, "but I hope I never see or hear from you again."

Sean smiled. "I understand. It's a bit of an occupational hazard: People are usually glad for us to arrive, but they're even *more* glad to see us go."

Arthur grinned, just a little. "I'm sorry about the hassle. But with ... well ..."

Sean waved it away. "Not a problem, Arthur."

Arthur nodded, then stood looking awkward for a moment before extending his hand. Sean shook it, then climbed into the back of the cargo truck. He gave a little wave, then stretched his sore body until he could grab the strap for the sliding door, and pulled it shut.

The metallic clap echoing through the trailer told the driver, who had been well paid to look the other way and not ask any questions, to move out, and Sean steadied himself as the truck rumbled to a start.

In the aftermath of the werewolves' attack on the town, Sean and Arthur had scrambled to get the Triumvirate out of the area as fast as they possibly could. But the inflow of authorities had made securing the plane, *any* plane, impossible. Trey had struck upon the idea of their sneaking out in a truck, one thing led to another, and now here they were — along with some bottles of water, a bucket for nature's calls, a space heater, a crate for Alistaire's coffin, and what seemed like a thousand boxes of smoked salmon jerky. Sean had no idea how long they would be in here before getting all the way down to Anchorage, but Sean was not going to complain.

One advantage was that, with only one electric light above them, it was very dark in the trailer. That's what Sean wanted right now — darkness, and Alistaire's counsel.

He wandered toward the other end of the trailer, where they had tucked Alistaire's crate out of sight. He passed Trey, who sat on some jerky boxes near the middle of the trailer next to the space heater.

"Ye all right?" he asked Trey, who was just staring off into space. Not that there would be much else to do on this trip.

" 'm fine," was the only reply.

Sean started to say more — Trey had been acting a little weird, not quite himself, since the showdown with the werewolf pack. The one *good* bit of news was that Trey appeared to be *healing* much faster than usual. Maybe the same cold which had pained his joints somehow worked to his advantage in this area?

Sean considered asking him about it, but then decided to let it go. Trey said he was fine, so he probably was ... especially now that they were returning to warmer climates.

Sean reached the crate, opened it, and rapped on the coffin inside. After their standard exchange of knocks, the coffin opened and Alistaire sat up, without assistance.

"I take it we are underway?"

"Just got rollin'."

Alistaire nodded. *"Good. I can still feel the white night out there, but the darkness helps."*

"Better than the cabin, I take it?"

"Much."

"Good." Sean sat down on a jerky box, folded his hands, hesitated.

Alistaire considered his friend. *"Was there something you wanted to talk about ...?"*

"Alistaire ..." God, but his heart was pounding in his chest. His hands were shaking, too. Maybe this wasn't such a good idea ...

He felt a cool, reassuring hand on his shoulder. *"Sean, what is wrong?"*

"I do need to talk about something," he said, more thankful than ever for the darkness (and trying not to think about how keen the vampire's night vision was). "I need ... well, I need to *confess* something. And ye're about the closest thing I have to a priest." Then doubt squeezed his chest and he started to panic and the words rushed out as he stood. "Look, never mind, I know the white nights are painin' ye, we can just talk about this later, I didn't mean to bother ye, ye can go back—"

"Talk to me, Sean."

Sean forced himself to sit back down and draw a deep breath. "This is very difficult."

"Confessions often are. But I think you will find the results ... liberating."

Sean breathed, breathed. Then, "Ye know how I've been ... sensitive ... to the suggestion that my sister might be a werewolf?"

Sean feared a teasing retort, but there was no trace of it in Alistaire's voice when he replied, *"Yes."*

And then it all flowed out of him, like the floodgate had been opened — hell, like the whole dam had been smashed to bits. He told Alistaire everything. About Theresa's actions the night Eamon had tried to kill him. About what happened between them during the red moon. And about the fact that he had killed his own sister. He told it all, and he kept his eyes to the floor the entire time, terrified of the judgement that this might bring down upon him from his religious friend. But he had to get it out — after his final exchange with the alpha, he had no other choice.

"... so that's it," Sean said at last, feeling bone-weary and emotionally exhausted. He wiped at the tears which wetted his cheeks, and did not remember exactly when he had started crying. "We stand together against the monsters, but *I* have committed sins far worse than most of the villains we face. Incest, sororicide ... I think I've topped the chart. I've hated myself for a long time, but I think that I'm ready to face the music. Finally." He wiped his cheeks again. "So whatever judgement ye want to pass, whatever ye think is fitting, I accept it."

"Sean ..."

"I know that ye might not want to work with me anymore, so I can clear out after we get back home, and Trey can always—"

"Sean, I forgive you."

Sean stopped talking, and for a moment, he thought his heart might stop as well. "What did ye say ...?"

"I said I forgive you, Sean. I know you do not hold to

the same religious Faith as me, so you may not seek forgiveness from G-God. And although I am warmed by this healing step you have taken, it seems you are unwilling to forgive yourself. So ... for what it is worth ... I forgive you."

"But ..." The tears ran unchecked now. "The things I've done ... the night of the eclipse, and ... and two years ago, and ..."

"Do you confess your sins because you wish to atone them?"

"... aye."

"Then if you will not seek the L-Lord's forgiveness, and you cannot find your own, then please, please accept my forgiveness. You are a good man, Sean Mallory. And I think you have punished yourself long enough."

Sean sat, stunned. And then the tears came in earnest, and he doubled over and shed them, and with them the pain and the shame of so many years. Alistaire placed a comforting hand on the back of his friend's neck, and prayed for solace to embrace him.

*   *   *

Sitting in the middle of the trailer, Trey heard parts of what was said, but much of it came too fast for him to follow. It sounded like Sean had done something bad, but it also sounded like Alistaire had excused him, so he guessed it was all right.

Picking up a piece of salmon jerky, he spent several minutes trying to open the wrapper with his clumsy fingers, and when he finally got it open, he took one sniff and knew that he couldn't eat it. This should have come as no surprise. Alistaire and Sean had tried giving him many different kinds of meat, but only raw beef had ever worked to subdue his hunger.

But now ... Trey was *really* hungry. He only *thought* he had been hungry before, but now he knew better. Now a true need, a deeper craving, had awakened in him. And he did not know if eating dead cow would be enough to satisfy it.

Because that living werewolf had tasted so good ... so good.

Trey Matthews sat in the darkness, with the rocking of the truck and the sounds of Sean's sobs and the dissatisfying smell of salmon jerky ...

... and his deep, profound *hunger*.

About the Author

CHRISTOPHER ANDREWS lives in California with his wife, Yvonne Isaak-Andrews, and their Pug, PJ. He is working on his next novels, and continues to work as an actor and screenwriter.

Excerpts from all of Christopher's novels can be found at www.ChristopherAndrews.com.

www.ingramcontent.com/pod-product-compliance
Lightning Source LLC
Chambersburg PA
CBHW061557100726

47898CB00002B/407